Promised Rewards

C. Flynt

www.darkmythpublications.com

Dark Myth Publications, a division of
The JayZoMon Dark Myth Company, LLC.
21050 Little Beaver Rd, Apple Valley, CA 92308

ISBN: 979-8-9863807-5-9

First Printing March 2023

Dark Myth Publications is a registered trademark of The JayZoMon Dark Myth Company, LLC.

10 9 8 7 6 5 4 3 2 1

Table of Contents

CHAPTER ONE

Sigurd and the Band of Thieves..01

CHAPTER TWO

Sigurd and the Demon Horse...23

CHAPTER THREE

Sigurd and the Lost Princess...39

CHAPTER FOUR

Sigurd and the Wandering Knight.....................................55

CHAPTER FIVE

Sigurd and the Three Ogres..75

CHAPTER SIX

Sigurd and the Two Trolls...89

CHAPTER SEVEN

Sigurd at the Inn of Entrapment......................................113

CHAPTER EIGHT

Sigurd at the Hall of the Mountain King........................139

CHAPTER NINE

Sigurd and the Long-lost Brother.....................................161

Table of Contents (Cont'd)

CHAPTER TEN

Sigurd and the Solstice Celebration..................................187

CHAPTER ELEVEN

Sigurd and the Winter of Discontent...............................201

CHAPTER TWELVE

Sigurd and the Long Trail...223

CHAPTER THIRTEEN

Sigurd and the Prince's Requiem.....................................245

CHAPTER FOURTEEN

Sigurd and the Plights of Princes....................................257

CHAPTER FIFTEEN

Sigurd and the Homeward Trek..279

CHAPTER SIXTEEN

Sigurd and the Councils of Kings....................................303

CHAPTER SEVENTEEN

Sigurd and the Field of Combat..321

CHAPTER SEVENTEEN

Sigurd and the Last Stanza...345

About the Author...357

Endorsements

Witty and clever, Bard weaves a delightful narrative as he and his best friend, the loyal, ax-wielding Sigurd, embark on a rollicking adventure through the Kingdoms of 9'th century England.
Shanelle Boluyt,
Author of *Intersections*

Bard and Sigurd are my new favorite characters. Their crazy romp through Anglo-Saxon Britain is just outrageous enough to make them real.
Carol Lynn
Baroness Gwynnyd in the SCA

This tale of friendship, adventure, love and battle kept me glued to the pages at every turn. I couldn't wait to see what predicament Bard and Sigurd would get into next.
Jeanna Janes,
Author of *Seas Apart*

Dedications

This book is dedicated to my wife Carol. Her encouragement and suggestions turned this from a one-joke short story into a novel. Her(frequent) grammar lessons are all that made it readable.

Promised Rewards

Chapter One

Sigurd and the Band of Thieves

ANGLIA'S OPEN SKIES were a clarion call for a young man to seek adventure and romance.

In my youth those skies called me to live my dream of being a wandering bard. A life of adventure, romance and sleeping beneath those open skies. However, as I neared twenty, The dream of sleeping beneath a lord's roof appealed more. The truth is the open skies tend to rain a lot.

Needless to say, my dreams were not real. A travel-tattered bard is not welcome in a court. He's barely tolerated in a tavern.

However, in deference to my advanced years, I kept

close to the trade roads where a man who travels lightly--a man who owns only his eating knife and lute--can reach an inn by nightfall. A bard sometimes receives a meal and a bed in exchange for an evening of song and story.

At worst there's space in the barn.

It was half past October when I stopped at a tiny inn where the trade path crosses the River Wier. The inn was built of stones borrowed from the long-abandoned Roman wall. The Romans constructed good, solid walls of well-dressed stone. Now that the legions have been gone for some five hundred years, those stones were finding better uses.

I entered the inn with a lutish flourish and a song on my lips.

I bring the news from far and near,
I'll sing the tunes you wish to hear.
A bard is welcome, far and wide,
For joy is always at his side

The innkeeper frowned at me. "Another penniless beggar. Stay out of the way and don't annoy anyone."

The scars on his face told me he'd been an armsman in his younger days. The thin gray hair on his head told me those days were not recent. The breadth of his shoulders and his huge hands told me that it didn't matter how long ago those days had been, he could still eject any bard who displeased him.

I retreated to the far corner and sang softly until he thundered. "If you're going to make noise, sing loud enough to be heard."

I obliged with a jaunty drinking song, and soon had several of the local farmers singing along and taking deep drafts of ale with each verse.

My host smiled as he refilled their tankards. Innkeepers favor a bard who increases their trade. He even gifted me a small mug of ale that was watered down just a bit more than necessary.

In hopes of being allowed to sleep near a fire, I sang my best sagas: *Sigurd and the Thirty Thieves, Sigurd Slays the Dragon,* and even *Sigurd and the Three Virgin Sisters.*

I tell myself that I am recognized for my Sagas of Sigurd. I sometimes sing the traditional sagas, but I prefer to present tales I've composed myself; adventures to thrill you, romances to enthrall you and moral tales to fulfill you. And, if my tales move you to bestow Christian charity upon a hungry bard, a blessing upon you.

Despite my best efforts, I ended the night in the stable. The stable was not well-cut stone. The walls were rough planks with gaps that let the evening-breezes flow freely. These breezes kept the stables as cold as outside without diluting the perfume of horse droppings.

Being the only traveler too poor to pay a penny to sleep by the fire, I pulled the loose straw into a pile and wrapped myself in my cloak. I fell asleep without being stepped on and counted myself lucky.

My luck changed shortly after moonrise. I woke with a start as the stable door creaked open, followed by the soft tread of footsteps. I cracked one eye and spied a figure approaching. The moonlight streaming through the open door glinted on shoulder-length blonde ringlets.

It's not unheard of for a young lady to sneak from her bed to visit a bard in the stable. For me, it happens after an evening of the tales of Sigurd. The door opens, a slim form slips in, and a hushed voice whispers, "Do you know where Sigurd is now? Will his travels bring him here?"

But I've sung enough songs about a quick dally in the stable that I kept hoping for some truth in the tales.

I admired the golden locks. The form beneath was more robust than I'd dreamed of, but even a bard sometimes prefers substance to an ethereal dream. A noise in the stables made my visitor turn, and moonlight gleamed on a full blond beard.

I prayed this was not a romantic visitation, merely another traveler without enough coins searching for a dry place to sleep.

"Bard?" the visitor whispered, "Are you awake?"

I considered pretending sleep and then mused about what my visitor might do to a prone bard.

"I am now," I grumbled.

"Good." He settled on his haunches near my chest and stared down at me. "I enjoyed the Sagas of Sigurd you sang tonight. They thrilled and inspired me."

How many times have I wished to hear a comely lass murmur those words. Not some hero-worshiping lad nearly as old as I.

"Thanks," I mumbled back, "may I go back to sleep now?"

"A moment of your time. As I said, the sagas inspired

me. Are they your own?"

"Yes. They are mine. Carefully crafted so none can fail to recognize my talen--"

"Wonderful. As I said, they inspired me. I wish to be Sigurd."

"Well, every man should aspire to do the best he can in the eyes of man and God. I aspire to sleep most deeply."

"You mistake my meaning. I do not wish to be as heroic as Sigurd. I wish to *be* Sigurd. Sigurd the Hero."

I grunted a querulous grunt.

He wasn't attempting to seduce me. That was the good news. The bad news was that he was obviously insane.

Everyone knows Sigurd is imaginary. Nobody could survive all the adventures I've composed of him. You might as well aspire to be Roland, or Lancelot or even a king like Charlemagne or Arthur. It's a grand dream, but I'd sing at court long before this lad became Sigurd the Hero.

I tried gently to explain this, but he interrupted me.

"I'm a sell-sword," he said. "A sell-axe, actually. Swords are expensive. But I live like you; wandering and earning money when I can. I guard a farmer's crops today, and don't know where I'll rest tomorrow."

"Aha, You have a story that should be a saga? In the morning I'll be happy to hear your tale."

Everyone believes their life would make a great saga. Too many are eager to relate every tiny detail in exchange for a portion of the coins they think I'll receive by singing of their boring lives.

"Alas, I only wish I had adventures like Sigurd.

5

Especially the one with the three maidens." He paused, gazing dreamily at the ceiling. "But that's not why I'm here. You sang that Sigurd is tall and fair-haired, like me. If I were Sigurd the Hero, I'd be paid with pieces of gold instead of chunks of cheese."

"So, tell people you're Sigurd. Tell them you're Hercules for all I care."

"No one will believe me if I claim to be Sigurd. But, if *you* declare me to be Sigurd, then I'll receive greater rewards for my services and your songs will be grander for my presence. We'll both sleep on feather beds, not in stables."

That pretty much settled it. The man was insane. Insane and armed with an axe. Not to mention upright while I was sitting, wrapped in my cloak.

Discretion is a bard's first weapon. I needed to remove this man--and his axe--from my presence.

"You have an interesting proposition. Let me sleep and consider it. We can continue talking in the morning."

"Thank you, Friend Bard. In the morning it shall be."

He rose and left the barn. I was surprised. I'd expected him to continue describing his grand idea.

As soon as he left, I checked my travel sack. My lute and the rest of my belongings were packed and ready to leave first thing in the morning, hopefully earlier than my would-be hero.

I learned years ago to be prepared the night before I intended to leave. Being prepared made it easier to slip away quietly before dawn. Before the innkeeper remembers you haven't paid and before anyone has collected the day's

6

eggs.

I woke shortly before cockcrow. The chickens were restless when I checked for breakfast, but it appeared they weren't laying today. It was lamentable, but not my first hungry morning.

I tip-toed across the yard and out the gate. I turned the corner and almost tripped over the blond axe-man. He had half a dozen eggs arranged in a circle around a small fire and was rolling them to bake evenly. In the daylight I saw the battered leather pauldron covering his shoulders above a dirt-brown tunic. His leggings were nearly as patched and ragged as my own.

"Good morning, Friend Bard," he greeted me. "I thought you might be an early riser. Would you care to share my breakfast? The eggs are fresh."

The road only gets longer when you start on an empty stomach. I sat down, knowing I'd regret it.

He picked up an egg, shook it gently and tossed it to me. It was hot. I peeled away the shell and bit into it.

"Nicely done." I complimented him. I'm always polite to my host. Especially when there are four more eggs I might share with him.

"Thank you, kind sir. Just one of the skills I've picked up in my travels." He cracked the shell between his teeth and nibbled the steaming egg. "And speaking of travels. Have you thought about my plan?"

"I considered it... But let us not discuss such things during breakfast." I stared at the remaining eggs.

"A good suggestion," he replied, picking up the eggs and wrapping them in a scrap of felt. "Breakfast is now complete. These eggs will be a fine luncheon." He carefully placed the eggs in his travel sack, "Of course, I mean a luncheon for Sigurd and his partner."

I'd learned early to be cautious when explaining unpleasant truths to axe-men. "Alas, good fellow," I said, "Sigurd is imaginary. Everybody knows that. There aren't any heroes today. They died out ages ago. If they ever existed then. If I point at you and call you Sigurd, people will laugh."

I ran my finger along the inside of the eggshell to collect the last remnants of an insufficient meal. "I thank you for sharing your breakfast, but I fear it is time to be on my way."

I glanced back at the inn. I recognized the first sounds of people waking and moving about. Soon I would hear them noticing which travelers and how many eggs were missing.

"An excellent suggestion. I believe we are both heading north, so we may as well walk together."

My stomach yearned for the two eggs in his pouch. I'd have to share the road with this youth for several hours to obtain my portion of those eggs. Or I could part company with him and eat nothing. Travelling alone was suddenly less appealing.

He stood and offered me a hand up. I rose without assistance. I may be almost twenty, but I don't need help to stand. He strode off at a strong pace. A soldier's pace, designed to get you where you need to be. Not a bard's pace, designed for watching the birds and trees while you search for the right couplet to complete a verse.

He slowed his pace to match mine and spoke. "People

want heroes to be real. That's why they pay you to sing the tales of Sigurd. They want to believe in someone better, someone who knows what he is doing."

He bit his lip, then continued, "That's why an armsman obeys a sergeant a sergeant obeys an earl, and an earl follows his lord. Nobody knows how a battle will flow. The lord is as confused as the earl, the sergeant, or the foot-soldier. But they all want to believe someone has a plan. So, they follow orders. Even when they know the orders are wrong."

He paused and stared through the tall oaks into a misty past. "Men will follow a hero to their death."

He shook his head, and I watched as he forced himself to relax. I hadn't noticed him tensing until his fists opened and his shoulders dropped.

This man had a story I'd never ask for and didn't really want to hear. It wasn't a grand tale like the Sigurd legend, but it would touch an old soldier's heart. I'd learn it if we traveled together. It might earn me a penny or two. Fodder for a new saga was a greater incentive to journey with this axe-man than even two eggs.

He continued speaking, barely glancing at me. "People want to hire a hero to guard their flock, not some nameless sell-sword. They'll pay a hero more than they'll pay a wandering axe-man."

He slowed and pointed at himself. "If you tell people I'm Sigurd, they'll want to believe."

He stopped and faced me. He wasn't looking into the past now. His eyes bored into mine as he offered, "You can keep the money you earn singing and I'll split the coins I earn with you. I'll give you one of every ten pennies I earn as Sigurd."

Now, he was talking sense. "Two pieces out of ten. From each task you do while we travel together, whether you claim to be Sigurd or not."

"Deal." He spat on his hand and held it out. I spat on mine and clinched the best and worst bargain of my life.

I wiped my hand on my tunic and stared back into his eyes. "I'm commonly called Bard, or sometimes, Bard the Lutist. How are you known?"

He grinned. "Why, you can call me Sigurd, of course."

There was no answer to that, so we continued walking without further conversation. The sun was high when we reached a fork in the path.

Sigurd glanced at the paths and then at me. "I choose my direction by flipping a coin." He studied me. "Do you have a coin?"

I smiled. I would show this youth the advantage of my years and experience, but not whether or not I had a coin. "Last night, a tinker told me the inn on the west fork had the best ale he'd ever tasted." I paused for drama. "We go east."

"East? If the best ale is west?"

"Any ale a tinker likes is too thin and sour for me."

We headed east, treading the narrow path between tall trees. The forest was dark and still and went on forever. I was starting to think thin ale was better than no ale at all when we reached a clearing. One moment we were wending our way between trunks so thick I couldn't encircle them with both arms, then we were avoiding the buckthorn crowding onto the trail. I was so busy dodging the thorns I barely noticed when we stepped into open fields of wheat and barley.

In the north was a plume of smoke.

"Someone must be clearing more land," I suggested.

"Better he then I," my friend replied. "I'd rather guard a harvest than plant one."

I squinted at a wooden building a few bowshots ahead. "Do I see a tin cup nailed above the door?"

"If it is, then it's probably an inn." He paused. "If we enter together people may realize we are acquainted and doubt our ruse. You go in first, and I'll come a moment later. We can recognize each other as if it were a chance encounter."

He settled beneath a huge oak as I sauntered to the inn. Now that I wasn't next to him, I was having second thoughts about declaring him to be Sigurd.

I do two things: I carry news, mostly true, and I present legends, mostly otherwise. Nobody pays me a penny to learn that a king has a new son or that a Viking band burned a village. I earn my pennies and sceats for the stirring sagas of my imagination.

Would my imagination be worth a penny if people thought I was merely reporting the real life adventures of a real live Sigurd?

More importantly, unlikely as it was for a traveling bard to gain a position in a court, finding a court willing to welcome both a homeless bard and a penniless axe-man was less likely.

By the time I reached the inn I had resolved to slip through the stables on the far side and hasten away from the town. However, one egg is not enough for a day's faring. I had time for an ale before departing.

I brought my lute to my chest and brushed my sleeve across the waxed cedar front to bring out the shine. I quickly checked the tuning, strummed a flourish, and strode into the inn. I glanced about the dim interior, scanning the rough wooden benches for potential benefactors. The inn was empty except for a lanky, gray-haired innkeeper.

"Good Day, Good Innkeeper," I called, "Would you spare a glass of ale for some news and song?"

"A small cup for a song," the innkeeper replied. "More will depend on how much I like the song." He wiped a modest copper cup on the hem of his woolen tunic, filled it and set it in front of me. A wooden cross swung from a leather strip around his neck. I considered an appeal to his Christian charity but gave up that idea when I saw the size of the cup.

He was true to his word. The cup was small, but the ale was wet and not too sour.

I sang him the first five verses of *Sigurd and the Seven Saracens*. Right up to my favorite stanza.

Seven jackals circled taunting.
Sigurd smiling, still undaunted.
Points he to the largest, laughing.
"You shall be the first to die."

I let my voice crack and nodded at the cup. "Perhaps a bit more, good Innkeeper. The dusty road, you know..."

He brought me a large wooden mug, and I did it some small honor.

"Would that Sigurd were real. We have only three thieves, but it would be a worthy saga if they were just driven away, let alone killed."

I stopped honoring the ale and started choking on it.

"Three thieves?"

"Three runaways from the King's Army. They camp back in the woods, take what they will and burn buildings when somebody protests." He nodded toward the smoke. "That would be Eadrick's farmstead. He never was one to part quietly with his possessions." He placed a stack of wooden mugs on the counter and nodded at my lute.

"Sing your songs of Sigurd tonight. It's worth dinner and all the ale you wish. Mayhap it will put enough backbone into our farmers to send them against the villains."

I was still choking. As soon as Sigurd announced himself, he'd be pressed into service. Three trained foemen would make short work of him.

My life would be simpler without him. There'd be no need to find a court with space for both bard and guard. But I didn't want to finish my sagas with *Sigurd and the Ignoble Death*.

I set down my drink, hoping to find it when I returned, and took a step towards the door. Before I reached it, the door swung wide, and Sigurd burst in.

"Friend Bard!" he cried, "I thought I saw you enter this

inn. Let us share some ale and I'll tell you my latest adventures. They will make fine sagas."

The innkeeper glared at Sigurd suspiciously. "You know this man?" he asked me.

I tried to protest that he was a stranger, but Sigurd was louder.

"Know me? Why he is my favored historian. I am the great Sigurd, and this is my trusted bard, the teller of my tales."

The innkeeper's jaw dropped. Sigurd was right. People wanted to believe.

"Sigurd?" he gasped, "*The* Sigurd?"

A bard should be in control of a situation. It's how we survive. But situations like this aren't what we practice.

I was still gasping when the door burst open and a peasant dressed in a rough farmer's tunic stumbled in shouting, "Mad bull! Run!"

He was followed by a large, brown bull.

Sigurd was still standing in front of the door. He'd barely turned when the bull burst in and paused, searching for the peasant he'd been chasing. The bull saw Sigurd, lowered his head, and pawed the dirt floor.

Sigurd was fast. He loosed his axe, grabbed it by the head and struck the bull on the nose with the axe-handle. He stepped in close, stuck his fingers in the bull's nostrils and twisted.

The bull bawled once and stopped fighting.

The innkeeper faced the peasant. "Friend Eadrick," he said quietly. "Would you kindly remove your bull from my inn?"

The farmer stared at Sigurd, still holding the bull. "Good sir, my thanks. My bull is well-behaved, but the robbers--" He paused for a breath. "Those villains burned my stable and chased my poor bull until he went mad. They stole three of my chickens and a firkin of ale." He glanced at the innkeeper. "We've got to stop those varlets. Drive them from our valley. Nobody is safe as long as they're about."

The innkeeper pointed at Sigurd, who now realized there was more than an angry bull in this village.

"We are in luck." the innkeeper said grandly waving his arm to include Sigurd and me. "Just now, the legendary Sigurd walked into my inn, obviously having heard tales of my fine ale. Such a hero would never let an opportunity to save our homes pass him by."

Sigurd glanced at me with an expression much like that of the bull he was holding.

"Three runaways from the King's Army," I summarized for him. "Hiding in the woods, living on pillage."

He paled but caught himself. "Three." He paused with enough drama to satisfy any bard. "Three is hardly worth my time, but I might give the farmers a bit of advice and training."

The innkeeper interrupted him. "I assure you; these three villains are worthy of your effort. They have been ravaging the farmsteads around this village for almost six months. None of the farmers have been able to defend themselves. I'm sure your bard will write a marvelous ballad about this adventure."

Eadrick began to lead his bull away, but Sigurd was still

staring at the innkeeper. The bull wheezed as Sigurd squeezed its nose harder. He finally noticed Eadrick and released the bull, wiping his hand on his tunic.

"Not a single farmstead in this entire village has fought the villains?" he asked.

"Oh, plenty have fought," the innkeeper replied. "But a single farmer is no match for three swordsmen. If you fight, they burn one of your buildings. If you let them take what they want, they burn none."

I glanced at Sigurd. His altercation with the bull and conversation with the innkeeper had given me a chance to think. It was time to get him off the hook.

"Sigurd, " I spoke slowly to emphasize my words. "Don't you have an urgent quest east of here? A princess in despair, wasn't it?"

He blinked at me, then squinted as he recognized my ploy.

"Of course. The Princess. I'm sorry, good host, but I really cannot tarry."

The innkeeper set a large mug of ale on the counter.

Sigurd grabbed the mug and took a hefty swallow. "Well, perhaps for a bit, but I truly can't take the time to search the woods for your knaves. It could take days to find them, you know."

The innkeeper set a half a fowl next to the ale. "It wouldn't take long to find them. I can direct you to the woods where they retreat after they steal from the farmers."

Sigurd tore a leg from the fowl and began eating. "Still, it would take me time, and I cannot afford it. I do wish your village well--"

The innkeeper interrupted him. "I know a hero expects a reward. This is a small hamlet, but we would not ask you to risk your life for nothing. Not that three knaves present a risk to a hero like you."

Sigurd took a large bite from the leg and stared at the innkeeper.

The innkeeper wrung his apron. "I offer you all you can eat and drink tonight, for both you and your bard."

Sigurd took another swallow of the ale and kept staring at the innkeeper.

"And a bed... for each of you..."

Sigurd swallowed the last of his ale, passed me the remains of the fowl, and cleared his throat. "I'm sorry, but my bard and I must attend to the quest. I do thank you for this meal."

The innkeeper looked ill. "I'll give you my horse," he pleaded. "It's the best in the town. Rid us of these villains and riding on horseback will make up for the time you spend here."

A horse was a serious temptation. Sigurd was a good bargainer.

"And trappings?" I suggested.

The innkeeper sighed. "Saddle, bridle and blanket."

Sigurd beamed at me, obviously pleased with himself. "I say we sample our landlord's hospitality tonight and rout the ruffians in the morning."

I nodded and wondered when it became we who were to do battle.

We spent the afternoon and evening sampling the innkeeper's ales and ciders. I sang when there were enough folks to listen and exchanged news of the kingdom and neighboring villages with the innkeeper when the inn was empty.

Among other gossip, I learned that Prince Wellach and his company had stopped here on their way north to pay court to King Elmar's daughter Beornwyn. This would be a fine snippet of news at the next inn I visited. I would love to winter in a king's court, but taverns were the finest buildings I'd ever been within.

A day with all the ale you can drink is a marvelous thing. It loosens the tongue, brightens the wit and by the end of the day it makes the path to the outhouse incredibly convoluted. I had almost reached my destination when I overheard two voices discussing an important matter.

The first voice said, "Sigurd is merely a bard's story. This lout is trying to cozen you."

"Not so, " the second voice responded. "I swear I saw it with my own eyes. He hit the bull with his bare hand, and it stopped dead in its tracks. He threw it to the ground with a single flip of his wrist. Ask the innkeeper. He saw it as well."

"He won't be a match for the gang in the woods."

"Hah! Didn't you hear the bard? Seven Saracens he slew, armed with only a dagger. He'll probably behead those three with a single swing of his axe."

"Go tend to your chickens. I need another cup of ale."

The footsteps departed in different directions, and I barely made it to the outhouse. The trail back to the inn was shorter and straighter. Something in the conversation I'd overheard was sobering, but I wasn't sure just what it was.

I sang the long version of "Sigurd and the Three Virgin Sisters." By the time I reached the last sister, only Sigurd, the innkeeper and I were left.

Our host apologized. "It's a fine song, but chores start early. Your beds are in the loft, up the ladder. Breakfast at dawn. I'll give you my horse after you've driven the bandits from the woods."

Sigurd and I helped each other up the ladder. It was straighter than the path to the outhouse but might have been longer.

The beds were clean straw tick over tight cords. Our host kept a good inn. I was asleep before I removed my boots.

Dawn came much too early and brought a headache with it.

Breakfast was eggs and oatmeal, washed down with watered ale. Sigurd and I dawdled over our meal, trying to make it last long enough to discern some way to leave without dying in the woods.

The longer we dawdled, the more villagers came to watch us search for the bandits.

I finally couldn't eat any more. The expression on Sigurd's face as he chewed a mouthful of oatmeal told me he'd reached the same condition.

We stood together and the villagers cheered.

"You see that corner of the wood." The innkeeper pointed to the left of where we'd seen the smoke yesterday.

"The knaves run there after they pillage. Their camp must be inside the woods. Bring back proof that you've driven them off and I'll give you my horse."

We set out slowly, with a few of the villagers trailing behind. The closer we got to the woods; the fewer folks accompanied us.

Sigurd glanced at me. From the side of his mouth he whispered, "I hope you have a plan."

I kept my head straight. "I assumed you'd slay them with a single blow, I'd write a saga, and we'd ride to the next town."

He stumbled and caught himself. "There are three of them. They're trained. They might even be sergeants or yeomen. If we're lucky, they'll kill us quickly."

I laughed at him. "You wanted to be a hero. This is your chance to be heroic."

Sigurd passed his axe nervously from hand to hand. "I wanted to be rewarded like a hero, not have to perform impossible deeds."

We'd walked over halfway from the inn to the edge of the woods where the innkeeper said the bandits retreated. The smell of the inn's cookfire had been replaced by the sour scent of a burned shed.

A game trail led into the woods just ahead of us.

"I have a plan," I assured Sigurd, nodding towards the trail. "We follow that path into the woods. Once we're hidden behind trees, we double back to the road and take the other fork. I'm thinking the tinker might know a good ale after all."

A dozen paces later, I glanced over my shoulder. I could no longer see the village. We were safely out of sight.

I smiled wisely at Sigurd. My plan had worked. We could slink away with our bellies full. We need not die fighting bandits nor need we ever return to this village.

Then I heard deep voices and footsteps. Sigurd's wide eyes told me he'd heard them as well. We had found the bandits. This trail must lead to their camp.

If we left the trail, we'd rattle the dry leaves and alert them to our presence. If we stood still, they'd find us when they next raided. If we retreated, we'd have to confess ourselves as cowards, and the innkeeper would be within his rights to demand that we pay for the food and drink we'd consumed. I knew I lacked the coins for that, and I suspected Sigurd had fewer coins than I.

I was unwilling to admit my cowardice, but I was even less willing to die proving my bravery. I saw no acceptable couplet to complete this stanza. I prayed this wasn't the last couplet of my saga.

Chapter Two

Sigurd and the Demon Horse

I PULLED SIGURD behind a bush, and we stared at each other, eyes wide. We'd be dead within moments if the bandits discovered us. Nervous sweat trickled down my ribs as my heart pounded and my stomach clenched.

"Sigurd is a legend," said a deep voice. "The villagers are trying to scare us away."

A younger voice replied, "He's not a legend. I saw him myself. He's almost seven feet tall. They say he killed a bull with a single blow of his bare hand."

"He's still just one man. He can't fight the three of us. Especially not if Olaf gets his rage."

"Olaf won't wake for hours. He must have drunk half

the firkin of ale. He's been nothing but trouble since we left the army. We should leave him here."

"We swore an oath to stick together. He was our friend when we needed him. We don't abandon him now."

"Be sensible. Sigurd's a legend. He could rally the villagers. We can't fight an entire village."

I'll confess to having a strange sense of humor. I see the world through a bard's eyes, and sometimes the world needs help to be as grand as the stories I sing. My fear-sweat had dried while we listened, my heart had quieted, and my stomach relaxed. I was ready to make the world what I wanted it to be, rather than accept what I feared it truly was.

I recognized what had sobered me at the outhouse the night before. The tales of Sigurd were growing. With each retelling, he became taller, stronger, and more heroic.

At least one of the bandits considered Sigurd a serious threat.

In order to deliver a song properly, a bard cultivates many voices. Thus, I had several to use as need arose. I stood up and shouted in the voice of an excited young man "Ho, Sigurd! They're over here!"

Sigurd grabbed me and pulled me down. I thrashed and kicked at the bushes while shouting heroically, "Onward! Attend me!" Then I called, in assorted voices, "Behind you, Sir!" and "Coming!" Between our thrashing and my shouting in different voices we made enough noise for ten men.

I made so much racket I barely heard the first bandit shout. "I won't leave him. Grab his feet."

Once the brigands left I stopped thrashing. We waited a few moments to catch our breath as the rustling of feet in dry leaves faded into the distance.

I brushed the dust off my tunic. "Shall we go see what proof they left us?"

Sigurd shook his head and followed as I walked in the direction of the voices. The camp was in a small glade about twenty paces further into the woods. A huge oak stood on one edge of the clearing, with arching branches making a green canopy. It looked peaceful and pleasant.

The odor was less pleasant.

Several rotting chicken carcasses had been thrown outside the glade into the woods.

The bandits had tied a cloak over a branch as a makeshift shelter. The fire in front of it was almost burned out. Two single-edged seax knives as long as my forearm and two iron shields the size of dinner plates leaned against the tree.

Sigurd cut down the cloak and spread it on the ground. I gathered the knives, shields, cooking utensils and bits of jewelry and stacked them on the cloak. We rolled the cloak into a litter, each took an end and headed back to the village.

"So," said Sigurd. "Did I slay them with a single blow and leave their bodies for the carrion eaters?"

"I think when they saw you appear from behind the trees, brandishing your shining axe, they lost their manhood and fled like frightened children. That way nobody will wonder why we left no bodies."

"That's almost what happened. I thought bards had

25

more imagination."

"I'll use more imagination when I sing of this adventure at the next inn. I assure you; you won't know yourself."

"Ah, but the villagers will. They'll want to recognize me." He shook his head and then grunted. "Tell me. Do you know how to ride a horse?"

I stared at him. "I assumed you knew how. You bargained for the animal."

He shrugged. "We'll find a use for it. Maybe we'll need it to carry all the gold we'll earn."

I had no answer, so we walked back to the tavern in silence.

That is, we were silent until we approached the inn carrying the rolled up cloak. The villagers who had cheered as we left the inn were even more jubilant when we returned. It was almost worth my moment of gut-wrenching fear to see the surprised expression on the innkeeper's face as we sauntered into his inn carrying the cloak. It was plain he'd never expected to see us again, let alone returning with the bandits weapons.

But he lived up to his word. He provided food and lodging while we traded on our sudden fame. We sold the knives and ironware to the smith, returned jewelry to the rightful owners, and regaled everyone who came to the inn with tales of our exploits.

There is much to be said for being a hero. The beer flows freely, villagers stop talking and listen when you sing, and you sleep indoors in a warm bed.

Nobody said it would last forever.

After a couple of days our glamour faded and the flow of visitors to the inn dwindled. When our presence stopped attracting more business, our gracious host reminded me pointedly that I'd mentioned Sigurd having an appointment to rescue a princess. Shouldn't we be on our way? In fact, shouldn't we be on our way now?

The horse we'd earned was a handsome coal-black stallion. This hellish hue reached deep into his cold, black heart. He was a fractious beast with no patience for a saddle and a tendency to bite, kick and generally misbehave. The innkeeper confessed he'd purchased the beast to draw a wagon but had never managed to harness it to one.

Sigurd knew enough about horses to get a knotted-rope halter onto it. He jerked the rope to lead it away, and it balked. After a few moments of testing each other's strength, Sigurd added a knotted loop around the beast's lip and we left town afoot, carrying our meager possessions. The animal wouldn't allow anything on its back, so we couldn't even use it for our packs.

I wondered why we were leading an animal we couldn't use for anything.

After several hours of dragging the grazing glutton away from every likely clump of grass, I began to compose a new ballad. It pleased me to discover that "horse" rhymed with "corpse."

Sigurd complained about being in charge of our reward.

"Bard," he said, "I can teach you to pull on the rope. I'd wager a gentleman of your skill would find it trivial."

"Ah, Sigurd," I replied, "Given your vaunted heroic prowess you must find subduing a simple beast easy as sleeping. I'd hate to interrupt your rest."

Sigurd planted his feet, grasped the rope in both hands and succeeded in getting our beast moving. The fact that the animal had finished swallowing the last clump of clover might have contributed to this.

"I've worked with horses before," he grunted as it veered to another patch of clover. "I've watched their hindquarters from behind a plow for longer than I'd care to admit. This is not a horse. It's a penance. Whatever possessed you to bargain for this demon when we could have asked for something useful, like a flask of wine, is more than a simple hero can fathom."

I motioned him to be quiet. A wider trail joined the one we were on. We might be approaching a village.

"Looks like a clearing up ahead. Can you make it seem as if we're in charge of the beast for a couple of minutes? Mayhap we can sell the animal if nobody recognizes it."

Sigurd conjured an apple from his pack. He sliced off a chunk and chewed it ostentatiously while our glutton sniffed and sidled closer. He put the remainder of the apple back into his pack and proceeded. The steed followed tight upon his heels, nuzzling the pack when it could.

We strode into a village slightly larger than the one we had left. It boasted a central well surrounded by a tavern, smithy, and a few houses. We angled around a two-wheeled wain filled with foodstuffs and headed to the tavern, leading our docile animal as if it were not a beast from the nether regions.

Sigurd led our noble steed to a tree growing by the tavern. He tied the lead to a stout limb and did the things horse people do. He removed the rope from the animal's nose and rubbed it gently. The horse shied from him at first but accepted his attention after he soothed its nose.

He spoke to the animal. "Your nose wouldn't hurt if you didn't fight so hard." He glanced at me. "I'll finish tending our hell-spawn while you find out whether there are any bandits we need to avoid. Greet me by name as I enter, and I'll know it's safe."

The door to the tavern stood open. Being mid-day, the inn was nearly empty, with only the innkeeper and a single patron, a dark-haired man about my age.

I loosened my lute and flipped it onto my stomach, strummed a lively jig and stepped in.

"Greetings, good fellows!" I called. "If my throat were a bit moister, I could share news and a thrilling tale or two."

The man at the bar, a young lord by his deep red, woolen cloak, tapped the bar. "I would hear something cheerful. Give him a small beer."

The innkeeper was a round-faced man sporting a fringe of short gray hair in a tonsure. His face fell into a natural smile as he drew a small beer for me.

A small song for a small beer.

Sing hi for the open road,
Sing hey for the flowing bowl.
A minstrel's life is free from strife,
Unless it is rainy or cold.

Sing hi for a sun-filled day
And keep the rain away.

With tales of joy, and girls and boys,
I'll chase your cares awa—

I croaked the last two words.

"Sorry," I apologized. "The road is dusty, and my throat is still a bit dry."

The lordling scowled. "A tale of love doesn't suit me. Do you know anything with bloodshed?" He nodded to the landlord, who drew a larger mug of ale for me.

"Certainly, good sir. Would you hear of *Sigurd and the Bandit Horde?*" I glanced to my host. "Are there any bandits nearby? I'd not want to frighten them."

He laughed. "No bandits in this village. The squire wouldn't tolerate them."

The lordling's scowl darkened. "Good to know his tolerance has limits."

The innkeeper's smile vanished. He matched scowls with the lordling and growled. "The squire tolerates more than I need to."

The innkeeper's greater experience in scowling prevailed and the young man dropped his eyes to his drink.

In a dispute between a man with money and an innkeeper, the bard loses. I needed to defuse this contention. "Is there news I should know? Mayhap it will fit with a stirring epic of Sigurd?"

The innkeeper continued scowling. "None, save that the squire's daughter has run off. He's offering a gold piece to the man who brings her home."

The lordling set down his beer. "And two to the man

who can keep her. It won't be me. Good day."

He stomped out, leaving a small pile of bronze coins on the bar.

I stared at my host. "I assure you, my singing has never driven a man from his beer before."

The innkeeper snorted a brief laugh. "His high-and-lordly was betrothed to the squire's daughter yesterday. Her father approved the match, but she did not. Today she's gone and soon the young buck will leave. Shortly after that I'll warrant the prodigal daughter will return."

Just then, Sigurd's shadow darkened the doorway, followed by Sigurd, ducking his head to enter the inn.

I set my mug onto the counter. "What ho, Sigurd. And how fares your famous steed?"

He relaxed and smiled. "The steed fares well, but I fear I should not force the animal to keep up with my deeds. T'would be a kindness to find him a less rigorous life." He dropped a bronze penny on the bar and motioned for a drink. "This seems a peaceful village. Mayhap my trusty steed will find someone needing an amicable mount."

I smiled at the innkeeper. "This evening, I could regale your patrons with the tale of *Sigurd's Race With Death*. Were my throat moistened."

The innkeeper nodded once as he poured Sigurd's drink. The mug was barely half-full when the pouring was interrupted by a crash and shouting from outside. Sigurd led as we raced out the door.

I gaped at the scene of growing carnage. Our hell-spawn had broken the branch Sigurd had tied him to and was galloping around the village green. Across the field, a bay mare reared and struggled as her master failed to calm her. The bay broke loose and galloped away before our monster reached her. He was unhindered by the limb he dragged. As he rounded the well, the limb wedged itself into a wheel of the cart we'd walked around. This stopped our hell-beast for a moment. Then, he reared and bounded forward, pulling the wheel from the cart. I gasped as the cart toppled against the well. Turnips, hams, and bags of grain tumbled out. Only a few fell into the well, but the splashes told me they would need to drain the well and clean it carefully before the water was fit to drink again.

It is a bard's talent to report events, real or fictional, so fully that a listener will believe they were present at the time.

Not all events lend themselves to this.

I confess to not remembering all that was said and done as the cart collapsed, the mare ran around the well with our stallion chasing her, the man who had been leading the mare became tangled in the branch our hell-beast dragged and more people than I believed lived in this village ran to help and hinder. There were a lot of words and actions and none of them were friendly. Claiming Sigurd and I did more damage than Norse raiders was an exaggeration, but I confess our monster contributed more than its share to the excitement.

In the end, Sigurd, I, and the infamous steed left the village significantly faster than we entered. And significantly less wealthy. Most of our coins were left behind to pay for the lost food and damaged well.

Neither of us spoke for a long time. I won't guess what Sigurd was thinking, but I was thinking I'd never been thrown out of a village when I traveled alone.

Sigurd spoke first "One who knows nothing of horses should not bargain for one."

The idea that I was responsible for the beast he seemed so fond of was one I hadn't considered. I started to suggest it was his beast, not mine, but remembered I wanted my share of any money we received from selling it.

"One who can't tell rotten wood from sound wood should hold onto a beast, not tie it up and leave it."

"Rotten wood! That tree was as solid as a mountain. An ox couldn't pull that tree apart." He paused. "This beast is stronger than an ox. And more stubborn."

The horse dragged Sigurd into a clearing and began to crop.

"Well," he said, rubbing his hands against his vest, "This is a fine place to camp. You gather some wood and I'll gather something to cook over it." He slipped a leather sling from his pouch and slid silently into the trees.

I glared at our beast. He was not hobbled, nor tied to anything. Still, he showed no interest in leaving the clearing, so I ignored him and gathered wood while he ignored me and ate more grass.

Sigurd returned carrying a handful of mushrooms and a pair of rabbits as I coaxed our fire to life. Once the rabbits had been skinned, cooked, and eaten Sigurd and I were ready to be civil to each other.

Sometimes it takes chewing half-raw meat to restore one's better nature.

Sigurd opened the discussion. "A strong, spirited stallion

33

must be worth something to the right person. I'm willing to sell the beast."

I nodded. "Making it known that the famous Sigurd rode this steed will make a buyer unwilling to admit he can't handle it and demand we refund his purchase." I strummed my lute. "You haven't heard *Sigurd's Race with Death* yet. It may help us find a willing buyer."

Sigurd cocked an ear, then gazed into the woods behind me.

"I should like to hear it." He stood up and walked towards the trees away from where he'd glanced. "Face this way and sing loud so I can hear you while I part company with some ale."

An unusual request, but I've had stranger.

The trick with *Sigurd's Race* is that it starts slowly and softly, almost at a dirge tempo, while the lyrics speak of speed.

My daughter's health is failing,
None can tell me why she's ailing.
Her doctor says that she
may never see another week.
But my daughter has a notion
that a distant wizard's potion
Will revive her if a hero rides
to bring her what she needs.

Sigurd leaped upon his steed
And cried "That potion's what she needs
I declare I shall not sleep

until the potion's in her hand.
Though the cure's a week away,
I will ride there in two days,
I'll return here with the cure
though I must travel halt the land."

Sigurd called from the woods "Can you sing louder?"

Luckily, the song's tempo picks up in the next verse as the song shifts to country dance rhythm.

Coal black hooves upon the pavement,
Feathered cap against the sky,
Sigurd rides away to gather
Potion so the girl won't die.

Two long days, he never falters,
Two long nights without a rest,
And the steed strains to run faster,
Each devoted to their quest.

With each verse, the tempo increases, but not so quickly as the listener wishes. They should be sitting at the edges of their stools by now, as Sigurd learns the Wizard needs a special flower that can only be found two day's ride from his hut. He gallops off and the rhythm becomes syncopated to match his steed's cadence.

By the mountains and the valleys
Through the village streets and alleys
Sigurd pauses and then rallies

As their destination looms

And he swiftly drops the reins,
Both hands gripping his mount's mane.
At a gallop, now he leans,
With his teeth he grabs the blooms.

I was surprised Sigurd didn't comment on this feat of courage and skill. How many heroes lean sideways from their galloping steed and pick flowers with their teeth? Not to mention the shift of scansion and verse style.

He didn't make a sound as I sang the next stanzas, continuing to increase the tempo and volume. As Sigurd rides back to save the girl, I stop playing the strings and just thump the lute body like a drum, as fast as I can in what my mentor called "the time signature of one."

Pound, Pound, Pound,
Hoofbeats thunder on the ground.
Crack, Crack, Crack,
Sigurd leaps off from its back.

Up the stairs he climbs the tower,
To the ailing damsel's bower,
It is near the fateful hour.
Has he won or has he lost?

I wondered where Sigurd was. His visit to the woodland latrine was taking much longer than it should. If he didn't come back soon he'd miss the last verse when the grateful father showers him with gold and praises the valiant steed.

Promised Rewards

As I started the last stanza, slowing to a majestic tempo and sonorous chords, I was interrupted by a thrashing in the woods behind me. Something shrieked like a wounded banshee as Sigurd shouted, "Got you, you little thief. Didn't hear me over the music, did you!"

I dropped my lute and twisted around in time to see Sigurd and a young man, little more than a boy, scuffling near the remains of the rabbit we'd been saving for breakfast.

As they wrestled, the boy sank his teeth into Sigurd's arm. Sigurd cuffed him above the ear, and the boy stopped fighting. He curled up on the ground, crying and whimpering. "Please, I'm so hungry. I just want a bite."

Sigurd stood. "Not a bite of me you don't. Not unless you want to lose those teeth. Stand up like a man, don't cower like a child!"

The boy stood, shaking slightly, and rubbing his head, but glaring defiantly at Sigurd. He appeared to be about twelve years old, with reddish brown hair tied by a leather strip. His homespun tunic fell to his knees above ragged leggings. He was skinny, as if he hadn't eaten in several days.

"A runaway," I guessed. "Looking for a life of adventure in the great wild world?"

The boy nodded. Something in the eyes made me study him. Our young boy might be more than he appeared.

"Sigurd, perhaps we can spare a swallow or two for our new friend."

Sigurd blinked at me, shocked at the suggestion. There was hardly enough meat for our breakfast, let alone to share. I sweetened the deal.

"I'm certain our fellow adventurer will care for our noble steed if we let him join us."

The boy studied the hell-beast and his eyes got wide. I couldn't tell if he were scared of our steed or attracted to it. Or maybe both.

Sigurd grunted. "If the lad can tend to that beast, he's welcome to do so." He pointed at the remains of the rabbit. "I can always get more tomorrow. Eat your fill."

The boy pulled a finger-width dagger from his belt and attacked the rabbit. In a few moments he'd skewered the meat and dragged several glowing coals away from the flames. He held the meat above the coals.

He saw us staring at him and glanced at his lap, embarrassed. "Meat cooks better over coals than over a fire. It cooks all the way through, instead of burning the outside and leaving the inside raw."

There was definitely more to our young companion than met the eye. I needed to distract Sigurd before he noticed it.

"Sigurd," I asked him. "What did you think of your *Race with Death*?"

He stared at me blankly. "My race with what? Was that what you were singing about? I wasn't listening."

I drew in my breath for a good solid tirade when a voice from the trail called "Ho, the camp. May I join you?"

Chapter Three

Sigurd and the Lost Princess

I GLANCED BACK and saw the lordling from the tavern bearing a pack on his shoulder. His cloak and shoes weren't made for dirt trails. He saw me and started.

"The bard? I thought you'd be singing in the tavern tonight?"

I decided to not mention our forced departure but play on his sympathy. A young lord might have more coins to spare.

"The innkeeper threw me out for driving off a customer. I thought you had a bed at the inn."

"Seems our host is adept at throwing folks out. I managed to insult his favorite niece. Since I'm unsuitable for her bed, I'm not good enough for his."

He dumped his sack onto the grass, A homespun tunic rolled out.

"At least I can get out of these fancy clothes and into something comfortable."

He yanked at the back of his doublet and cursed. "These things need a servant to get you in and out of them."

He turned to our new friend, who had finished cooking his rabbit and was stripping it from the skewer. "Boy, give me a hand getting out of these clothes."

The boy's eyes widened in sudden fear. "Um, I need to get more wood-- The--the fire..." He trotted into the woods away from the lordling.

Sigurd watched him scurry off and shrugged. "I've undressed men before. But not live ones." He fingered his dagger. "I normally just slit the laces, but I think I can manage to undress you."

The lordling blinked, but Sigurd was as good as his word at helping him disrobe. He had no trouble getting into the homespun and leather garments by himself. Once he was dressed, he swung his arms about and grinned. "This feels more like it!" He didn't look like a lordling now. He looked like the son of a prosperous farmer. Well-fed and well-muscled.

Sigurd studied him and announced, "You work for your living."

The farmer's son nodded. "Someone has to, eh? Fields don't plant themselves and herds needs herding."

He reached into his travel sack. "I've got some bread and

cheese. I'll share these, if you've got meat to spare." He glanced at the boy, who had come back carrying an armload of wood just after he'd finished dressing.

The boy nodded shyly. He split the cooked rabbit into two piles. The farmer pulled a couple slabs of bread and cheese from a leather bag he'd carried in the pack with his clothes. He scooped the smaller pile of meat onto his slab of bread. "You did the cooking; you should get the man's share."

The farm-boy took a huge bite from his bread and meat, chewed twice, glanced at me, then studied the fire.

"I apologize for costing you a bed. I should keep my ill temper to myself." He swallowed. "If you'd care to continue down this trail, we'll reach my father's lands. I can promise you a bed, an audience and the best ale within a two-day walk."

"And meals?" I prompted him.

He laughed. "Aye, we'll feed you. We've never let a guest starve and we don't intend to start." He waved at the boy. "We'll even feed you, youngster. Feed you better than rabbit meat!"

While he was talking, he finished the last of his meal. The boy had eaten half of his. I glanced at Sigurd, who nodded at me.

"We'll happily accept your offer. And since we'll be traveling together, we should share names. I'm called Bard, and this is the famous Sigurd."

The farmer glanced at Sigurd. "Rishley." He waved a greasy hand at himself. "The Sigurd of the 'Bandit Horde' and the 'Race with Death'?"

Sigurd beamed, "You've heard of me?"

"No," replied Rishley, "I've never even heard the songs. But I've heard *of* them." He glanced at the boy. "And you, youngster, do you have a name?"

The boy shrank back and swallowed hard. "Um, Dale."

Rishley smiled at him. "Well, you cook a good rabbit. You'll make some man a fine wife, eh?" He tapped Dale on the shoulder and the boy shrank back further.

I nodded at the boy, "You can travel south with us for a few days to taste adventure, or we can return you to your home. Which do you want?"

Dale's eyes darted between me and Rishley, then settled on the stallion. "I'll travel south. For a few days. Maybe."

Sigurd grunted. "A few days' worth of adventure. If they don't sit well with you, we'll see you safely back home. That's the fairest bargain you'll ever see."

The boy nodded and shrank back on himself even more. He was obviously embarrassed by the attention he was getting.

Sigurd broke the sudden silence. "Perhaps a song would help fill the evening."

I can resist anything except a request. I decided against *Sigurd and the Three Virgins*. I'd already sung *Sigurd's Race with Death*. If Sigurd wouldn't listen to it before, I wasn't going to waste it on him again.

I chose *Lament for Lost Loves*. A slow song, most often requested late at night by gentlemen who have reached an age where their past is brighter than their future. When sung at jig-tempo in a major key the doleful, maundering lyrics are silly and frivolous.

Rishley and Dale were uneasy when I began, but by the end of the song they both laughed as I jigged while singing the last verse.

Alas for the last lass that ever I'll love.
I never believed I'd be leaving her love.

Followed by a quickstep away from the fire and a joyful caper.

By then everyone was ready for rest. Sigurd and I each had our cloaks. Rishley shook a sleep-sack from his bag and rolled his cloak into a pillow. Dale watched us wrapping ourselves for warmth and then curled near the fire.

Rishley noticed this and sat up.

"This won't do," he said. "The fire won't keep you warm. It'll barely heat one side of you." He held his sleep-sack open. "Come, crawl in here and you'll be warm."

Dale's eyes got large, and he shook his head. "I'll be fine. I've been sleeping like this since-- all my life."

Rishley tossed his cloak at the boy. "Here. At least take this. I don't want you freezing to death before I find out how well you can cook a breakfast."

Dale squared his shoulders in rebellion and started to speak. His breath puffed white in front of him. He considered the cloud and decided he'd rather be warm.

"Thank you, sir," he muttered, wrapping himself in the cloak and folding the edge over his head.

I woke shortly after dawn dreaming of baked apples.

The dream was so intense, I swore I smelled their warm sweetness. In fact, I still smelled them when I was certain I was awake.

I opened one eye, and saw the boy was no longer curled near the fire. Instead, four apples rested near the coals.

The boy was next to our steed, slicing an apple with his dainty little dagger. Our hell-beast gratefully accepted each apple slice and let him rub the white star on its forehead. It seemed to be enjoying the lad's attention.

Sigurd had lost a sleeve trying to gentle the beast.

Rishley woke next. He sniffed audibly. "Why, our little man *can* cook a breakfast!" He grinned. "If you were a girl I'd marry you just for making this meal!"

Dale glowered at him. " *If* I were a gir--!" He shouted and stopped. "I didn't make them for you. I made them for me, Bard and Sigurd, but there was an extra."

Rishley observed the apple in the boy's hand and the happy mount. "Two extras, I'll warrant. But I won't complain about getting a horse's breakfast leftovers." He rolled out of his sack and juggled one of the hot apples.

"Watch out!" Dale barked. "You'll dump the stuffing. See the leaves there. Use them to pick up the apples so you don't burn your fingers."

Rishley had dumped some stuffing from the apple onto his leggings. He dropped the fruit onto a large maple leaf and scooped the stuffing into his mouth.

"You filled them with chestnuts, didn't you! Mmm. I might marry you even if you aren't a girl!"

Dale fed the last of the apple to the horse and showed

him empty hands. Our monster gently butted his head against the boy's chest as he rubbed its ears and murmured something soothing.

By now, Sigurd was awake and holding an apple wrapped in a green leaf. He bit into it and burned his lip.

Dale scooped the last two apples onto leaves and handed one to me. His dainty dagger sliced off a sliver. He blew on it and popped it into his mouth.

"I've had better," he said. "But this will do."

Sigurd pulled a seax as long as a short sword from his belt and sliced off a quarter of the apple. He popped it into his mouth and his eyes grew wide.

"Small bites, so they cool." Dale chided him. "Haven't you ever eaten fresh baked apples?"

Sigurd swallowed hard and took a slurp from his flask. "The innkeeper bakes them at dawn. I generally eat them long afterward. Where did you learn to cook like this? Were you apprenticed to a baker?"

Dale glanced past Sigurd into the woods and huddled in on himself. "Umm, I've been inside a kitchen before." He glanced around. His eye lighted on the steed, eying him hopefully. "What do you call your horse?"

Sigurd grunted. "*I* call him Mis--"

"Midnight," I interrupted him. "We call him Midnight Star. For his black coat and the star on the forehead."

Announcing that the animal's name started with Misbegotten and went downhill from there would not be a selling point.

Sigurd blinked at me. "Of course, Midnight Star." He

popped the last of his apple into his mouth. "Good breakfast. But we'll need to be moving."

Sigurd and I travel light. Breaking camp consisted of kicking out the fire. Rishley shoved his fancy clothes and sleep sack into his shoulder pack. The lad had nothing to pack or carry, so he watched us prepare, then swept a branch over the ashes. We were ready to fare onward within moments of finishing the apples.

Sigurd grabbed the horse's lead, but the hell-beast snapped at him and backed away, eyes wide and ears flat against his head.

Rishley laughed, "Mayhap the boy is the better man for this job. The stallion seems to prefer his company."

Sigurd glared at him. "I've never met a horse I couldn't--"

Rishley swallowed his laugh. "I'd say you've never met many horses. This beast is not some plow-horse or lady's gelding. He's a stallion, with pride and a mind of his own. It was obvious as soon as I came into your camp last night."

He walked past Sigurd, cooing to the animal as he approached it slowly holding his hand out. The beast's ears raised a finger's width as he edged towards Rishley to sniff his hand. While he snuffled Rishley's right hand, Rishley lifted his left to the steed's neck and scratched it vigorously. Our steed relaxed. Even I recognized the tension leaching away as it blinked and brought its ears erect.

Rishley nodded to Dale. "You bought his favor with an apple. I'll wager he'll let you lead him."

Dale edged up, giving Rishley more leeway than the horse and took the rope. He tugged gently and Midnight took a step towards him. Within moments we were trooping down the lane, Sigurd first with Rishley and I walking abreast each other. The lad bringing up the rear, holding the rope halter as the horse ambled behind him. He didn't need the lip-loop Sigurd required to lead our spawn of Satan.

Rishley interested me. Farmer or lordling, he knew horses. His red woolen cloak--from the continent, I'd wager--and white linen tunic indicated he had money. Perhaps he'd like to buy a mount.

"You certainly know your horses," I offered, and paused for him to answer.

"Me? No. Me Da is the hostler; Earl Acton's head groom for twenty years. The earl gifted him with land so he could breed and train them from birth. The earl comes to our very home every year to buy a new horse. Won't ride anything me Da didn't train."

"So, your da might like to buy a horse."

"Well, he asked me to see to a bay mare that was ready to breed while I was up to town, but I'm guessing you mean a black stallion with a white forehead?" Rishley nudged me. "I think that horse already has a master, but me Da could be interested. Your stallion needs to be tamed and trained before it's fit for a saddle."

"So, were you up here scouting for horseflesh?" I was determined to figure this man out.

"No. I was on a fool's quest seeking a different type of filly."

I raised my eyebrow.

"Looking for a wife. I saw the squire's daughter at last winter's dance, and... well, it was a foolish thought. Her father approved of me, but Miss High-and-Mighty preferred running hiding to being courted by a groom's son."

Dale had edged closer while we discussed the horse, listening intently.

"You certainly appeared the lordling," I replied.

"That's me Da. He said that if I intended to court above my station, I should dress above my station. I guess a well-dressed fowl is still a fowl."

"Garbed like some foolish fop," Dale interrupted. "As if I-- a woman wants to wed a fool who wastes his money on linen instead of wearing good homespun wool."

Rishley laughed. "So, lad, I should come to you for courtship advice, eh? Me Da may have been wrong, or he may have been right. Either way, he managed to get himself a wife. How many women have you wed?"

The lad and stallion dropped back a few paces. Rishley was quiet for a few moments.

"Do you think the lad was right?" he asked me. "Could she have objected to my clothes, not my parentage?" He shook his head. "Probably not. The lad's too young to know much of women, hmm?"

I changed the subject back to our horse, extolling his virtues, which I borrowed from the best ballads of rider and steed.

The rest of the day passed uneventfully. Rishley assured us we'd find no taverns until we reached his father's lands, but he knew a camp site with good water and another apple tree.

Sigurd detoured into the woods as we neared the site and joined us bearing a brace of rabbits and a hat full of mushrooms. He tossed them to the lad to prepare while he chopped a fallen log into firewood and kindling.

The lad cooked the rabbit and mushrooms on spits. Truly, hunger is the best spice. The wild sage and bay leaves the lad added to the mix didn't hurt either.

Once we'd eaten, I tuned my lute and played *Sigurd and the Three Thieves*. When I finished, the lad's eyes were wide, staring at Sigurd, while Rishley grinned.

"Felled three with a single blow," he marveled. "That's very impressive axe work."

Sigurd examined his feet. "Well, they were three small villains."

Rishley laughed. "I'll wager they were." He waved at the stack of firewood. "I'll not dispute your skill with an axe. Could you split me something as thin as a roof-shake?"

Sigurd was as willing to show his skill as any other man. After two swipes of his axe, he presented Rishley with a shake tapering from as thick as your thumb to barely thicker than a fingernail.

"Perfect," Rishley agreed, as he applied his dagger to the narrow edge of the shake.

I played *Blazon of an Evening Sky*, a quiet song for the end of the day while he worked on the shake. Sigurd dozed and the lad petted our suddenly tame hell-beast. He came back as I finished the last verse.

"I think the horse has something in its fur." he said.

"Coat," Rishley corrected. "It's a burr. I noticed it this

morning." He lifted the shake he'd been carving, displaying a series of triangular teeth in the narrow edge. "What does this look like to you?"

Dale stared at it. "It's like a misshapen comb."

"Misshapen!" He examined the shake. "Well, I've done better when I had more time. Anyhow, you should learn to care for a horse. You're not man enough to adventure with these vagabonds forever and grooming is a useful skill for a lad. You hold the head while I work out the worst burr, then I'll show you how to comb the rest of the burrs out of his coat."

Dale held our monster's head while Rishley worked at the burr with comb and dagger. After several beats, Rishley commented "Better suited to that lady's toy you carry." They switched places. By dusk, our steed looked cleaner than I'd ever seen it. Rishley came back to the fire while Dale worked knots out of the stallion's mane.

He assessed the lad and stallion and observed. "It's not a bad animal, but it's not trained, and it's been mistreated."

"A good horse for a man who can train them, then."

"We'll talk to me Da tomorrow." He wandered off to gather apples, and I began composing a new thrilling saga, *Sigurd and the Lost Princess*. I was considering a dragon or an ogre, and counting likely rhymes for each when a hopeful Rishley returned carrying a double handful of apples. He told Dale to let the animal sleep, and we settled down for the night.

The next noon saw us at Rishley's farmstead. His Da, aptly named Ryder, was a blocky man whose long rectangular face matched his horses. He welcomed us with a pitcher of excellent ale and a downcast expression when Rishley admitted he would not be wedding the squire's daughter.

"There be other fillies in the field." he finally conceded, running a work-worn hand through his bristly gray beard. He was still talking softly as he and Rishley went to study our beast.

When he came back he announced that Sigurd and I were welcome to guest as long as we wished. He shuffled his feet as he admitted his farmstead was too new to offer the accommodations we were used to.

Any roof is better than I'm used to, but I did not mention this.

A small steading has more work than workers. Soon we were helping with chores, Sigurd at a woodpile, me weeding a garden and Dale in the kitchen.

Ryder set an adequate table. Nothing fancy, but plenty of stew, heavy bread-trenchers the size of a double-fist and an ale that lived up to Rishley's description; dark brown, rich and nutty. The kind of ale a man who works hard wants at the end of a day.

After hours in the farmstead's fields, Sigurd and I were both willing to cut the guesting short and continue our travels.

Rishley's father was not surprised at the decision. He nodded to Dale. "My son says you've got a knack for horses. If you want, I'll offer you a bed, and train you. I don't brag, but you'll find no better groom to learn from."

Dale stared at his empty plate for a full measure, then at Sigurd and me. "Are you heading north?" he asked.

I nodded. "If you've had enough adventuring, we'll take you back to your master."

Dale nodded back, staring at me, but avoiding Rishley's and Ryder's eyes.

Rishley's father shrugged. "Better be a good master you've got lad. I could train you to be groom for an earl, mayhap even the king."

When the last of the gravy had soaked into the last trencher, Rishley glanced to me. "I promised you an audience." He waved at the small table, his da, two field-carls and the house-carl. "Will this do?"

His Da frowned at him. "These are guests. I'll not ask my guest to sing for his meal."

I stood and bowed graciously. "You need not ask, good master. A bard lives to sing. A willing ear is all the encouragement I need."

Ryder did not refuse my offer. In distant holdings everyone is starved for entertainment. He and his carls had likely recited every Edda they knew so many times they had each memorized them.

I tuned my lute and sang. A full tavern, loud with conversation, is where a bard earns coins, but a small, attentive audience is what fills his soul.

Halfway through singing *Sigurd and The Band of Bandits*, I noticed that nobody was watching me. They were gazing behind me. I glanced back and saw Sigurd pantomiming the actions described in the song, sneaking up upon the bandits, leaping upon them and valiantly slaying them.

I didn't interrupt my song but resolved to discuss this with Sigurd. For ten years I'd been traveling and performing by myself. I had absolutely no interest in becoming the musical accompaniment for a mummer.

I finished the evening singing *Sigurd's Race with Death*. Sigurd, Rishley and Dale yawned and left after the twentieth verse, but Ryder stayed to the end. He chuckled at intervals and laughed out loud as I described Sigurd picking the flowers with his teeth.

When I finished he clapped briefly and told me, "I can see you know nothing of horses, but you've got a grand imagination!" He picked up a candle and dripped a bit of wax onto a small chunk of wood. He pressed his ring into it and gave me the token with his signet embossed.

"The earl loves his horses and loves a good song. Show him this. He'll give you a warm bed and a good meal for a song about riding all night and gathering daisies in your teeth. I daresay his youngest will be in the paddock trying it before you've finished."

I slept deeply, dreaming about a winter spent in an earl's warm keep without Sigurd. Once we'd returned the lad to his master, Sigurd and I would part company.

Chapter Four

Sigurd and the Wandering Knight

IN THE MORNING, Sigurd and I were ready to leave before breakfast. To be accurate, before being asked to help with the first chores. Ryder's morning meal changed our mind about an early leave-taking: eggs, bread, cheese, apples, and more ale. Ryder's family and carls worked hard but they ate almost well enough to make up for it.

Over breakfast, we discussed the horse. I invented new virtues, while Rishley's father described all the problems he found, most notably the lack of training.

After a great deal of discussion, we settled on five Mercian silver pennies and two days' worth of cheese, dried meat and bread.

As we prepared to leave, Ryder called to his son. "The lad has no cloak. Fetch him your old one. It's too small for you but will suit him."

The brown woolen cloak barely reached Rishley's thighs. It was large on the lad but appeared serviceable. The weather had turned chilly, and he'd need a cloak by evening.

Rishley joined us as we left the farmstead. He motioned me to let Sigurd and Dale lead, while he and I trailed behind.

"Me Da knows his horses."

I nodded.

"He's a bit of a harder trader than he needs be."

I nodded again.

"If you and Sigurd ever return, we've got a roof and meals for you."

I thanked him. I'd not be eager to work so hard, but it's good to know where a meal can be found.

"Some bardic wisdom for you," I whispered. "When you've saddle-trained that hell-beast you bought, ride it north and call on the squire's daughter again. You may be better received."

He smiled and we shook hands. I rejoined Sigurd and Dale, and we headed north.

Dale kicked a stick from the trail, glanced behind us, kicked another stick, then asked where we'd be camping.

I suggested the same places we'd stopped before. He sighed in relief.

"Do you have to recover something hidden near our first campsite before you go back to your master?" I asked.

He nodded.

"Linen or homespun?"

"Homespun!" he blurted, then took a deep breath. "I mean, of course."

Sigurd laughed. "No secrets among adventurers. I've wrestled both boys and girls. I know the difference."

Dale blushed.

I grinned at him. "No boy ever carried such a dainty dagger or blushed so prettily. We've known who you were from the first night."

Dale glanced behind us.

"He never twigged to it," I assured her. "But he'll be back, riding Midnight, in a few months. You might not let him know you've already met."

Sigurd was still chuckling and glanced at me. "Silver pennies for a horse we couldn't ride, a gold piece for returning our 'lad' here, and a few days of not eating rabbit. I told you teaming up with me would be good for you."

I remembered my terror of being killed by bandits, then being run out of a town behind a half-tamed horse. Still, in the interest of a pleasant jaunt on a fine fall day I didn't mention those incidents.

Overnight, the leaves had turned golden brown. They tumbled to the earth like huge snowflakes with every breeze. The sun was butter-yellow and warm, but it would be a cool evening.

Now that she wasn't hiding her sex, Dale skipped

through the leaves joyfully, kicking up brown and yellow fountains. Sigurd marched deliberately, leaving a straight furrow behind him.

I strolled thoughtfully, considering my future.

When the weather turns cold my thoughts turn to finding a warm castle for the winter. This is preferable to wandering from tavern to tavern in the cold rain and snow.

Fresh white snow is a fine metaphor for pure, virginal love, but I prefer snow in my lyrics to snow in my boots.

I was also brooding about Sigurd's miming to my song last night. Our bargain was to travel together and share money he earned. I had no need for a partner without musical skill. I did not intend to train him to entertain an audience, or in the gentle art of being persuasive without being obvious.

It was time we went our separate ways.

Once we returned Dale to her father and collected the gold piece, I'd part company with Sigurd. I didn't know where he would go, but I intended to visit the earl and see how far I could stretch his hospitality.

Thanks to Sigurd's attempts to hurry us we reached our campsite before the sun touched the horizon. Another traveler was setting up camp. The wood Sigurd had chopped burned brightly as the wayfarer split more.

"Good Even, trail-mate!" I called. "Would you enjoy some merry company?"

The woodchopper spun, pulling a dagger from his belt. He wore a polished leather cuirass. I saw a metal cap lying on the ground nearby. When he saw us waiting, holding no weapons and hands at our sides, he visibly relaxed.

"Well met." he called back. "Come and enjoy the fire. I've some bread and venison to share." The armsman was a few years older than I, with close-cropped, light brown hair still matted and sweaty from wearing his armored cap.

Dale glanced at the slab of meat he had sitting on a rock near the fire and offered to cook. As she glared at Sigurd and me, I winked back. We'd not reveal her secret.

Sigurd volunteered to collect apples and mushrooms as Dale began slicing the venison.

I studied our campmate. "I'm known as Bard the Lutist," I told him, "and my companions are Dale and the famous Sigurd."

He studied me intently. "Ector." he replied. "You are a bard?"

I nodded.

"Are you trained to read and write?"

Few bards learn to record their songs. Most rely on their memory. Having been raised in a monastery, I'd been trained to read and write a bit, despite my best efforts.

I nodded again, wondering why that skill interested him.

He frowned and pulled a scrap of parchment from his wallet. "I'm charged to deliver this message to Ryder the Groom. But, neither he nor I read, so I don't know what to tell him."

I stared at him. "You were sent to deliver a message you couldn't read to a man who can't read?"

Sigurd returned carrying a double-handful of apples and mushrooms before Ector answered. Dale had sliced the venison into thumb-sized chunks and began arranging the meat, apple slices and mushrooms on skewers.

Ector admired the preparation. "The lad knows how to cook. Is he yours?"

Dale bristled at the suggestion she was a slave. I didn't want to explain that she was a runaway we were returning. It would be easier to believe we aided her escape. I changed the discussion as deftly as I could.

"I read church Latin." I told Ector. "I should be able to read your message."

He handed me the parchment, upside down. I righted it and puzzled out the words as he explained.

"I was to get the message read by the squire a day north of here, to have less time to forget it. But he was too distressed to even glance at the parchment and sent me off. His daughter has run away. He offered me a gold piece if I should find and return her."

"And two if you'd keep her?" I jested.

Ector blinked at me. "Why should I want to keep her? I've no means to keep a wife."

Dale raised her eyes. "Some folks lack the wit to recognize humor." I assumed she meant Ector, until she paused and glared at me. "They should stick to their music and not attempt jests."

I directed my attention back to the parchment. "It says you are to request Groom Ryder to have a pony trained by spring. It is to be presented to Earl Acton's youngest son. It should be trained to respond to bridle and leg commands, like a warhorse." Ector repeated this. "It also warns the groom to be wary of strangers. There are three villains ravaging the roads and villages."

Ector scanned Sigurd, Dale, and me. "Three villains?" he asked. His hand descending back to his dagger.

He could not read, but he could count. At least, he could count to three. I knew we were not the three bandits, but I needed to convince Ector of this before our lives became too interesting.

"Sigurd, would those be the three bandits we drove off last week?"

Sigurd nodded at me. "Yes, *I* drove three bandits away from Barleytown You must sing of my exploits once we've eaten."

Dale was kind enough to distract us by announcing our dinner was ready.

Dale's cooking skill allayed Ector's suspicion faster than my attempt to describe us as heroes who drove off villains. Her meal convinced him we were good company to have fallen in with. The venison with apples and mushrooms pleased me as well.

With a full belly, I was willing to forgive Sigurd for taking credit for driving away the bandits.

Almost.

I'd never been a hero before, and although it was short-lived, I enjoyed the pleasure while it lasted. I doubted I'd have a chance to be a hero again.

Bards create heroes, but we are seldom heroes ourselves. In truth, being a hero is dangerous and I prefer comfort to danger.

So, having eaten, I tuned my lute and began proclaiming

the great feats of Sigurd. In deference to Dale, I skipped *Sigurd and the Three Virgins* and sang *Sigurd and the Band of Bandits*.

Ector was unfamiliar with my sagas. By the time I'd reached the middle of *Sigurd's Race with Death* he was leaning forward, eyes wide and hands clenching his knees as Sigurd re-mounted his horse to seek the fabled flowers of healing.

I plucked a verse with ornamentations to rest my voice and build the tension. As I inhaled for the next verse Sigurd whispered in Ector's ear "The next part is best. I gallop through the fields picking flowers with my teeth."

Songs have a magic in them. They can make the imaginary more than real. It takes practice and patience to coax a song's magic out of the air. But a song's magic is timid. With the least disturbance, it vanishes as if it were never there.

With Sigurd's whisper, my music's magic faded. Ector relaxed and enjoyed the rest of the song, but it did not stir him the way it had. The loss of the magic drained my enthusiasm for playing as well. I finished the song and set down my lute, resolving once more to have words with Sigurd and travel alone in the future.

"Time for wanderers to rest," I announced, and wrapped my cloak about me. I lay down on one side of Dale. Sigurd took the other side, as Dale draped herself in Rishley's cloak.

In the morning I repeated Ector's message to him, so that he might deliver it to Ryder, and we parted company. Once we were away from the messenger, Dale shed her shy demeanor and was once more a bouncing young girl.

After spending the night wrapped in Rishley's cloak, she appreciated the gift. She kicked her way through the golden oak leaves and raised a corner of the cloak to my face.

"Does it smell of Rishley?" she asked.

I sniffed warily. "It smells of horse," I replied. "Which may be the same thing."

She was serious for a brief moment. "I'd like to keep the cloak," she said, "but I don't know how to explain to my father how I got it. Could you tell him you gave it to me?"

I examined at my patched, travel worn garments. Rishley's old cloak was well-used, but not as well-used as mine. It was also too small for me.

"You father wouldn't believe I had a cloak to gift you with, but--"

"I can gift it to you," Sigurd interrupted. "I can claim it as a treasure I found when I drove off the bandits."

It was a good suggestion. I'd been about to make it myself. I looked forward to being able to finish my sentences once I was traveling alone.

We walked briskly. Dale was as anxious to get home as she'd been eager to leave it a few days earlier.

We reached the clearing where we'd first met when the sun was near the zenith.

Dale surveyed the campsite, then glanced at Sigurd and me.

"Will you wait here for me. I... I need to collect some things." She paused. "Promise you won't follow? I'll be right back."

We nodded as she slid into the woods and vanished.

She vanished for a long time.

I began to wonder if she'd slipped back home and deprived us of our reward when a young lady stepped out of the woods. Her red-brown hair was wrapped demurely in a lace snood. She wore a pale gray homespun gown, belted tightly around her waist. As a boy, he was skinny and frail. As a girl she was slender and lovely.

Sigurd and I both stared.

She stopped and blushed. "Am I dressed properly?"

We both nodded. Sigurd spoke first. "Very properly," he agreed.

I swallowed hard. "Um, how do we present you to your father. It's been four days. He'd have every reason to believe we abducted you for...hmm... Maybe we can tell him you got lost and we found you?"

She snorted. "Lost in my woods? I know this forest as well as I know my own kitchen. Mayhap you found me heading east and convinced me to return to my ailing father?"

"You left an ailing father?" I was shocked that a daughter would abandon a sick parent.

"Of course not! He was never sick a day in his life." she laughed.

Sigurd grinned. "I could truss you up and carry you home over my shoulder."

"And I could bite your fingers clean off if you tried."

Sigurd had a young man's pride in his strength. He grimaced, "The day I can't out-wrestle a wen--"

This dispute needed to be redirected before we were

chasing our reward through woods she knew better than we did.

"If your father reconsidered betrothing you to Rishley, would you return?"

She considered my suggestion for a moment and nodded.

"Then, Sigurd shall go to your father and announce he has found you, but you won't return unless the betrothal is canceled. Once your father agrees, Sigurd will return, and we'll escort you home."

Sigurd was obviously still enjoying thoughts of wrestling with our lass, but he nodded and strode toward the village. I admired his pace, as long as I wasn't required to match it. While he visited her father, I spent a delightful half hour chatting with Dale.

Mostly, we chatted about Rishley.

She was guessing how long it would take him to saddle-train Midnight when Sigurd strode into the clearing. He was smiling and pleased with himself.

"The marriage is canceled!" he called. "We can take you home. I told him we found you deep in the woods and promised to intercede if you'd come with us."

The trip from the clearing to Dale's home was short. The squire met us at the door. He had the broad shoulders and broader belly of an armsman who had earned the right to live well. He glared at Sigurd and me and then studied his daughter.

"Are you well?" he demanded. "Did they..." his eyebrows met as he glared at Sigurd and me.

"I'm fine father. These gentlemen, Bard" she dipped her head at me, "and Sigurd," she nodded at Sigurd, "treated me with grace and respect."

"Good. That is, they told you the marriage to the farmer is canceled." His shoulders and hands relaxed. He no longer stood like he was on a battlefield.

She smiled and thanked him.

"In the future, you might tell me if a lad fails to please you, rather than showing your heels."

She nodded again, demure, and contrite.

He stood aside, and she slipped into the house.

"I'll fix supper for you and our guests." she murmured.

The squire glanced fondly at her, then faced Sigurd and me. As soon as his back was turned, Dale grinned at us and skipped from the room.

"You have my thanks. It appears you'll be getting a free meal for returning my daughter. Ermindale is an excellent cook."

Sigurd bobbed his head, "We kn--"

I nudged him and interrupted. "We've heard that. She promised us a meal if we escorted her home."

"And a meal you shall have. A meal fit for a king. Or at least fit for a squire and two wanderers who have been of service." Once assured of his daughter's safety, and that her rescuers were not knaves, he changed from the protective father to the gracious host.

He led us into his common room where a shoulder-high foundation of field stones supported the rough log walls. A double-mouthed fireplace, shared with the kitchen, warmed the spacious room which was dwarfed by a trestle table large enough for twelve. Strips of leather, knives and punches covered most of its surface. The squire did more than steward his land and daughter.

There was an open space the end of the table wide enough for three people to eat. And a fine meal it was. Ermindale was truly a mistress of her kitchen. She did not eat with us, of course, but kept a steady stream of soups, meats, breads, sauces, and even a pitcher of honey-sweetened wine sent to the table.

Sigurd and I made certain her efforts were not wasted, keeping our mouths too busy for speech.

Finally, we had eaten all we could manage. Perhaps we'd eaten all the kitchen contained.

Sigurd looked up from his plate to our host. "I understood there is a reward for returning your daughter."

The squire had been counting dishes as they passed our palates. "And you and your friend have certainly received a fine meal for your service."

"A gold piece was mentioned."

"A gold piece! I never--"

"Your brother, the tavern keeper, told us you had offered a gold piece for your daughter's return, as did the earl's messenger."

The squire shifted his feet. "I might have said something like that in the heat of the moment. But, surely, you understand--"

"I understand you offered a reward."

"Perhaps in jest. A jest between a man and his brother."

Sigurd scowled darkly. "Oath-breakers are not well thought of."

Before Sigurd finished speaking, the squire was on his feet, leaning forward, hands on the table in front of Sigurd. The gracious host had vanished, and the man who commanded armies was back. "I'll not be called an oath-breaker at my own table by the likes of--"

Sigurd was rising to the challenge when I put my hand on his thigh and pressed him back down. He hadn't gotten his weight over his feet yet, so he sat back hard.

"Good squire," I smiled sweetly. "We are not greedy men. None can deny that your daughter is a gem beyond reckoning. In returning such a treasure to your household we have done you a great service." I patted my stomach. "This meal is a grand reward, but in returning your daughter, we have secured many such meals for you. Surely, more meals like this are worth a more generous reward."

The squire paused and glared at us, his eyes bouncing between me and the door to the kitchen. I kept my hand on Sigurd's lap to remind him to keep silent.

For the second time in a single day Sigurd's brashness had come close to costing us our reward. I was relishing my plans to travel alone again. That is, I'd travel alone once I acquired my share of the reward.

Our host settled back onto his bench.

"I'll not quibble over my daughter's value. She is truly a gem beyond price."

He glanced at Sigurd. "Ermindale called you Sigurd. Are you the Sigurd who drove the vandals from Barleytown?"

He glanced to the west. Sigurd followed his eyes and nodded.

"A gold piece is a lot of money in a small holding, but I may be able to make you an offer worth more than a gold piece."

Sigurd and I leaned forward. The squire knew how to command our attention.

He waved his hand grandly in a circle. "It being harvest season, my villagers have gathered their wealth. I must send a goodly share of it to the earl. The road from here to the earl is safe, but it would be worth more than a gold piece to have my taxes guarded until they reach Earl Acton's castle."

Sigurd grunted. "More than a gold piece?"

The squire smiled. "The earl is a generous man and much richer than I. Surely more than a single gold piece."

He appealed to our greed, but my plan to visit the earl's castle without Sigurd hinged on Sigurd *not* traveling there with me.

"A promise of gold never filled a man's stomach." I would remember the phrase. It sounded like an ancient aphorism despite my having just invented it.

Our host paused. "Excellent point," he conceded. My hopes for silver coins and parting company with Sigurd rose. "I'll have Ermindale prepare food for you. I'll give you one of my special smoked hams. They are the best hams in the valley. One of them will feed a family for a week." He glanced at our plates. "Or you two for a day."

My hopes collapsed. Sigurd and I would travel together to the earl's castle. I'd have to wait to be free of him.

Settling the details took longer than I expected. By the time we'd agreed to guard the squire's taxes in exchange for a ham, a few bronze coins and whatever the earl granted us, the sun had set.

As we discussed the details, Ermindale returned from the kitchen and perched on a three-legged stool near the fire, embroidering the hem of a linen gown. As soon as her father, Sigurd and I shook hands she stood.

"Good bard," she asked, eyes cast down demurely, "Would you be willing to share a small song with us? Do you know a song of a hero? Or of a horse?"

Her father stared at her and frowned. "Surely any bard knows at least one hero saga, but there's no sagas of horses." He glanced back to me, "I'd not ask." he said. "Not of a guest. But I'll not refuse, either."

I lifted my lute and motioned towards my throat. "There has been much dry talking, perhaps a bit of moistening would help."

I tuned my lute while Ermindale gathered cups of wine and ale. She grinned at Sigurd and me whenever her father wasn't watching. She greatly enjoyed her joke that we had first met this afternoon, not shared several days together.

Turnabout is fair play, and a bard is a master of jests. Despite certain claims to the contrary.

"I know several songs of heroes and horses. There is *Odysseus Tricks the Trojans*, and the tale of *Alexander and Bucephalus*, but this song might amuse you more."

I strummed a single dark chord and let it ring to silence.

Slow the ogre stalked her.

Promised Rewards

Slow the ogre treads.
Slow the sunlight dwindles
As the sun drops to its bed.

When the princess felt the evening chill
Come creeping through her cloak.
Twas then she knew she'd wandered
Much too far from hearth and home.

Round eyes
In the forest.
Huge eyes
Coming closer.
Large feet,
Treading silent.
Huge hands
Reaching forth.

Small feet, fast feet, shod in dainty shoes.
Large feet, slow feet, chasing after food.

Except for my song, the room was silent. Ermindale's eyes got as large as the ogre's and even Sigurd held his tongue.

After six verses of racing through the woods, the lost princess encountered Sigurd, who attacks the ogre and defeats it in just ten more verses.

But now both Sigurd and the princess are lost. As they wander aimlessly, they encounter a large black dragon.

Tail slashing, teeth gnashing,

71

C. Flynt

Claws as sharp as swords.
Mouth snapping, scales rapping.
Hear it rushing towards
Sigurd and the princess,
Will he live or will he die?
If he can't defeat the dragon,
Then in honor he will lie.

Then the dragon sees the princess,
And the dragon slows its tread.
Now it crawls upon its belly,
'Neath her hand it slips its head.
She caresses it behind the ear,
And mounts upon its back.
And the dragon bears her homeward,
Leaving Sigurd with his axe.

Ermindale's father looked up from the fire when I finished. "The dragon takes the princess home and leaves the hero behind? Not much of a song. A true hero would slay the dragon, carry her home and collect the reward."

I stared guilelessly into his eyes. "True, but I sing the tales as they are, not as I would have them be."

He grunted, and announced it was time for bed. He left the room as Ermindale collected pallets and furs for us to sleep on and piled them near the fire.

"I liked the one about the horse better," she said. "Especially the flowers. But the dragon was nice. Did it have a white star on its forehead?"

I smirked and nodded as she kissed me on the cheek.

"Good dreams, friend Bard." She tripped over to Sigurd and kissed him also. "And friend Sigurd."

She left the room and I fell asleep dreaming of dragons, maidens, and leaving Sigurd behind.

Chapter Five

Sigurd and the Three Ogres

IN THE MORNING we were eager for another of Dale's breakfasts, but before the table was set the squire announced that the taxes were ready to be transported. He observed pointedly how it would be better to leave sooner rather than later.

I should have expected the wealth and taxes from a small squire's hold would not be a sack of gold and silver. The taxes were the cart filled with foodstuffs we'd seen on our first visit to the village. The wheel had been replaced, and the cart loaded with sacks of grain, cheeses, smoked hams, a few casks of ale and lots of turnips. The cart was attached to a huge brown horse, complacently chomping the grass growing alongside the road. The steed's head was nearly the size of my torso and its hooves were as large as a steel buckler.

"You'll not need to bring the horse and cart back." the squire announced as if he were doing us a favor. "They are part of the taxes."

Sigurd glanced at the horse and shook his head. "The earl appreciates fine horses. He won't be pleased with this lump."

The squire bristled. "That's the best dray horse in this county. She'll pull a cart or plow all day with no rest. And what's more, she will not get you run out of any villages. She's so gentle, my daughter rides her."

It was time to divert the discussion before Sigurd angered our host further. "Sigurd is ready to guard your treasure. Where is the cart's driver?"

The squire raised his eyebrows in surprise. "Why, you two are the drivers, of course. What better way to guard the taxes than to be in the front seat."

This time Sigurd bristled. I didn't blame him, but I also didn't want him to back out of this deal. The sooner we reached the earl and collected our payment, the sooner we would part company.

"Among Sigurd's many talents, he is a master at handling horses." I climbed into the cart. "We'd best be starting. I'll take the first watch while you drive."

Sigurd glared at the squire, then at me. He opened and closed his mouth several times. He finally shrugged and stepped onto the cart. "If this is our bargain, it's the bargain I'll keep," he muttered, flicking the reins, and spurring the horse into a slow plod.

76

He turned to me. "There will be plenty of time to teach you to handle a horse." he muttered. He made it sound like a threat. I'm certain that's how he meant it.

As soon as the cart was moving, the squire was back indoors, probably to enjoy his breakfast. I was lamenting the missed meal when we slowly turned a corner and found Ermindale standing in the road.

"You left before breakfast!" she called. "So, I brought you baked apples and eggs. I can't send my fellow adventurers off with no food." She giggled. "I know it wasn't an adventure for you two vagabonds, but for a squire's daughter it was a grand lark. Thank you for keeping my secret from Rishley and my father." She shoved a wicker basket up to me. "I must run. Father will miss me."

As I accepted the basket she dashed down a deer trail that must have led to the squire's farmstead by a shorter route than the road followed.

I glanced at Sigurd, who stared at the trail with a slack jaw. "She moves quickly." He finally said.

"Like a deer," I agreed. "Would you prefer apple or egg?"

He grinned at me. "Or? I'd prefer apple *and* egg."

Dale had packed enough food for both of us.

We ate in silence. I didn't know what Sigurd was thinking, but I was still bristling over him interrupting my performances and his lack of tact.

"The squire would have given us the gold piece if you hadn't stopped me," he grunted as he swallowed the last egg.

"You can't eat a man's food and call him an oath-breaker.

Especially when the oath wasn't sworn to us."

"If I'd waved my axe at him, we'd have gotten a gold piece."

"If you'd waved your axe at him, he'd have had us whipped out of town."

"We still should have held out for silver coins. Not another trip with a horse." He flicked the reins for the fifth time in as many minutes. The horse did not change its pace.

"At least we're riding, not walking. You said you'd watched a horse's hindquarters in the past."

"And swore I'd never watch them again." He lapsed into silence.

I tuned my lute and continued working on *Sigurd and the Lost Princess*. I wasn't happy with the real world Sigurd, but the Sigurd of legend was how I earned my meals.

It was almost sunset when I finished the verse in which Sigurd tracks the Lost Princess, but the dragon finds her first. I was staring thoughtfully into the distance, hoping to see the next verse, when a man stepped into the road ahead of us. He was as tall as Sigurd and more heavily built with dark, rough-cut hair and beard. He spun his quarterstaff in the manner of an expert.

"Uh-Oh," Sigurd muttered as he passed me the reins and grabbed for his axe.

A second man stepped from the woods beside me. He also wielded a quarterstaff. His staff swung at my head and missed me by an inch. The breeze rustled my hair and knew he would have hit me if he'd intended to.

A war-cry rang out on Sigurd's side of the cart. A third

man, larger than the other two, burst from the woods brandishing long staff with a sharpened end. He waved it as if it were a light javelin. His straw-colored braids and mustache streamed behind him as he raced forward, the spear-point aimed at Sigurd's chest. Just before he skewered Sigurd he dropped the spear-point and shoved it into a wheel.

The spear jammed the spokes and the cart stopped abruptly. Sigurd and I tumbled from our seats into the shafts and reins. By the time we sorted ourselves out and stood, the three men were spread around us with weapons at ready.

Sigurd glanced at his axe on the ground between us.

"I'd not go for the axe, friend," said the man who had been spinning his quarterstaff. "Not unless you fancy a cracked head."

He surveyed the cart. "So, what have our new friends brought us?"

"Nothing of value." I replied. "Just some foodstuffs. We're poor merchants, delivering--"

"Food!" said the one with the spear. "Want food!"

The leader spun his quarterstaff again, perhaps to remind us it was there.

"I'm certain our friends will share their food with us. It's a strange assortment for a merchant. I'd wager our friends are taking a village's taxes to the earl."

The one with the spear muttered. "Hate tax collectors! Hate. Hate!" He bit his spear, working himself into a frenzy.

"Relax, Olaf," said the leader. "Tax collector or no, these

are our new friends, and they're going to share their food with us." He motioned to the man who had been silent. "Take the reins and lead our new friends away from the road. We don't want to be disturbed."

The silent man grabbed the reins and yanked. The horse docilely followed him. I wished we were still traveling with our hell-spawn. Midnight would not have been led so easily.

Olaf prodded us in the back with his spear and we decided to follow the cart. The leader collected Sigurd's axe and my lute from the road and carried them behind us.

In a few moments we reached a clearing similar to the one Sigurd and I had scared three bandits from a week ago.

"Olaf, make the big one hold still. Shawn, bind his legs."

Olaf placed the tip of his spear under Sigurd's chin. "You move, even a little, tax collector and I'll carry your head on this."

Sigurd stood motionless while Shawn the Silent wrapped deer-hide strips around his ankles and knees. When this was done, Olaf removed his spear as Shawn kicked Sigurd behind the knees. Sigurd fell forward and struggled up to kneeling.

The leader pointed at me. "Now the other." Olaf and Shawn repeated the procedure while he stood back, ready for any attempt to fight or escape.

When we were trussed and kneeling the group's leader loomed over us.

"How shall we guest our new friends?" he asked the other two.

Olaf shouted. "Carve the blood eagle on their backs and sacrifice them to Odin!"

"Perhaps later. First, they should work for the dinner they are sharing with us." He waved Sigurd's axe. "Which of you is the axe-man?"

I stared at Sigurd, and he nodded.

"Excellent. We have a log to be split into firewood. I'm certain you can do that while you are kneeling. Don't think of being clever. Olaf would rather spit you than watch you do his work."

He faced me. "You must be the lutist. What tune were you playing when we met?"

"I was composing *Sigurd and the Lost Princess--*."

"Sigurd!" shouted Olaf. "Sigurd, Sword-Thief! If I'd been awake, he'd be Sigurd, Raven's Feast. Hate Sigurd. Kill Sigurd when we meet!"

"Calm, Olaf, calm and peaceful." The leader's voice was smooth and soft. He was obviously practiced at soothing Olaf. "Sigurd is not here, no need for berserkergang."

Olaf stopped shouting but continued muttering under his breath as Sigurd chopped the log into billets.

"Tales of Sigurd are not welcome here. Perhaps you have a song about the joys of life in the greenwood? One where noble bandits relieve thieving tax collectors of their ill-gotten gains?"

I sang my song of the joys of being a wandering bard, changing "bard" to "bandit". It damaged the scansion, but a man must adapt.

While we spoke, Shawn rummaged through our cart.

81

The leader called to him. "What have you found?"

"Food, Harald." was the reply. "Many turnips, sacks of barley. A couple hams and three kegs."

Olaf shouted. "Ale! We drink tonight!"

The leader grinned. "We *feast* tonight! Shawn, build up the fire and roast five turnips, we'll warm the ham and have a meal fit for a king."

Shawn was not as good a cook as Dale, but he soon had the fire roaring with a turnips buried below and a ham on a spit above.

Long before the turnips were half-cooked, the scent of warm ham filled the clearing.

Olaf was the first to succumb to the odor. "I don't eat turnips. I want ham and ale!" He grabbed the axe from Sigurd's hands. "Enough wood. I need a cask-opener."

He leaped onto the back of the cart, smashed the top of a cask with the axe and dipped his hand in, slobbering as he tasted the ale. "Thin and sour," he called, "But it's ale. No ale is bad ale."

He shifted the keg to the end of the cart. Shawn and the leader jostled each other getting wooden cups into the cask and tossing off the ale.

Harald wiped the foam from his lips. "Not the best ale," he agreed. "But ale, nonetheless." The three of them huddled near the fire, carving strips of meat from the ham, and going back to the cask for more ale.

"Give us music," called Harald. "A merry tune for a merry meal."

He tossed a strip of meat at me. It bounced off my

shoulder and into my lap. I scooped it up, chewed quickly and swallowed. I've sung for my supper before, but I've never begged for scraps like a dog. I was angry, but I had to keep smiling and singing. We would live as long as I kept them from deciding to kill us.

I sang one of my feasting songs. The chorus is simple, and they were soon singing along, albeit with three different tunes.

When Olaf crawled awkwardly onto the cart to broach the second cask I had the glimmering of an idea.

The thieves refilled their cups while Sigurd sat near the log he had been chopping, settled on his haunches with his head low, his shoulders slumped. He shuddered as if sobbing. He would be no help. It was up to me to save us.

I sang *Drink, Drink, Drink and Be Merry*. When sung properly, the singers drain a cup at the end of each verse.

Our new friends knew the proper way to sing the song. Before long, Olaf cracked into the third cask. It took him two tries.

I sang a drinking-challenge dance tune and soon had them in a line, stepping and twirling. And stumbling. Whenever anyone missed his step, he had to drink a cup of ale. On the twelfth verse, Harald dropped out to lean against the cartwheel, cheering his companions.

Shawn joined him a few verses later, while Olaf jeered at them. He quaffed another cup of ale as he stumbled in his twirl. He took one giant swallow, rolled his eyes to the sky and slumped into a heap.

Harald and Shawn giggled at this. They toasted each other and nodded as they stared into the fire.

By now it was fully dark, and the fire had burned low. I sang a lullaby, softly and gently. Within moments the song had worked its magic and all three were snoring.

I set aside my lute. My legs were numb below the knee, so I clumsily hopped and crawled to the fire. Sigurd's dagger was still stuck in the ham. I pulled it out and sliced my bonds. My legs throbbed and tingled, and would not hold my weight, so I crawled to Sigurd to free him.

He massaged his legs briefly, then rose to his knees to massage mine.

"What do we do now?" he whispered.

"It's too dark to drive the cart." I whispered back. "We could leave it here, and head into the woods, but we'd lose any chance of reward. We might even be accused of stealing the cart."

Sigurd nodded. "Let's wait for dawn, hitch the horse and drive away before they wake."

A bard wants a world peopled with grand deeds. Stealing away like cowards was the wise choice. It was what I intended when I sang the drinking songs. But now that we were free to leave, the idea of escaping didn't satisfy me. This tale needed a finer finish.

"Could you tie them up without waking them?"

Sigurd chuckled. "Three casks of ale for three men? I could dance on their bellies without waking them."

"Then, let's take them with us. There may be a reward for three runaways from the king's army. At least we can deliver them as thieves and let them take the blame for the missing ale and turnips."

We rummaged around the campsite and found more scraps of leather. We had their hands bound behind them and legs hobbled hours before the sun peeked through the leaves.

As soon as we had enough light to see by, we hoisted them into the cart and gathered everything of value from the campsite. There wasn't much to gather. The most valuable item was the remaining half-ham the squire had given Sigurd and me.

The horse wasn't bothered by the extra weight and soon we were racing down the road at a sedate plod.

After a sleepless night, Sigurd and I were too tired to talk. I was even too tired to play my lute.

I was not too tired to think. Mostly, I thought of how shamed I was to have had to play my lute and beg like a dog while Sigurd, so boastful when there were no foes nearby, sat silently sobbing.

Eventually, the sun was low in the sky. I suggested we find a place to camp. The discussion woke our passengers.

They were not happy.

After several minutes of cursing and complaining about headaches we reached a clearing and Sigurd drove the cart off the road. Once the cart stopped rocking the leader called to me.

"Friend. There was a lot of ale consumed last night. It desires to see the outside world. We'd be most grateful if you'd let us relieve ourselves."

Sigurd stopped the cart and brandished his axe.

"One at a time. I'll watch the man relieving himself," he

waved his axe, "And the bard will guard the other two." He handed me his dagger. "If they try to stand, or even move, kill them."

Olaf swore he would eat our livers, but he stayed still until Sigurd and Harald returned and it was his turn to visit the bushes.

After they had relieved themselves, we made them lie on their stomachs, hands tied behind their backs as Sigurd, and I took our turns. Once we'd taken care of our immediate needs, Sigurd prepared our camp, while I watched the bandits.

Harald never stopped talking, Olaf never stopped swearing, and Shawn never said a word.

We were eating the last of the ham when I finally listened to Harald.

"Friend," he said. "We treated you better than this. You had your hands free, and we gave you food. This is most unfriendly behavior. At the least you might share the scraps with us."

I glanced at Sigurd, who winked and carved the last slivers of ham off the bone. Then he tossed the bone to our prisoners. It landed at their feet, just out of reach.

"That was most boorish," the leader rebuked us.

Sigurd smiled and passed me the handful of meat. "You feed them; I'll keep watch." He hefted his axe.

I brought the meat to our prisoners, requested they open their mouths and tossed slivers of food between their lips, keeping carefully clear of teeth.

Eating was the one time Harald stopped talking. Food

even made Olaf stop swearing.

When they'd eaten the meat, I turned to Sigurd to discuss how to split our watches during the night.

As I took my second step, Harald called "Friend. A swallow of ale would wash down your gracious scraps. We'd even welcome water, if that's all you wish to share."

I was unwilling to release their hands to hold a cup, and I didn't want to stand close enough to lift the cup to their lips. Perhaps Sigurd had a plan for how to offer them water without providing an opportunity to escape.

"Sigurd, " I called, "how can we--"

Behind me, Olaf yelled "Sigurd! Sigurd-Sword Thief? Kill Sigurd!"

Olaf snapped his bonds as if they were spider threads. He rolled forward, grabbing the ham bone as he rose to his feet. The bone flew in a great arc and slammed into my face just below my ear. My head pulled the rest of me into a tree. My other cheek struck the trunk almost as hard as Olaf's blow. The world flashed white, like a lightning bolt as the ground rose to greet me. Blackness flowed over me, dark and smooth as a woolen blanket.

Chapter Six

Sigurd and the Two Trolls

I AWOKE WITH lights dancing before my eyes and blood dripping down my chest.

Sigurd crouched near the fire, sobbing. "So much blood. I never knew. So much..."

I shook my head to see around the dancing spots. Olaf lay sprawled on the ground facing Sigurd. His legs twitched. Harald and Shawn sat with their eyes and mouths open. Olaf's head lay between them.

I crawled to my feet and stumbled to Sigurd.

"Are you all right?" I croaked. My neck hurt and my throat was tight. Sigurd raised his face, tears streaming down his cheeks.

"Bard? You're alive? I thought-- Your head made a noise--" He stared at the body in front of him. "I never meant... but I thought he'd killed you."

I sat next to him, and Sigurd buried his head in my shoulder and sobbed convulsively.

While he shuddered and sobbed I listened to the bandits speak in low voices.

"Olaf has left us."

"True, friend, we kept him as best we could, but his wyrd has found him."

"With Olaf gone, our fellowship is sundered. I was never suited to the life in the wildwood."

"Nor was I. We kept our oath, but still, the pact is broken. It is time to accept what fate has for us."

Sigurd stopped shuddering and stared at my face.

"You are bloody. Are you sure you're all right?"

I nodded. The ham bone had cut me where it hit, and the tree had scraped me when I hit it. I'd suffered worse.

Sigurd shuddered. "I thought he'd killed you. I truly thought... I never--" he gasped. "I was angry. He charged at me-- But I didn't intend--"

The bandit leader spoke up. "It was a good blow. Well struck. It was the death Olaf wanted."

I stared at him in disbelief. No man wants to die.

"Truly." Harald nodded at the corpse. "He worshiped Odin. A death in battle against a worthy foe sends him to Valhalla."

Shawn broke his silence. "The first blooding is hard,

Axe-man. It never gets easy, but it gets easier. Honor your foeman and it will ease the passing. Both his and yours."

Sigurd still sobbed at intervals. He stared at the ham bone lying near Olaf's right hand. It had been the berserker's final weapon. He shook his head and hurled his axe into the fire.

"A weapon for a warrior." he cried.

We were all silent as the haft burned brightly.

"Well spoken, friend." the leader said gently. "Olaf will bear your axe proudly at Ragnarök."

He fell silent, staring at his feet as Shawn chanted a quiet Gaelic dirge.

Sigurd and I dragged Olaf's head and body to the edge of the clearing and discussed what we would do. We resolved to collect stones for a cairn and entomb the corpse at sunrise.

For the rest of the night, we were silent and sleepless. I was thinking of Sigurd.

When a man's first blood is shed to avenge your death, it forms a bond, whether you were dead or not.

I saw how I'd misjudged him during the past days. When we were tied and I watched him shudder, he wasn't sobbing. He was flexing his legs and loosening his bonds. That was why he was able to walk sooner than I.

When he needed to fight, he did. There's a difference between guarding a wagon or even standing in a shield wall and killing a man in single combat. You don't stare into a dying man's eyes in a melee as you do when you slay a single opponent.

I wondered if Sigurd had ever seen combat. It's possible to spend years as a guard and never be attacked. The simple presence of a large man with an axe will convince most thieves to find an easier way to gain coins.

I would have sworn I stayed awake all night, but I woke with the sun in my eyes when Harald whispered to Shawn, "Olaf broke these bonds. So can we. We could escape while they sleep."

I held motionless and reminded myself to breathe. Sigurd's axe was burnt. We had no weapons other than our eating daggers. Two against two was an even match, but I'm a bard, not a warrior. I doubted Sigurd could best two trained armsmen.

Shawn replied. "Our fate would find us. We are doomed to die by axe or gibbet," he paused. "I've tired of life in the wildwood. I will accept my fate."

"We are agreed," Harald replied, "Surrender to the king's justice and pray for an honorable death."

I opened my eyes at those words. Sigurd's tunic rustled as he rose.

He stood over the two bandits.

"You will surrender?" he asked. "Truly?"

Harald nodded. "It's time to confess our sins and make amends."

He glanced at Sigurd and then me. "I'll travel with you to the earl and take my punishment. I give you my oath."

"Your *oath* ?" I said, somewhat pointedly.

He looked me in the eye. "My oath is good." He paused and lowered his eyes. "Was good. I only forswore it once, and never stopped regretting it." He nodded to Shawn. "This was not the life we sought."

Sigurd recovered his axe-head from the ashes and found a branch to make a new handle for it. While he attended to his axe I dragged and rolled rocks to Olaf's body. The sun was warm on my back as we piled them onto the corpse.

Once we covered Olaf with stones the size of my head and larger we paused and panted. Harald intoned a Latin prayer I recognized from my youth in the monastery while Shawn chanted his Gaelic dirge. Sigurd and I stood silent until they finished.

I tossed one last rock onto the top of the cairn while Sigurd boosted Harald and Shawn into the cart. We trundled along the trail in deep silence.

A silence can be soft and comfortable: the silence between friends who don't need to fill the air with words.

It can be cold and brittle: the silence between friends who have quarreled and need to reclaim their friendship.

Finally, there are deep, solemn silences: the silence after you've performed a sacred rite or are riding to your death.

The silence in our wagon was all of these and more. We each had too many thoughts to speak.

It is truly rare for a bard to be silent. Harald being silent was even rarer.

It was late afternoon when we topped a rise and spotted the earl's holding in the valley below. From the hilltop we gazed over the man-high log stockade deep into the hold. Homes, shops, and kitchen gardens were scattered inside the wall, with larger fields and flocks outside.

When Sigurd stopped the cart to admire the village Harald finally broke his silence. "Friend. I own myself your prisoner, but I beg a boon. I would walk to the earl's justice like a man, not be carried like a sack of grain."

I cocked my head at Sigurd. He studied our prisoners for two beats. then nodded.

"Your oath to not run?" I asked Harald.

"My oath." He replied.

"And mine," Shawn echoed.

Sigurd nodded to me. I cut the bonds and helped them out of the cart.

Harald rubbed his wrists. "Thank you, friend. If you drive the cart and Sigurd guards us with his axe, all will see we are your prisoners."

I nodded. I'd studied Sigurd and had taken brief turns at driving the cart. The horse recognized my skill and ignored me, doing what it was supposed to do.

As we approached the gate a guard wearing leather mail and a metal cap stepped forward, readying the poleaxe he carried.

"State your business with Earl Acton," he called.

"We bring taxes from Squire Bolton and two captured highwaymen." Sigurd replied.

The guard studied Harald; Shawn then turned back to Sigurd. "Prisoners," he asked, "with no bonds?"

Harald replied. "We own ourselves captured. We've given our oath to surrender to the earl's justice."

The guard stepped aside and pointed to a stone keep in

the center of the stockade. "The earl receives his taxes at the keep. I guess he receives prisoners there as well."

We were met outside the keep by two more guards wearing light leather armor, and a white-bearded scribe in a long grey robe. The scribe accepted the package of reports and tally sheets from the squire and began checking the cart's contents.

As he counted, Harald spoke. "You'll find three casks of ale, several turnips and a ham missing. We took them. We'd have stolen the whole cart if we weren't defeated and captured."

The scribe and guards ogled us, perplexed. Harald nudged Shawn and they stepped forward, with their hands crossed at the wrists.

"We," he waved at Shawn, "confess to being thieves and villains. They," he indicated Sigurd and me. "captured us when we tried to steal the cart from them. We surrender ourselves to the Earl's justice."

The guards and the scribe faced each other. Apparently nobody had ever brought them a prisoner before.

The scribe cleared his throat and spoke. "The Earl is inside. He should accept your surrender himself. I'll present you."

I climbed off the cart as he led the four of us into a large hall with long, rough-wood thick-legged tables in the center. At the end of the hall, near a huge firepit, several men stood around an oak trestle table.

A burly man with a salt and pepper beard sat at the center of the table. He wore a gray, homespun tunic, embroidered with Celtic knot patterns. He frowned while herders, farmers and millers clustered about him, each demanding his favor. Within the babble were the phrases "seed," "bread," "flocks" and "mutton." They were disputing how to prepare for winter--how much wheat they should grind to flour and how many sheep to slaughter. These decisions would determine how well his people ate this winter and how rich next year's harvest would be. The farmers wanted to save seed and eat the lambs. The shepherds preferred to eat bread during the winter and save the lambs for next year's flocks.

I remembered the monks spending hours every fall deciding how much seed to save, how much fodder to store, and how many of the flock to slaughter. Guessing wrong meant running out of food for the livestock or even the monks if spring came late.

As we approached, faces turned to us and the babble quieted.

The scribe cleared his voice. "My lord, Squire Bolton sends his taxes: one dray horse and cart, the cart filled with barley, turnips, and hams." He paused. "Here are also two thieves, captured and surrendering themselves to your justice."

After he spoke the hall fell silent. The entire assemblage stared at us.

The earl pushed himself to his feet. "Gentlemen," he spoke to the crowd around him. "We'll finish the discussion tomorrow. I fear I must hold court today."

Two guards stepped forward and placed his chair on the table. The earl climbed up and took his seat. His frown was no longer harassed. His face was stern and sorrowed. One of the guards thudded the butt of his poleaxe against the floor three times slowly. The blows echoed in the silent hall like a somber bell.

The scribe stepped forward in front of the table.

"Earl Acton will deliver justice. Come forward and speak."

Harald stepped to the table.

"My Lord. I come before you as a thief and deserter from the king's army. I was captured by the warrior Sigurd and his companion bard."

Shawn stepped next to him. "My lord. I also confess to being a thief and deserter. Also captured by Sigurd and the bard."

The Earl glared down at them. He intoned, "You are aware of the penalty for deserting your liege."

Harald nodded. "I understand. I beg to be allowed to confess to a priest and be shriven before you deliver justice."

Shawn raised his face to the earl. "I would spend a night beneath an oak and make my peace with my gods, if it please your lordship."

The earl addressed his guards. "Feed them first. I'll not have it said that any were mistreated in my home. Escort the Christian to the priest, then confine him in the root cellar. Take the other to the great oak and guard him. I'll deliver justice at dawn."

He stood as the armsman knocked on the floor three times and called "Justice shall be done." After the third thud, two guards escorted the repentant villains out, other guards removed the chair from the table and the counselors returned to their clamoring.

The earl waved them silent. "You" he pointed at Sigurd "will eat at my left hand tonight. I would speak with you. And bard, you shall be fed now, that you might entertain us."

This pleased me. We had eaten well at the squire's, but food had been scarce since then. With Sigurd sitting at the earl's left hand, he would not mime while I performed.

A guard escorted me to the kitchen. The smells of cooking meat, smoke and sour ale filled the room. The guard spoke with a portly man wearing a long grease-stained apron over his smock. He motioned to a pretty, round-faced young wench with coal-black hair barely contained by her lace snood. "See that the bard is fed well enough to entertain."

She came to me, curtsied, and said softly "We have fowl, ham, and venison cooked. As well as a leek soup, lamb stew and bread." She paused. "Master Kenley is noted for his breads and stews."

I recognized the suggestion. Meats and sauces were for my betters. I requested the bread and stew. In a moment she brought me a half a loaf of crusty bread, hollowed, and filled with a savory stew.

I hadn't realized how hard Olaf hit me until I opened my mouth to take the first bite. My jaw creaked and the pain made me gasp.

The wench ran her fingers lightly over the side of my face. "Did you get this fighting the bandits?" she asked. The news of the prisoners had traveled quickly. I must compose a song before the Earl's dinner.

I nodded and she whispered, "How brave!" I was ready to forgo the meal at this point to spend time with her. Except I was starving, the earl expected entertainment, and I needed to compose at least twenty verses describing the battle with the bandits.

I suggested "Perhaps we can meet after dinner and I'll tell you the tale."

She nodded, blushed, and ran off, returning in a moment with a generous mug of ale and a damp rag.

She gently blotted my face with the rag. I winced the first time she touched the bruise where Olaf hit me, and again when she padded the scraped flesh where I struck the tree. By the time I finished the ale, however, I felt much better and marveled at how round and blue her eyes were.

While I ate and had my face bathed, the surrounding hubbub increased. I was almost finished eating my stew when I noticed the servants lining up by the door carrying platters of food.

A horn blared in the hall as they paraded out. I gave my lute a quick tuning, strummed three chords and followed them singing.

I sing of dinner, rich and fine.
Of meat and bread and ale and wine.
Earl Acton is known for the bounteous fare,
In all of the kingdom, there's none to compare.

It's a jaunty tune, and I can squeeze the name of anyone who feeds me into it.

I had snippets of news to relate, including the courtship

of Princess Beornwyn and a prophesy of a wedding at the Squire's next spring. I sang forty verses of *Sigurd And the Seven Saracens,* which occupied most of the meal. When the kitchen servants brought out fruits and cheeses the earl motioned for me to pause and had a mug of spiced ale carried to me.

I sipped the ale, "I carry good news." I paused dramatically. "There are three fewer villains on the roads."

I strummed a dramatic chord. A bard keeps a collection of generic verses ready for need. Just as I had a several songs suitable for entering a tavern or feasting hall, I had dozens of verses about Sigurd fighting bandits. I'd composed a few new stanzas to link these together while I was eating, and now I was ready to sing.

Sigurd travels from town to town.
Performing heroic deeds.
Saving maidens, slaying dragons,
Wherever adventure leads.

Once Sigurd was guarding a wagon of gold.
When three huge ogres leaped onto the road.

In just twenty verses Sigurd slew the largest ogre and had the others begging to be spared. The earl smiled as I sang, and Sigurd sat with eyes wide. It was a truthful telling of our trip from the squire's village to the earl's.

Except for a few minor details.

The Earl applauded. "Excellently done." he cried. "Tell me, bard, do you know any songs about horses?"

"Please your lordship," I dug Ryder's sigil from my pouch and handed it to him. "I have a song I'm told you will favor."

He glanced at the sigil and leaned back. His face was an open book, harassed and troubled when we met him, stern when he administered justice, and now as eager as a child awaiting a present.

By the time I finished *Sigurd's Race with Death,* the hall contained only the earl, his young son, the blue-eyed servant, Sigurd, and me. The earl laughed so hard the tears ran down his face, while the boy stared wide-eyed at me and then at Sigurd.

"Truly?" he asked. "Picked the flowers with his teeth from a galloping horse?" I nodded and the earl patted the boy on the head.

"You go to bed and dream about that feat. When you find a horse to run for three days and nights, I'm certain you'll be able to pick flowers with your teeth as well."

He glanced at Sigurd then at me.

"And now we talk. Your song told the story well, but I need truths." He motioned to his guard. "Send for the priest, I would speak with him also."

He faced us. "Were these the villains who menaced Barleytown?" I nodded and he turned to Sigurd. "You drove them away?"

Sigurd dipped his head. *"We* drove them off, Bard and I."

"The squire's report says they stole food and burned buildings but did not kill anyone. Is this true?"

I nodded. "The tavern keeper said they had fought but did not mention any deaths."

"And when they captured you. Were you tortured or mistreated?"

I had to own we were not.

He studied my face. "Did you receive those wounds when you were captured or when you escaped?"

"Olaf, the bandit Sigurd slew, attacked me before attacking Sigurd."

The earl noted the wounds on both side of my face. "He struck you twice?"

I pointed to the left side of my jaw. "He struck me here." I rubbed the other. "I struck a tree here." I paused for drama. "The tree did not strike back, so I spared it."

The earl smiled at my jest and returned to question Sigurd. "And you killed a man armed with a ham bone?"

Sigurd dropped his eyes and stared at his feet. "It happened so fast. His berserkergang took him and he charged me. I thought he'd killed Bard."

The earl nodded. While we spoke, the guard had returned with the priest.

The earl motioned to the cleric. "I won't ask you to betray a confession, but I wish to know about this man."

The priest looked him in the eye. "I have taken his confession and prayed with him. He has sinned most grievously and repented most sincerely. He is willing to accept justice."

"And what kind of man was he, to desert his king and turn bandit?"

"A man pushed beyond what he could bear. I'd have called him a good and moral man, save for that sin."

We spoke for hours. I tried to excuse myself but failed. The blue-eyed maiden finally blew me a kiss and departed, blushing. Shortly after she left Earl Acton told the priest to return to the prisoner.

The earl continued questioning us. There was not one minute of the previous week he didn't ask about.

Then it was dawn. Time for justice.

The earl stood and motioned us to stand as well. "You are part of this, you shall see it end." A guard brought him a great-sword and helped him belt it across his back. "Fetch the Christian. I'll administer justice beneath the oak."

He treaded slowly out the door, with Sigurd and me behind. Step, pause, step, pause, step until we reached the oak.

Shawn sat cross-legged with his eyes closed, weaving, and chanting in a quiet monotone.

He opened his eyes when Harald arrived. The earl motioned and both of them knelt before him, heads bowed, staring at his feet.

"I will not deliver justice until 1 have full truth." he said. "What was your rank in the king's army?" He pointed at Harald.

Harald swallowed. "Sergeant, your lordship."

Shawn whispered "Yeoman, please your lord."

"How long had you served our king?"

"Ten years."

"Five years, please your lord."

"And after so many years, you broke your oath and deserted. I will know why. You must have seen battles. You must have served well, or you'd not have your ranks. Why did you suddenly become cowards?"

Harald flushed and he raised his face. "I'm no coward." he said firmly, and then more quietly, "well, maybe. I've no fear of battle. No fear of an honorable death. But we were to be sent by boat. I was on a boat once and swore I'd never board one again. There's no honor in drowning, begging your lordship's pardon."

Shawn nodded. "The sea is not my friend." He turned his face back to the earl's feet.

The earl shifted and stared down at the two prisoners.

"You are weapon trained?" he asked.

Harald looked up again, confused. "Yes, your lordship. Axe, polearm, sword and shield."

Shawn nodded, "Spear, bow and quarterstaff. Please your lordship."

The earl raised his face, staring over them at the great oak. Deep brown leaves sliced through the dawn's pale glow as they tumbled to the earth, their day in the summer sun finished.

He studied the prisoners as he loosed his sword and drew it. "It is time for justice." he said solemnly.

Harald and Shawn lowered their heads. The morning sun glistened on the sweat beading the back of their necks.

"The penalty for desertion is death." the earl intoned. "The penalty for banditry is also death."

He raised his sword. Its shadow crossed the shadow cast by the prisoner's necks. A brown oak leaf dropped by Harald's head and joined its shadow to molder in the earth.

The earl took a deep breath. "Taking a man's life is also a sin. The Lord does not approve of wasting his clay." He held his sword firm, still crossing the shadow of their necks.

"Harald, Do I spare your life, do you swear to serve me and never again sin against our God?"

Harald looked up, eyes wide and mouth open. "I..." he paused and swallowed. "Please your lordship. No boats. If it's to be boats, I'd rather the clean death."

The earl was still stern. "No boats. My domain has no seashore."

"My oath to serve your lordship. I bless your lordship's mercy."

Shawn was still kneeling with his neck stretched out.

"And you. Will you serve me, or would you rather receive the punishment for your deeds."

Shawn stared at the earl's feet, then lowered his head until his forehead touched the ground. "My oath to serve you."

The earl looked at Sigurd and me. "You have held their oaths. Did they break them?" We shook our heads. "You hold them to be men worthy of their oath?" We nodded.

The earl turned back to Harald and Shawn. "A man I trust has given these men," he glanced at Sigurd and me, "his trust and these two men have extended that trust to you. By this shared bond, I accept your oath and your service. Do you break these oaths, your lives and the lives of your sponsors are forfeit. Do you acknowledge this debt?"

Harald glanced at us and swallowed. "Your lives are safe with me." he said.

Shawn pulled a tiny dagger from his boot.

He slashed across his palm and let the blood drop onto the ground by the earl's feet.

"Your land holds my blood. I am yours." he murmured.

"Bind that before it festers." the earl commanded him. He addressed the guard as he sheathed his great sword. "Find them quarters and duties."

He stepped toward the hall and called to us. "You two, attend me."

As we walked to the hall the enormity of what had happened sank into my stomach. The sigil I hoped would buy me a meal had just bought two lives. I saw in Sigurd's wide eyes and pale face that this realization had struck him as well. He'd taken one life and saved two.

The earl sat at the center of the long table and motioned us to sit across from him. As soon as he sat down, the kitchen servants brought us food.

The earl took a swallow of ale and waved the cup at us.

"The squire's report suggests I reward you for delivering the taxes to me." Sigurd nodded and the earl continued, "I'll not deny it. You delivered the bulk of his taxes and a bit more.

"I don't know whether to thank or curse you for bringing those men to me. They will be good armsmen, but they present a problem."

He paused and tore a large swallow from a loaf of bread

before continuing.

"I have never taken a blow I did not return. You brought me both treasures and problems. I'll return your blow with the same."

He shifted his gaze from Sigurd to me. This did not bode well. I prefer treasures to problems. In the past weeks, I'd had plenty of problems and only promises of treasure.

"It must be explained to my king that I have forsworn his law, pardoned two criminals and taken them into service. He must understand why I did this." He faced Sigurd. "You have shown yourself to be honorable and just to those who earned no mercy from you." He glanced at me. "And you have a bard's eye for remembering detail, with a bard's tongue for describing what you wish people to see." He examined both of us together.

"I have decided you shall be my emissaries to King Elmar, to explain my actions and obtain his forgiveness. You will be rewarded for your success."

I waited a moment to see what Sigurd would do. He sat still and finally said. "I trust to my lord's generosity."

The earl smiled. "And well you may." He waved a hand and the scribe we'd seen yesterday came, bearing two thick leather belts. He handed them to the earl who dropped them onto the table with a surprisingly loud thunk.

"Five gold pieces are sewn into each of these belts." he said. "I would have you relay my message to the king and use this gold to ransom the men I have taken into service. You may bargain as you will. Such gold as the king does not demand is yours."

I gasped, as Sigurd took a sudden breath. Ten pieces of

gold was more money than I'd ever seen, let alone possessed.

Earl Acton smiled at me. "This is the message I would have you deliver to the king." He then explained the events we'd told him, and why he had elected to spare the villains lives. He never chastised the king for wasting good men, but the intent was clear.

"And do you want these words repeated exactly as you've spoken them?" I asked.

He laughed. "A bit rough, is it? Well, my cousin is used to plain talk from me. But you may soften the message as you will." He pushed the belts to us. "I won't tell you when you should leave, but I'll point out that it's late in the year. The sooner you head north, the more likely you'll be under a roof when the snow falls."

I nodded as Sigurd pulled his axe from his belt and set it on the table. The handle was the rough branch he'd jammed into the axe-head. "Please your lord, I'd keep your gold safer if this were better mended. May I ask your smith to attend to my axe?"

The earl looked at the makeshift repair and laughed. "Sigurd, you are a man of many talents. Both warrior and drover, but definitely not a weapon-smith." He motioned to a guard, who took the axe and headed out of the hall. "Follow him, he'll lead you to the smith. Tell him you need a new axe quickly."

By now, we'd finished eating, and the counselors were crowding around the edges of the table. "I must work." the earl spoke to me. "You may make yourself free within the village. I'll welcome your entertainment with dinner."

108

I slipped back as the counselors started talking about two extra mouths to feed and the need for storage bins.

I found a corner to curl up, gently strummed my lute and fell asleep. After the last few days, I needed the rest.

I woke late in the afternoon with an empty belly. If I were to entertain during dinner, I'd best eat quickly. I found the kitchen and the blue-eyed maiden smiled at me.

In a few moments, I had another bread-bowl of stew and was chatting with her while I ate. We each apologized for missing last night's assignation and promised to meet after tonight's dinner.

When the servants carried the food to the head table, I joined them, and once more entertained the earl. I played my lute softly while folks ate and talked among themselves. I was no longer a novelty, and they wouldn't be ready to pay attention until they finished their meal.

Once the eating slowed, I sang the new song that had come to me while I slept.

> I'll sing you a tale of a noble earl.
> An earl so brave and bold.
> Now listen to how his sword did whirl
> On the day he met two trolls.

The earl set down his cup and the hall fell silent except for my song. Even the kitchen noises died down as the cooks crowded into the hall to listen. I didn't name their earl, but everyone knew it was a song about him.

In the next verses, the earl tracked down two trolls who had been pillaging and burning his villages. He attacked them with his sword, and when it broke, with his bare hands. In just ten more verses, he bested them, and they dropped their weapons. After the trolls surrendered, the earl offered to spare them if they would swear fealty to him. Upon giving their oaths, the trollish skins fell away, and two mortal warriors served the earl for the rest of their days.

I finished the song to silence. It was scary. I was afraid I'd gone beyond the bounds and offended the earl.

He raised his drinking horn slowly, then slammed it onto the table. "YES!" he bellowed and slammed the horn again. "Yes. Yes! YES!" The rest of the listeners cheered as he reached into his robe and pulled out a small leather sack which he tossed to me. It clinked when I caught it and was so heavy I almost dropped it. "I have chosen a worthy emissary!"

Approval does not fill a bard's belly, but it certainly makes a meal sit more lightly. There's no approval more sincere than a pouch of coins.

I bowed as the earl rose and left the hall. The kitchen serfs began clearing the tables, as the rest of the diners faded from the room.

I crossed to where Sigurd sat on one of the benches and settled next to him.

"Excellent song," he said. "Well chosen, well-constructed and well played."

I thanked him as he stood. "I would check how the repair of my axe is proceeding. We should travel in the morning." I agreed as he left.

The blue-eyed kitchen wench scurried to clear the tables.

A bard is not a servant, but I lent her a hand. We soon completed her after-dinner chores and she had no more duties.

We claimed a half-empty crock of ale and settled into a quiet corner. We talked for hours. Her name was Corliss, and her tale was much like mine. An orphan, she was raised in a convent instead of a monastery. She had been trained as a Lady's maid while I learned to sing in the choir. When she was of age she had been released to the earl's service, instead of running away during the night as I had. We knew each other's lives as nobody else could know them. The fire had burned low when we fell asleep, leaning against each other.

We woke with a start in the morning when the drudges lit the fire, and the breakfast preparations began. She ran to the kitchen while I arranged myself for travel. The belt with the gold hung heavy around my waist. My pouch bulged with the bronze and silver the earl had gifted to me.

Sigurd arrived about the same time as the earl. Breakfast for all was brought a moment later. Soon my belly was as heavy as my belt and money-pouch.

We paid our respects to the earl, while his counselors argued about how much wood they needed to keep warm during the winter.

As we passed through the outer door, Corliss appeared and pulled me aside. She handed me her kerchief, tied to make a pouch. "To keep you fed... until you return." she whispered. I raised her fingers to my lips and smelled the perfume of her hair in the kerchief.

"I'll think of you with every bite." I whispered back, kissing her fingertips.

As I turned to leave, Sigurd was speaking to a tall blonde maiden. She handed him a shiny axe with a gleaming black handle that glinted in the morning sun. She murmured "I just finished polishing the haft." Sigurd kissed her hand and replied back. "I'm indebted. I'll thank your father when I return."

Thus, we strode from the earl's domain. I, cradling my lute and a packet of food, and Sigurd admiring his new axe.

The day had started well. We were well rested and well fed. And, it appeared, well respected and perhaps even well loved.

The snow didn't start until several hours later.

Chapter Seven

Sigurd at the Inn of Entrapment

SIGURD DIDN'T STRIDE today. He meandered along the trail, staring through the trees that blocked the horizon. I ambled beside him, lost in thought as well.

Since meeting Sigurd, I had greeted several mornings with a full stomach and begun my journeys carrying food to eat along the road.

And I had stolen none of it.

For the sake of the story's moral, I didn't include the first breakfast of stolen eggs he and I shared.

Two of our leave takings were punctuated by food from a damsel. After years of maidens avoiding me unless my fingers were busy on my lute this was a strange and welcome change.

Sigurd had irked and annoyed me. He acted like a misbehaving child or a pesky younger brother who needed discipline. Mind you, I'd never had either of these, but I'd sung songs about them.

However, after our encounter with Harald, Shawn and Olaf, Sigurd had been less boisterous. In fact, he had been nearly silent since he slew Olaf. I marveled at how humbly he accepted Earl Acton's generosity after his brazen attempt to extract a gold piece from Squire Bolton.

And now, we were being sent to a king to plead for two men's lives and the honor of an earl.

Sigurd interrupted my thoughts.

"I never expected to be an emissary to a king." he said.

I nodded. "It's an honor and a burden."

We were silent for another fifty paces or so.

"We could take the gold and go elsewhere." I suggested.

"But we won't."

"No. A month ago, I would have. But a month ago, nobody trusted me with two silver pennies, let alone five gold pieces."

"Why? Why would an earl trust two vagabonds like us?"

I was silent. Why indeed? We were two homeless wanderers selling our skills for a meal and a roof for a night. But somehow, we'd become more.

"Because you're the hero Sigurd." I whispered. The idea scared me.

He stopped dead in his tracks and stared at me. "You

114

know I'm not."

"True. And they know you're not. But you *act* like Sigurd. You chased three bandits away from a village, rescued a lost maiden, captured the villains, took one life and spared two." I kicked a twig off the path. "You said it when we first met. People *want* to believe. If you live up to their expectations, they *will* believe. At least a little."

Sigurd was silent. "That's a large burden for a man to carry."

I nodded. *"You* wanted to be a hero."

"Not really." He smiled for the first time since he broke our silence. "I just wanted to be paid like one."

"It appears the two are connected."

He was silent for a few moments.

"You must help me learn to be a hero."

Now I stopped. Dead in my tracks. Me? Tutor a hero? I know how to compose doggerel, how to flatter a landlord and how to steal eggs, but being a hero, or even a hero's bard was never what I aspired to. I never even imagined I could aspire to such.

I must have said something out loud, for Sigurd answered.

"Yes, you. Who better? You know the lays of every hero since Gilgamesh. There must be a verse describing how a hero handles any situation." He paused and swallowed. "When we started traveling together you treated me like a younger brother. I resented it. I tried to play the hero to spite you; bragging, posturing, threatening. To pretend I'm more than your lesser companion. I understand now.

You've been trying to help me grow up."

If he'd seen this, why hadn't I?

"I wasn't acting like a hero, I acted like a spoiled child. I want to be a hero. I need to be the man people think I am."

I guessed the people he was concerned about had blonde hair and polished his new axe.

I remembered a pair of blue eyes and a whispered "How brave." I knew exactly what he meant.

It was good to be larger than life in someone's eyes, and a huge burden to live up to it.

"It's a harder task than either of us can handle," I replied. "I'll help you if you'll help me."

This time he stopped. At this rate, we'd never reach the king's castle.

"Me?" he replied. "I'm just a farmer's son with an axe. I wasn't trained in a monastery or taught to read. I don't know an Edda from a chant."

"Perhaps true," I replied as I glanced at the sky. Clouds blotted out the sun and the brown oak leaves swirled about our feet. The weather would change soon.

I set a brisker pace and continued, "But, as the earl said, you have honor, and you treat others justly."

I hung my head. My cleverness had been a point of pride, but I viewed it differently today. The woodland bandits had shown more virtues than I could claim.

"I left my honor at the monastery," I told Sigurd. "I need to find it again."

We walked in silence, each lost in our thoughts. My

thoughts led me back the monastery where I was raised. The gray granite walls I remembered mirrored the gray skies above me.

A burst of cold, driving rain struck my face.

Sigurd nudged me, "It feels like it could turn to snow. Should we make camp while we can or keep walking and hope for better shelter."

I decided to share the wisdom I'd gathered in my years of wandering. "Inns and taverns are spaced about a day's walk apart. Moreover, they are closer together the nearer you get to a castle. Finally, it's too early in the year for a serious snow. Even if this rain turns to snow, it won't stick."

Two hours later, it was dark, and we were slogging through three inches of *not sticking.* We'd pulled our cloaks over our heads and wrapped them tightly around our shoulders. The cloaks were heavy with snow *not sticking* to them.

My companion showed incredible restraint in not pointing this out. I would have never been so restrained. I resolved to purchase the finest, warmest accommodations available once we found an inn.

Sigurd stopped abruptly. I bumped into him and almost knocked us both over. He pointed to the right, away from the trail.

"I see a light," he croaked. "Not close, but it's our best hope."

I tried to see where he pointed, but the snow had crusted around my eyes, and I couldn't open them wide enough to see. I nodded and followed as he led us off the trail.

The glimmer Sigurd saw was nearby, blurred and swallowed by the blowing snow. With each step it grew brighter. In a dozen steps we stumbled into a log wall. The light we followed came from candle-glow behind the snow-covered joint where two crude shutters almost met. We felt our way around the wall until we discovered a door.

We didn't care if we'd found a tavern, church, or thieves' den. No one would deny us in this weather, and we were eager to accept any shelter.

We stumbled into the light and blinked, warmth caressed our faces as the wind and snow swirled around our waists.

"Close the door," someone shouted at us before we'd fully entered. Sigurd leaned against the door, forcing it shut against the wind. We glanced about a small, daub and wattle inn. The fire pit was almost hidden behind a dozen or so men in homespun and leather.

I let go my cloak. It fell from my shoulders and clattered as the sheet of ice and snow broke away. I sucked the warm, smoky air into my lungs and shivered.

"Clear a space by the fire," called the voice that demanded we close the door. A pair of large hands dragged me to the fire and shoved me onto a bench. I pushed my fingers toward the fire and felt the snow melting off my face and dripping onto my chest.

I blinked the snow off my eyelashes. I could see again! Even better, I saw a plump pair of hands offering me a mug of warm cider.

A heavyset balding man pushed Sigurd onto the bench next to me. "Fetch warm cider for this one, too." he called to the wench. I blinked more of the water out of my eyes as a plump girl in a shapeless, dirty garment dipped a cup into a cauldron hanging over the fire. When she offered the cider to Sigurd I saw her face. It too was round and plain, much like the innkeeper, who I guessed was her father.

A raggedly dressed man near the fire nodded at us. "Best get out of those wet clothes and wrapped in warm blankets," he said, "or you'll catch ague, and we'll have to keep you on ice until spring."

The balding man was apparently our host. "We wish to spend the night," I told him. Several patrons laughed-- everyone had decided to stay at the inn, rather than brave the storm. "Have you room?"

He shrugged. "The spots by the fire are all taken. There's space in the barn for a bronze penny. I've a room upstairs with a brazier, but I want a silver sceat for it."

I turned my back to the crowd circling the fire and opened my money pouch, letting the innkeeper see it was full. I selected a silver sestertius and handed it to him.

"We'll take the room. Make up the fire and send your best dinner."

I'd never taken a room at an inn before. Nor paid for a personal fire and a good meal. Between the money from selling Midnight and the gift from the earl, I was rich. I intended for us to enjoy it.

The faces around the fire stared as this happened.

I stood and bowed grandly to them. "I'll return after we've eaten. I have songs, news and tales to amuse."

Sigurd and I climbed a ladder to the private room in the loft. The room was small, the straw smelled sour, and the brazier was tiny. Tiny as it was, it soon warmed the space. Within moments Sigurd and I had shrugged out of our clothes and had them drying by the fire.

"So," said Sigurd. "Is this how heroes travel? I could learn to enjoy being a hero."

"It's how we travel." I replied. "At least, it's how we travel until we run out of money. Then we'll be back to barns and egg stealing."

Sigurd tapped the straw pallet on the floor. "I'll enjoy sleeping under a roof while I can." We listened to the sleet striking the thatch above us.

The wench brought two steaming bowls of stew with little meat and many turnips. "Please, gentles, me Da would be most grateful if you'd join him by the fire and share your tales with us."

I nodded graciously and agreed to return once we'd finished eating.

In truth, I could hardly wait. I had new songs, a marvelous story about the earl's new armsmen, the rumor of the squire's daughter's impending marriage, tales of Princes courting King Elmar's daughter and enough coins to keep my throat moistened without needing to beg.

By the time we'd finished eating, our clothes were dry enough to wear. Sigurd climbed down the ladder while I tuned my lute. He reached up to hold the lute as I descended. The inn fell silent as everyone stared at us, eager for song and news. I didn't need to sing any of my usual tunes to get attention, so I plucked a single chord and stepped forward.

"We come from Earl Acton's keep. The earl sends his

blessings to his people and thanks for a bounteous crop." I paused and strummed softly. I picked up the tempo as though leading into a song and declaimed.

"The greatest news is this. The brigands who have been terrorizing the villages and roads have been captured and reformed by Sigurd the Hero!"

I sang the tale of *Sigurd and the Three Ogres*, not as I sang it for Earl Acton two nights ago, but as it should have been. While we trudged through the snow I composed new verses to replace the ones I'd stolen from other songs.

The entire tavern chanted with me.

Thrust, parry, parry, swing.
Axe and dagger, dance, and sing.
Cleave, parry, parry thrust.
Heroes do as heroes must.

I stopped playing and tapped the lute as we chanted the chorus one last time and raised my lute over my head as they cheered.

These folks knew the fear of walking the woods-roads, and the story of dispelling the ogres was musical magic at its best.

When I strummed a new chord, they fell silent, eager for more news or another song. I played a full measure, whetting their appetite.

"In truth," I proclaimed, as I plucked a single grand chord and let it ring. "Sigurd slew one bandit, captured the other two and delivered them to the earl's justice." I nodded to our host. "Landlord, a fresh ale for everyone that they may drink to Sigurd's health. Gentle listeners. I present to you the man who made the roads safe again: Sigurd." I finished with a flourish and a crescendo.

Sigurd stood, slightly embarrassed, and greatly pleased. He bowed as the villagers cheered, and graciously accepted the toasts and well-wishes.

As the cheering died down, I strummed loudly as Sigurd settled back onto his stool.

"But, what of the bandits? What of the Earl's justice?"

And I sang the tale of the earl and the trolls. Again, the magic flowed. A tale of redemption is powerful, for we have all sinned against one god or another, and we all hope to be admitted to Valhalla, Heaven or Tír na nÓg when our time comes.

I finished the song to a thick silence. This time I recognized it as the time it took for the listeners to leave the world of my song and return to the tavern. There's no greater compliment a bard can receive than those few moments when the song's mirage is more real than the tavern's ale.

This was enough news and serious songs. I sang *Sigurd And The Five Virgins* and drove the blushing serving wench from the room while even her father laughed. I sang of sharing a haystack during harvest, and finally sang a mother's lullaby for her child.

By then we'd drunk most of the available ale and cider, laughed, cried, cheered, and repented. Everyone was exhausted and many missed the lullaby's last verses for the snores of their neighbor.

Sigurd and I climbed to our private room in silence and

fell into deep sleeps. Between bandits, earls, and maidens, we had hardly slept for three nights.

We woke when the serving wench tapped on the door.

"Please, sirs. Me Da wants to know if you'll be eating here or join the other guests downstairs."

I glanced at Sigurd, and he pointed down.

"We'll join you in the common room," I told the wench.

As we pulled on our outer clothes, I noticed my money pouch was missing. I'd left it on the rack by my blouse and trousers, but it was gone now. Even worse, Corliss's kerchief was also missing.

"Sigurd," I whispered. "Did you pick up my pouch?"

He stared back at me, wide-eyed.

"No, I was about to ask if you'd taken mine."

We searched the room but did not see our pouches.

"Now what do we do?" Sigurd whispered. "You gave our host a silver piece, do you think it was enough?"

I moved the clothes rack aside and found nothing beneath it. I shook my head. "Not with the ale I bought for everyone, the fire and meal." I paused. I didn't like the only idea I had. "The thief didn't take our belts. Perhaps we can use one of the earl's coins to pay for our lodging."

He glared at me. "Would Beowulf do that? Or the real Sigurd?"

I sighed. He was right, and I knew it. "No," I admitted. "A real hero would die defending his liege's treasure."

I shook my clothes, hoping for a pouch to fall from a pocket or sleeve. Nothing fell out. "We might try to sneak out without paying what we owe."

Sigurd shook his head. "This inn is small and poor. The innkeeper and his child would suffer greatly for the loss. A hero does not cheat the innocent."

He turned over his sleeping pallet and found nothing but dust beneath it. "If we find the thief, we might force him to return our coins. My purse was a plain leather sack. Can you identify yours?"

I nodded. "Mine came with me from the monastery. It had a cross embroidered on it. I plucked out the threads, but the needle holes remain."

After exhausting places to search, we descended the ladder, intent on breakfast and studying the travelers. I'd recognize Corliss's kerchief in a moment. She had embroidered crosses and roses along the edges.

The breakfast was simple, but ample. We dawdled over it, studying each of the remaining travelers as he paid for his food and night's lodging. None displayed a corner of the kerchief or a pouch I recognized.

At last, we were alone with the innkeeper, his daughter, and the remnants of the morning's fare.

"So," he said, wiping his hands on a greasy rag. "You'll be wanting to be on your way soon, I'm thinking." He pulled a tote board from under the shelf, and counted hash marks, x's, and o's.

"The total is three Roman silver denarii and five sceats." He smiled. "I can give you ten bronze triens in exchange for an aurie."

Sigurd waved to me. He obviously thought this was a task for a learned, clever bard, not an ex-farmer with an axe.

If I were truly clever, this would be a task for someone else.

"Good friend. I am aggrieved to report that one of your guests was a thief."

He scowled. I don't know where innkeepers learn to scowl, but they all learn the same expression. It reminds you they keep a cudgel near their right hand.

"A thief?" he growled. "I'm thinking there were two thieves here last night. Are you refusing to pay your bill?"

"Not refusing," I replied. "We are more than willing to pay for the fine meals and lodging. But, our purses were stolen during the night, and alas, we have no longer have money."

The scowl did not budge.

"I've heard that tale so often I'm surprised it has no tune. How do you propose to pay for the food and lodging?"

I swallowed and offered, "Sigurd and I are charged to deliver a message from Earl Acton to King Elmar. We will be rewarded for delivering it and can return to pay you."

The scowl faded as I spoke. He replaced it with raised eyebrows and a burst of laughter.

"*That* story I've never heard," he laughed. "You wish for me to simply let you continue your travels. But I needn't worry, for you'll be back with a king's reward to pay what you owe." He wiped tears from his eyes, and the scowl returned.

"As if I'd believe two vagabonds like you would be trusted with a message for the king," he growled. "If you and your companion cannot pay for your lodgings, you may work for them. The inn needs more work than the two of us can manage. There is plenty for two young men. In the evening, you may sing and beg for pennies. Perhaps you'll earn enough to pay your bill."

We talked and argued for nearly an hour. In the end, Sigurd and I agreed to work for a week to pay what we owed. We would sleep in the barn and be fed such food as remained after the paying guests finished.

The daughter led me to the kitchen to wash and trim turnips while Sigurd was sent to chop wood.

He stopped at the door.

"Friend innkeeper, do you have a wood-chopping axe?" he asked.

The innkeeper stared at him with narrowed eyes. "Isn't that an axe you carry? And a fine looking axe it is."

Sigurd cradled his new, black-handled axe. The shiny curved blade had no nicks or scratches.

"Yes, I have an axe." He paused, "But it is a war axe, not a woodsman's axe. The blade is not shaped for chopping wood."

The innkeeper shrugged. "Very well. You may use my axe, but don't damage it, or you'll work longer to pay for a new axe." He nodded to his daughter, who sauntered into the kitchen and returned with a battered axe.

It soon became apparent that the innkeeper and his offspring were adept at watching someone else work. The girl only visited the kitchen to fetch more ale for her father and complain about how slowly I prepared their lunch. The "Please, sir" vanished from her vocabulary as soon as I became her kitchen drudge.

I finally finished slicing the turnips and relaxed, listening to the chunk and tear as Sigurd chopped and split the logs. Once the storm passed, it was a bright, sunny day. Not a bad day to be working, I thought, happy it was Sigurd working instead of me.

I didn't hear the daughter's footsteps, but I heard her voice.

"What are you doing sitting and staring into space?" she shouted. "Gather the scraps and take them to the trash heap." She shoved a bucket at me to fill.

"Where is the midden?" I asked.

She pointed behind the inn. "Fifty paces, just beyond the rail fence."

She took another wooden cup of ale to her father, as I lifted the leather door and stepped outside into the mud. It wasn't as warm as I expected.

I saw a single set of small footprints in the mud, leading to the back fence. Those would be from the daughter's feet when she discarded the breakfast scraps. I followed them.

Once I neared the trash pile, I didn't need directions to find it. The odor of rotting meat and vegetables declared its location loudly. I paused several paces away, took a deep breath and raced to the trash heap to dump the scraps as quickly as possible.

As the turnip peels left my bucket I saw a strip of white cloth half hidden beneath the breakfast scraps. I tossed the empty pail behind me and waded into the trash, still holding my breath. I clawed through the fresh turnip peels and the older breakfast garbage. My lungs wanted to burst, but I recognized the slip of white cloth and was determined to retrieve it.

I exhaled slowly as I tossed aside the garbage until I reached a soiled white kerchief buried below the breakfast scraps. It had crosses and roses embroidered along its edges.

With the kerchief were two leather pouches, one of which had a cross marked out in old needle holes.

I waded back out of the midden, clutching my prizes and nearly passing out for lack of air. I stumbled several steps away and gasped.

After wading in the midden, there was no air suitable for breathing near me, but I filled my lungs anyhow. I carried the stench on my boots and trousers, as well as in the pouches and kerchief. Corliss's perfume no longer scented her gift.

I carried my treasures to Sigurd. I approached him from downwind to spare his nose. Given the hours he had spent chopping wood in the warm sun, I need not have bothered.

I waved the pouches and kerchief at him. He stopped in mid swing.

"Where did you find them?" he asked.

"In the midden, below the breakfast scraps, but above last night's dinner remains."

He glanced at the clouds. "That would mean they were stolen and discarded before breakfast. Perhaps by someone who departed without eating?"

He studied his boots, ankle deep in the mud. "We might identify the thief by his footprints, if we weren't sworn to remain here for a week. He will be miles away before we

128

can even start searching for him. We'll never find him, even if we weren't also sworn to deliver the earl's message to the king."

I smirked. I'd held back one piece of information for this moment.

"I think we can find our thief, even if we spend a week here."

Sigurd stared at me, puzzled.

"There was only one set of tracks in the mud. The daughter's."

He clenched his teeth. His lips thinned and his eyebrows crouched low over slitted eyes. "You're saying we've been victims of theft, and then forced to work to repay the money they stole themselves?"

I nodded. Sigurd set down the wood-chopping axe looked at his black war-axe.

"What would a hero do?" he asked.

I thought.

"When Theseus discovered Procrustes forcing travelers to fit his bed by stretching them or amputating limbs, he made Procrustes fit the bed himself.

"Hercules did similar by applying the same violence to others as they applied to him."

I paused and studied the mud we stood in. "The innkeeper stole coins from us. A hero would return the favor by stealing coins from him."

I pulled my dagger, sliced the threads on my belt, and extracted a gold piece.

"Run inside and tell the innkeeper you found this by the woodpile. I daresay he and his daughter will be out quickly. While they are out here, I'll ransack the inn and steal back what was ours, and maybe a bit more to repay our host for his hospitality."

Sigurd nodded, grabbed the coin ran to the front of the inn, shouting. As he barged through the main door, I ducked into the kitchen. As soon as they left, I dashed through the common room and into the private room the tavern keeper and his daughter shared.

This room was better appointed than the rest of the inn. An ornate tapestry decorated one wall and a large chair piled high with furs set near the fire. A stack of empty wooden cups told me this was where the innkeeper had spent his morning.

I dug through the furs and found nothing.

I turned the two pallets, but only dirt hid beneath them.

I examined items on the mantel, but none of them contained coins.

I finally reached under the fur-covered chair and felt the floor. I stretched until my fingertips touched a flat rock that tilted when I pressed it.

Outside, Sigurd swore he'd found the coin right where he pointed. He loudly claimed that since he'd discovered the coin it was his. The landlord shouted back that it was found in his woodpile and thus belonged to him.

I pushed the chair, sliding it closer to the fireplace. I lay down next to it and stretched my arm as far as I could. My fingers barely reached the loose stone. One of my fingernails broke as I pried up the rock. Under the rock was a hole filled with coins.

I pulled out a handful of bronze and silver coins. I considered emptying the horde, but decided this didn't fit with my new-found honor, so I only took a few more than had been stolen from us.

That this was all the coins I could hold did not influence my decision.

Much.

As I pulled the chair back over the hideaway a new voice echoed outside calling for order and demanding to know what was happening.

By the time I scrambled out the kitchen door and around the inn, a man on a horse was staring down at Sigurd, the tavern keeper, and the daughter. All of whom were gesticulating and shouting at once.

I recognized the man on the horse.

A bard is trained to project his voice. After all, he must be heard over the hubbub of a court or tavern.

I took a deep breath and called, "Ho, Ector. Well met again!"

Sigurd, the innkeeper, and his daughter fell silent as Ector stared at me..

"Bard?" he called. He studied Sigurd more closely. "And Sigurd. What brings you into dispute with this man."

The landlord spoke quickly. "These vagabonds pretended to have coin to pay for their keep. They had no coins and refuse to work to pay what they owe. This one," he pointed at Sigurd, "has stolen a gold piece from me and claims it for his own."

Ector had a spear and a sword mounted on his saddle. He rested his hand on the sword's hilt.

"Bard, what say you to these claims?"

"I call them false knaves who prey on weary travelers, stealing their money and forcing them to work without payment."

The landlord bellowed denials while the daughter called me a liar, thief, and rapist.

Ector drew his sword and shouted, "I am the King's Justice and I will have silence!"

It would have been more impressive if his voice hadn't cracked in the middle, but it was sufficient to quiet the landlord and daughter.

Ector glared at me.

"Can you prove your claim?" he asked.

I lifted the soiled kerchief.

"This was given to me by a maiden in Earl Acton's keep. I found it, with my money pouch beneath the breakfast scraps in the midden."

The innkeeper broke in, "Any thief could have discarded them there. That's not proof my child and I are thieves. And don't forget the gold piece. That's my gold!"

Ector waved his sword and the landlord fell silent.

"There are only two sets of tracks in the mud and snow leading to the midden. One is mine, and one is hers." I pointed to the daughter.

The girl fell silent as soon as I showed the kerchief.

The landlord shouted that these items were never in his

midden, and if they were, I'd placed them there myself.

Ector slammed the pommel of his sword against his saddle. It made a satisfactory thud, caused his horse to rear, and quieted the landlord for a moment.

"Bard, Sigurd. " he said. "Hand me your belts and the gold piece."

I took off my belt and handed it to him. He studied the slit seam and the gold piece. He pulled a second gold piece from my belt and compared it to the one the landlord claimed. Both had the Earl's rune stamped on them, signifying that he attested to the gold's purity.

The landlord stopped shouting when he saw the coins in my belt. His face paled and beads of sweat dotted on his forehead despite the day's chill. The girl moaned and bit her fingertips.

Ector glared at me. "This is the Earl's gold. How did it come to be in his possession."

Sigurd spoke. "I used the gold to lure them out here so Bard could search for our missing coins."

The landlord regained his courage. "There is no money in my tavern. I'm a poor man with a child to raise, her sainted mother dead these past five years and nobody but--"

Ector glared at him. This time, it was enough. Landlords practice the scowl. A mounted knight with a sword in his hand need only glare.

Ector addressed me, "And did you find stolen coins?"

I held out my cupped hands, displaying bronze and silver.

"Earl Acton gifted these to me yesterday. They were concealed under a rock beneath a chair. There were many more."

With this revelation the landlord lost his bravado. He knelt before Ector and wailed how he was a widower with a young child to keep. He begged for mercy, if not for himself, for his child. The girl wept and moaned piteously.

Ector swung from his saddle.

"Sigurd, hold the man and girl here. Bard, show me where you found the coins."

I led him into the tavern, and to the chair. He tossed it aside flipped over the rock. The hole held enough coins to fill his metal cap.

"Find something to hold these and bring them out. I shall administer justice."

I found a rabbit hide on the chair and wrapped the coins in it.

When I exited the inn, the innkeeper and daughter were on their knees before Ector. He stood erect. his sword point first in the ground in front of him, his hands on the pommel.

He pronounced his verdict slowly and carefully. This might be the first time he had been called upon to be the voice of the king.

"I find proofs for Bard's and Sigurd's claims. I find no proof to support the innkeeper's claims. I know Bard and Sigurd to be Earl Acton's trusted messengers. I have no witnesses to the innkeeper's honor or honesty.

He pointed at the tavern keeper. "Do you wish to confess

and repent?"

The landlord sobbed. "My child. I done it all for her. A poor girl with no mother, she needs a dowry and there's too much work and not enough money to be made in a tavern."

The daughter nodded dumbly.

Ector turned to me. "The coins you had in your hand. Were they what the earl gave you, no more and no less?"

I started to nod and thought better of it. "Very nearly. I've not counted it, but the earl gave me a small pouch filled."

He nodded. "You and Sigurd have worked for half a day."

We agreed. Ector appraised the pile of firewood. The billets Sigurd chopped gleamed white above the older, weathered gray wood. It was obvious he had been busy with his axe.

"I say you have each earned a silver piece." He extracted a two silver pennies from the rolled fur I'd given him and handed them to me. "In the King's Name, I fine the landlord half of these coins." He spilled half the coins onto the ground, wrapped the fur securely about the rest and placed them in his belt pouch.

The landlord crawled to the coins. He was busily grubbing them from the dirt when Ector spoke again. The daughter had not moved since her single nod.

"I saw the maid Corliss embroidering cloths for the earl's wife. I recognize this pattern." He glanced at the tavern keeper's daughter. "You will wash this until it has no stains, and you will sew the gold coins back into Bard's belt."

She was still staring dumbly at him.

"NOW!" Ector shouted, and she scrambled to her feet.

"Please, sir," she said to me, "It were so pretty. I wanted to keep it inside, but he wouldn't let me. I'm sorry it's got so stained. It were so pretty and white, an' I don't got no pretties."

Ector rested with us while she washed the kerchief in a bowl of hot water. The tavern keeper fetched us food and drink as we supervised her replacing the two gold coins in my belt. After the tasks were complete we gathered our possessions and were ready to travel once more.

Ector unrolled the fur and extracted a silver piece. He tossed it to the tavern master. "This for the food and drink. Be aware. More of the king's men will stop and question anyone they see working here. The next time you steal from travelers your daughter will be an orphan."

The innkeeper nodded and we left. Ector mounted his horse.

"There is an honest inn about three hours walk. You should reach it before nightfall. I shall tell the landlord to expect you."

He waved at us, slapped his horse's flank, and galloped away.

I held the kerchief to my nose. It did not smell of midden, but it no longer smelled of Corliss's hair either.

Sigurd shrugged. "A three hour walk," he said.

"A shorter ride," I agreed.

As we strode away, I heard the landlord and his daughter blaming each other for being caught and lamenting the lost coins.

I hummed and chanted:

Long ago and far away
Procrustes had a bed.
And folks too tall
To sleep on it
He'd shorten by a head.

Had Sigurd met Procrustes,
As the evening sun grew dim.
With hacks and whacks
From his coal-black axe
He'd have made the bed fit him.

Most innkeepers are honest folks,
Providing rest and meals
But there are some,
False, thieving scum.
Abusing trust to steal.

When Sigurd met this latter type,
And got tricked into slavery.
He stole back gold
From a hidden hole,
And thus repaid the knavery.

Sigurd laughed and picked up the pace. We had a long
way to go, and you never know when it might start
snowing.

Chapter Eight

Sigurd at the Hall of the Mountain King

ECTOR HAD SPOKEN truly about the distance to the next inn. It was almost dark when we approached a well-constructed wood and stone building. The wide open door and windows gleamed orange and yellow from the fire pit and candles. The sound of merriment drifting from the door into the cool evening made it clear this was a well-frequented inn.

The innkeeper stepped out of the doorway as we approached. He was a huge man, tall and broad. His mass of red hair and unruly beard made him even larger. The apron he wore over his tunic didn't cover his broad chest and fell only part-way to his knees.

"Welcome to my inn!" he boomed. "You must be Sigurd,

the Hero of Barleytown, and you, the earl's most favored bard. I am honored to have you choose my humble inn. A great honor it is, to host two such notable patrons. Please, come eat and drink with us. Perhaps you will deign to share a marvelous tale or two of your adventures. I have had fresh straw placed in the pallets awaiting your arrival."

A bard thrives on attention and craves adulation. Even so, I was taken aback by this boisterous welcome.

I've visited many inns. Innkeepers do not welcome me with open arms. They grudgingly admit me, watch how much ale I consume, let me sleep in the stable and count the eggs in the morning after I leave.

However, a bard's honor does not allow him to be bested in a contest of compliments.

I nudged Sigurd, who had stopped dead in his tracks with his mouth hanging open.

"Friend Innkeeper. Joyously well met, you are. We have heard tales of your marvelous ale and journeyed far to sample your famous hospitality. We have no doubts our travels are well spent, for all sing the praises of your lodgings and your board."

It would have been better to include his name or the name of his inn, but this was adequate. Once I knew his name, I'd stitch it into a verse of praise and consider him bested.

The innkeeper backed into his establishment, holding the stout wooden door for Sigurd and me to enter. The inn was larger than our previous lodgings as well as cleaner and serving more patrons.

The innkeeper swept his arm in a circle. "I let it be

known that the famous Sigurd and his equally famous bard would be visiting me this evening. All have come to pay their respects to my honored guests."

I reconsidered stitching his name into a single stanza. I'd need at least one verse of praise for each item we ate, drank, or slept on.

He stepped behind a rude table holding a large cask.

"Friends, " he called. "I bring you the famous Sigurd and Earl Acton's most favored bard! A free ale for everyone that we may drink their health."

I was speechless as he thrust a large wooden mug of ale into my hands and a second into Sigurd's. The other patrons crowded about the table holding out their cups.

Free ale from the innkeeper? This was beyond any of my wildest dreams. Praising his food and drink wasn't going to be sufficient. I'd need to compose a saga in which Sigurd is near death and is restored to health by a single sip of our host's ale.

I considered reworking the saga of Thor guesting with the giants. My host was large enough be a giant. The drinking flask that could not be drained and the groaning board of foodstuffs would be suitable. I'd skip the verses about wrestling with old age and lifting the Midgard serpent.

I nodded to Sigurd and then at the table. He gave me a boost, so I stood high above the rest of the patrons.

I strummed a flourish, and the crowd quieted. They raised their cups me and Sigurd, drained them, and proffered them to the innkeeper for refilling.

"Good friends. Good welcome. I bring you Sigurd, the

Hero of Barleytown. Sigurd Thief-catcher, Sigurd the Rescuer of maidens, Sigurd who made the road between Barleytown and Earl Acton's keep safe to travel once more."

The innkeeper led the crowd in a cheer and toast after each title. His patrons were quick to drain their cups and accept another refill. Sigurd looked a bit embarrassed, as well he might. It was most fulsome praise. He'd earned it.

Now it was time to return our landlord's favors.

Here in the Danelaw, everyone was familiar with the saga of Thor being tricked into a drinking contest in which the alehorn was constantly refilled from the ocean, and a competition against fire to see who could consume a meal the fastest.

I tapped the base of my lute, timing the taps to my heartbeat, and declaimed in the Norse style:

Sigurd, questing,   traveled northwards.
Follows footsteps   to an inn.
Seeking food and   ale and slumber.
Giant Redbeard   welcomed him.

Redbeard offered   him an alehorn,
Sigurd slurped   a doughty draft.
Spitting sea foam   from his whiskers.
Saw the alehorn   was still full

Sigurd took a   stouter swallow,
Making honor   to the ale.
Finished, gasping,   whiskers wetted,
Still the alehorn,   brimming full.

Sigurd said "I   am not thirsty,
Bring me to   a groaning board.
I've not eaten   in a fortnight.
I could eat   two goats and more"

Redbeard offered   food a-plenty,
Meat and bread   and spices rare.
Sigurd fell   upon the feast.

Ate until the	board was bare.
Redbeard's other	guest did smile.
He had also	eaten well.
Ate the foods that	had been offered.
Also eaten	up the board.
Sigurd called, "My	host is gracious.
Never have	I been so fed!
Meat a'plenty,	ale unending.
Still, I wood not	eat a board!"

Our red-haired innkeeper laughed at how I compared him to the trickster giant Utgard-Loki. He allowed that his ale barrel, though large, was not bottomless. I conceded his ale was much more flavorful than seawater. We toasted this quip and each other.

The innkeeper waved his arm and a lady nearly as tall as he with long blonde braids, carried a board of food from the kitchen. The board was so heavily laden she could barely hoist it onto the serving bench.

"Feast, my friends." The landlord motioned to Sigurd and me. "But do not eat this board. I'll need it in the morning for your breakfast."

I glanced at the tray of food and back to the landlord. I'd been outdone again. My own song had been used to best me.

I resolved to provide the best entertainment this inn had ever seen. The best drinking songs, the funniest tales, the bawdiest verses to *Sigurd and the Seven Virgins*. This night would be remembered long after we'd departed.

I'm quite certain I succeeded, though I don't recall the latter part of the night.

I awoke the next morning on a sweet-straw pallet with

my coin-pouch beneath me and both of Thor's legendary goats dancing inside my head. I never realized their hooves were so sharp and loud.

Rustles and thumps from the common room roused Sigurd as well. He levered himself into a sitting position and held his head. I think he feared it would fall off if he moved too quickly. Mine was only attached by a single thought.

We stumbled into the common area and found our host setting chairs and tables upright, occasionally kicking a sleeper awake to make space. It pleased me to note his eyes were as red as his hair and beard.

He was smiling, but it was a painful smile.

"Good morrow," he whispered. "A marvelous night. I thank you, gracious bard. Those who were not here will rue the fate that kept them away." He set another bench upright. "Would you break your fast?"

Sigurd moaned and my stomach twisted.

"Perhaps a small ale," I suggested. "To settle the stomach."

After an ale and egg, followed by some cheeses and fruits, I was ready to consider living. Sigurd and our host were also recovering and showing signs of relishing life.

"Friend innkeeper, " I called. "We should settle our tab and be on our way. How far is the king's castle?"

"The feasting was paid by the king. Arms-man Ector gave me a handful of coins when he passed and told me to make you welcome." He waved at the villagers still unconscious on the floor. "I trust his coins were well spent."

I nodded, wondering briefly why my head did not fall off with the motion.

"The king's castle is about five hours walk. I'll give you bread, apples and cheese to stay your hunger. You will find more inns to slake your thirst."

Sigurd and I thanked him, accepted the sack of food, and walked northward, placing our feet carefully to keep our heads balanced.

The snow was completely melted by now. The road was dry and the sun was warm and bright. The sunbeams drove themselves into my eyes and out the back of my head like slender seax blades. A few miles later, my troubles passed and I could once again enjoy the brown and gold tapestry the sun created from the oak and elm leaves carpeting the trail.

Sigurd broke the silence.

"So, was that a hero's welcome?" he asked.

"It will do until a real hero passes by," I replied. "Next time, I intend to be a bit less welcome."

Sigurd nodded. "I won't feel the need to honor every toast by draining my cup again." He massaged his temples. "But it truly felt grand to be welcomed. I could very much enjoy being a hero."

"Being a hero's chronicler is pleasant as well," I agreed with him. "We must find more heroic quests for you to fulfill."

He glanced aside at me.

"I prefer tasks with maidens and treasures, rather than chopping wood or heads."

145

I nodded. "Next quest: no exploring the middens, no hell-spawn horses, and no brigands. I'll compose it as a lullaby. It will surely lull everyone to sleep."

He laughed. "With your talents with truth, I'm certain a walk to the privy would enthrall the listeners and include battling a dragon or two."

We strode along, joking and laughing. After the troubles we'd had, it was good to simply enjoy each other's company on a fine autumn afternoon.

Proving my observation that taverns got closer together as you approached a village, we passed two more inns before reaching the king's castle. At each, the innkeeper smiled to see us, asked if we were the hero Sigurd and his bard, then offered ale, bread, and cheese in exchange for our tales and news.

Since they knew of us, they must have known my news as well. But there is a cachet to be gained by telling your guests how you hosted a hero and got the tales directly from his bard. The ale and bread we ate would become bronze and silver when his patrons waited for him to relate the next tidbit of gossip "from Earl Acton's favorite bard."

We left the second inn well-fed and pleased with ourselves. We weren't celebrated as joyously at these taverns as at Redbeard's but being welcome instead of shunned was a pleasant change in our lives.

The woods ended abruptly. One moment we shuffled through mounds of leaves and the next we strode between fields of golden grain. The trail flowed uphill, and atop the hill a stone-walled fortress perched, gray and white against a deep blue, autumn sky.

146

Promised Rewards

I resolved to craft a verse describing the king's castle on this bright clear day. A painter might show stark gray walls against soft blue sky, but I would make the listener understand how it feels to step from the dark chill of the woods into warm, golden farmland with a king's welcome awaiting you.

We strode across the farmlands, waving to the peasants. Some harrowed fallow fields while others dug turnips. We slowed our pace as we trudged uphill to the castle gate. Four guards stood by the gate, armored in chain, and armed with long-handled axes.

Two armsmen lowered their axes to block the gateway. One stepped beside us, while the last stood in our way.

"State your names and business," he said briskly.

"Sigurd the hero, and his bard," I replied. "We bear messages from Earl Acton to King Elmar."

The guard tensed and shifted his poleaxe. "Sigurd who slew Olaf the Berserker while his rage was on him?"

Sigurd nodded as a cold breeze slipped down my neck. Olaf had been in the king's army. If this were one of Olaf's friends he might wish to avenge his death.

The guard shifted his weapon and grasped Sigurd's forearm. "That would have been a blow to see. Olaf in his rage was a match for three men."

He released Sigurd's arm and pointed to a stone-paved road within the wall. "The cobbled path leads to the castle entrance."

The roadway was crowded with handcarts, oxen, pigs, horses, and people. Everyone was pushing to go in one direction or another.

After being shoved off the cobbles into the mud twice, I let Sigurd lead and stuck close to his heels. There are certain advantages to being a head taller than everyone else and carrying an axe.

When we reached the keep, we met another pair of guards. We explained who we were, and they nodded.

"You're expected. You may enter."

King Elmar's keep resembled Earl Acton's, except larger and more ornate. Instead of sitting at the same table he ate at, Elmar sat in a deeply carved chair on a raised platform. Rich tapestries hid the wall behind him. Two guards with great swords flanked his throne.

King Elmar resembled his cousin. He was tall and broad, with graying hair and beard. He wore a heavy, deep red cloak lined with wolf-fur and trimmed with ornate embroidery over a white linen tunic. His expression said he'd rather be wearing chainmail over leather.

The guard who had admitted us followed us in. He raised his poleaxe and hammered it against the stone floor with a hollow thud.

"Messengers from Earl Acton to see the King!" he called in the silence following his thuds. He whispered, "Step forward and relay your news."

Sigurd and I took two steps, stopping just short of the woven rug in front of Elmar's throne.

"Sire," I began. "Earl Acton sends his regards and best wishes."

The king yawned, bored already. I realized my message must be short and succinct.

"Earl Acton sends us to inform you that he has apprehended three runaways from the King's Army. He has had one slain and accepted two as armsmen. He--"

The king leaped to his feet and shouted, "My cousin is raising an army against me and sends assassins to my court!"

The guard closest to us leaped forward, swinging his sword high and down in a diagonal sweep at Sigurd's collar bone. The blow would have split him in half had it landed.

Sigurd jumped back shouting "Sire! No!"

The guard stepped forward, completing his downward swing, looping back up, and coming down in another diagonal sweep at Sigurd's other shoulder.

I fumbled for my dagger, but somebody behind me grabbed my arms.

I fell forward to break his grip, but my attacker knew my trick and I ended up with my arms pinned behind my back.

Sigurd raised his axe to parry the second blow, still protesting.

I kicked backwards to free myself from my captor. I proved a man wearing soft leather boots should not kick a man wearing iron greaves.

The swordsman stepped close to Sigurd and brought his sword up into a defensive posture. In two sudden moves, he slipped his weapon behind Sigurd's axe head, then leaped back, pulling the axe forward. Sigurd was thrown off balance and stumbled as his opponent stepped aside.

The swordsman kicked Sigurd's feet as he shuffled past, then swung his sword at Sigurd's unprotected back.

A dull clang echoed in the hall. I twisted again, looped my foot behind my captor's knee to pull him off his balance. My opponent knew this trick as well and trapped my foot.

Sigurd was on his hands and knees, with his axe beneath him when King Elmar called "Hold and report."

"He fights like a farmer," the swordsman replied. "But he's strong, fast and knows enough to keep hold of his weapon. He'll do."

I realized the sword's clang was not the sharp crack a blade makes slicing into flesh. It was the dull thud made by the flat of a sword striking a tender backside. Sigurd rose and rubbed his afflicted area.

Behind me, my captor reported, "This one fights like a tavern rat. I don't know what he expected to do with a dagger against a swordsman, but he was game to try."

He whispered. "Relax, you're safe." and released me.

I stumbled as he let me go and looked up. The king smiled at me.

"My cousin claims a good eye for a man's potential. Let me see if his ear is as good." He waved his left hand. A slight, gray-haired man in a long gray robe, carrying a shoulder-harp strode from behind the tapestry.

"Attend me and repeat," he said.

He plucked two strings on his harp, the notes the monk's used for "Amen."

I stared at him.

"Sing them then play them." he commanded.

I sang "Ahhhh-Men," then played the notes on my lute. To be fancy, I then strummed the two chords.

He smiled and plucked a tune I'd learned from the monks when the abbot wasn't about. I'd sung it in many taverns since then.

I sang it and continued with a line I'd added.

He plucked the tune Shawn had chanted while he waited to be executed.

I'd never played this tune, but I'd heard it once. I sang the notes, then plucked them on my lute.

He nodded and said, "Complete this verse."

Fire is needed	by him who has come
And is benumbed	to his knees.
Food and clothes	are needed by one
Who has traveled	over the mountain.

This was part of the Norse guesting rules. It's well known in the Danelaw, though the brothers at my monastery never repeated them.

I finished this verse easily.

Water is needed	by the one who thirsts.
More needed than these	is honest welcome.

Then he sang a strange melody I'd never heard before. Three fast notes followed by three slow ones and unusual steps between them. I could sing it back to him, though I fumbled a bit. I could not find the right notes on my lute.

He sang more melodies; some I knew and could copy

but several were strange to me.

He finally turned away from me and back to the king, who had not yawned once during these challenges.

"He is church trained, but they didn't damage him. He knows Latin forms, some skaldic, and has been exposed to Celtic chants. He is unfamiliar with other musical styles. His ear and voice are good. I will accept him, if my liege wishes."

King Elmar nodded.

"Very well," he spoke to Sigurd and me. "My cousin has sent you with ten gold pieces to ransom the criminals he pardoned. I will accept them."

I'd intended to tell him we had eight gold pieces, to keep the others as our reward. But he knew exactly how much gold we had to barter with and demanded all of it. We had made a long journey for nothing.

I opened my mouth to protest.

"In exchange," the king continued. "I will give you gifts of greater value than ten pieces of gold."

I closed my mouth.

"You shall guest with me this winter. Sigurd, you shall train with my arms master and learn to use your axe for something other than firewood. Bard, you will study with my scald. He has traveled widely and knows many of the world's musical forms."

His face grew stern as he finished, "If you grow to become the men my cousin thinks you can be, there will be positions for you in my household. If not, you will at least be better prepared to make your way in the world."

He nodded us dismissed as the poleaxe knocked against the floor and the guard announced the next visitor claiming his attention.

The guards shoved us gently out a narrow doorway. A gray-haired scribe lounging beyond the door demanded our belts. He slit them open, counted the coins and returned our belts. He told a boy to show us our quarters.

The runner led us through a maze of stone corridors, pointing at side passages and announcing, "armory," "granary," and "stable." Eventually he led us to a large room with a fire pit in the center and twenty pallets on the floor.

"Barracks," he said, and left before I could demand more information.

Sigurd stared at me, slack jawed. I stared dully back at him.

Last night, we had been heroes, welcomed and celebrated. Now we were apprentices. Or something. I wasn't certain what we were, or what had just happened, except we had been tested and found wanting.

"Church trained, but not damaged." The phrase irked me. The brothers had taught me well, and I'd learned even more in the years on my own. Then I remembered the strange triple-beat tune Terrel played, and the others I hadn't known. I ached to embrace those forms and make them my own.

I glanced about the room and back to Sigurd.

He spoke first.

"At least we have a dry place to spend the winter and we'll eat regular meals."

I nodded, "If we can ever find the great hall again."

He opened his mouth to speak when the boy who'd led us to the barracks ran back. "Sigurd," he said. "Practice yard. Bard. Master Terrel's cell."

He spun around "Follow," he called over his shoulder and dashed away.

We dropped our cloaks on two empty pallets and ran after him.

The runner sent Sigurd down the third corridor, and he led me an even merrier chase. We went up four or five levels until he paused before a large tapestry of a young man playing a harp in a woodland glen.

"Master Terrel, I bring the lutist," he called softly.

"Send him in," said a gentle voice behind the tapestry.

I lifted the tapestry, revealing a narrow doorway, and stepped into a cell three paces wide, with a hand-sized, parchment-covered window.

And musical instruments. The room was filled with musical instruments. On shelves, hanging on walls, in boxes and loose on the floor. I saw wind instruments with reeds, metal horns, ox horns, various drums, bells, wooden flutes, bone flutes, harps, and things I didn't recognize.

The gray-haired man who had acknowledged me as "not damaged" was almost invisible in the clutter of musical instruments.

"Do you play anything besides your lute?" Terrel asked.

I nodded at the shepherd's pipes and a hand-sized drum.

He handed me one of the shepherd's pipes. "Play me a

tune you know."

I puffed a soft breath into the instrument. It had a fine tone. I ran it by my lips to get its feel and played a shepherd's lullaby I'd learned a year ago. It's a lovely, lilting tune, well suited to a pipe's soft tone.

I stopped after just a few notes. It was horrible. The notes were wrong. The tune sounded nothing like what I intended to play.

I examined the pipes, counted the number of tubes, and carefully blew into each one.

"The notes are wrong," I told Terrel. "The tubes are the wrong lengths."

He laughed at me.

"The pipe is fine," he assured me. "It's for Greek shepherds, not ours." He held out his hand and I passed him the pipes. He played the song with three long notes and three short ones. The tune was strange but compelling. It fit these notes. The strange rhythm captivated my ears.

He stopped playing. "That's a Greek warrior's dance." he told me. "Do not interrupt or join a man while he performs. That is a challenge to fight." He reached to the harp in his lap and softly plucked the strings. "There are patterns and traditions for all music's. You've learned church traditions and our Celtic patterns from hearing them. You'll need to understand the rules behind the tunes to use them."

He handed me the pipes, and another set from a shelf behind him.

"Take these two pipes and play them. Tomorrow you should be able to sing the notes of either pipe in any order. When you know the pipes, I'll teach you the phrases that go

155

with them. Each land has its own musical language, as distinct as its spoken language."

I accepted the pipes, wondering how I would carry both them and my lute as he continued.

"It's time for us to eat, so we may entertain during the king's meal. I play for the king's table. You will play at the other end of the hall, below the salt."

He led me down the corridor more slowly than the runner. I had time to notice different tapestries on the walls and memorize how to return.

I trotted to be abreast of Master Terrel.

"Please, sir," I began. Politeness is always good when cajoling someone. I respected the minstrel after the few minutes we'd spent together, and I wanted him to think well of me. "How did you learn the languages of music?"

He smiled. "I traveled in my youth. I walked to Londinium to hear the Roman tunes. I listened to sailors sing songs I'd never heard, so I traveled to Gaul. Travelers in Gaul told tales of more types of music further south and then to the east. In the end, I spent almost twenty years traveling and learning." His eyes got a far-away look. "I walked the entire breadth and length of the Roman Empire and a bit beyond. I think the caravan to the spice lands of the far east was the most instructive. So many things I still don't know."

He glanced back at me. "After enough years in the dry, sun-scoured east, you miss a cool, foggy morning and that shepherd's lullaby you tried to play. So, I came home and settled here."

I gasped. He had spent nearly as many years learning

156

music as I'd lived. I wanted to know everything he'd learned and despaired of ever knowing a tenth of it.

We rounded a corner and entered the kitchen by a back entry. A huge fireplace dominated one end of the room. It crouched against the outer wall, its bright amber fire glaring at us behind iron racks, and spits filled with pots, and meats. The cooks knew Master Terrel and had a bowl of stew and a fresh loaf of bread waiting for him. At his gesture, another bowl was brought for me.

King Elmar's kitchen was larger and more orderly than Earl Acton's, but I missed Corliss's personal attention.

As I swallowed my last morsel, Terrel rose and motioned for me to follow. We strode together into the great hall. Unlike the earl's keep, we entered before the food servers. Terrel promenaded to the king's table and pointed me towards the others. He played as the serfs distributed food to the nobles.

I glanced at the king's table before approaching the armsmen's and servant's benches. King Elmar wore a white linen tunic with embroidery about the neck and sleeves. On his right sat the guard who had attacked Sigurd, now wearing supple black leather armor. On the king's left sat a young lady as dainty and fair as Ermindale. Her red-gold hair was bound and tied in a complex braid held in place by a silver and bronze tiara. She stared at me with frank curiosity, and then looked demurely at her plate when she noticed how I stared back at her.

The lady I was admiring was Princess Beornwyn! I should not be staring at a king's daughter. I dropped my eyes and fled to a spot in the lower end of the hall where all could hear me--and most could see me--and sang *Sigurd and the Three Thieves.* Many eaters fell silent and listened. I was new and had tales and songs they hadn't heard. In a day or so, unless I had a new tune, I'd play my lute while they ignored me; talking, eating and drinking.

Once the meal was complete, most armsmen and castle attendants left for evening duties or sleep, but some stayed to listen as I played and told tales.

I was in the midst of *Sigurd and the Seven Virgins* when a hush fell over the crowd. I scanned the listeners to see what had happened.

A new peasant had joined them. He was a large man, wearing simple homespun, but he wore it as though it were trimmed with ermine. He concealed his face within his cloak, but I saw enough to recognize the resemblance to Earl Acton.

Nobody bowed or acknowledged the king, but a space appeared on the bench nearest me.

He sat and listened as Sigurd finished with the seventh sister in a most lewd manner and laughed as heartily as the others.

"Good bard," he called when I'd finished. "Do you know a saga of horses?"

I wished I'd never written this song. I didn't consider it my best, but it was developing a life of its own.

After *Sigurd's Ride with Death,* the king left, as did everyone else. I followed a crowd to the barracks, and found Sigurd lying face down on his pallet, being pummeled and massaged by a burly woman. The strong odor of horse liniment encompassed him, and dark bruises marred his ribs and arms.

I settled myself on the pallet next to him as he greeted me.

"Tell me, Bard, do you know how many ways there are for an axe-man to be struck by a wooden sword?"

I admitted I did not.

"Neither do I. I learned many this afternoon, and I fear I will learn more--ouch--tomorrow. I hope you fared better with the minstrel than I fared with the armsman."

"I learned I know nothing about music."

I dug out one of the flutes Terrel had given me and played the notes up and down. They sounded strange, wrong. The idea of wrong notes being right was hard to understand, though it made sense when he played the melody meant for this instrument.

Sigurd grunted. "That's an ill made set of pipes," he said. "Even I can tell the notes are wrong. You may use my dagger to shorten the ones that aren't right."

He grunted as the matron slapped more liniment between his shoulders and ground her fists into his back.

It would be a long winter.

Chapter Nine

Sigurd and the Long-lost Brother

I WOKE THE next morning with the notes from the Greek pan pipes echoing in my ears. They still sounded strange, but not so utterly wrong.

The music in my head was quickly drowned out by the groans and curses of twenty men rising for breakfast. Sigurd was loudest, swearing each time he moved.

I lifted my head to a view of the bruises across his ribs and arms as he pulled his tunic over his head. I hummed my new notes, settling them in my mind and throat as Sigurd grunted and moaned his way into his leggings.

Like most days, I was happy to be a bard, not a warrior.

We followed the crowd to the great hall. I was not

required to play during breakfast, so I ate with everyone else. The king's table was not lavish, but there was plenty of cheese, bread, and porridge.

I was nearly done when the runner came up behind us.

"Practice yard," he said. Sigurd groaned and stood.

"I don't know whether my bruises or muscles hurt the most."

I felt sorry for him, but content in knowing I only had one more set of pipes to memorize and all morning in which to do it.

Yes, being a bard is the best life.

"Both of you," the runner said, and headed away between the tables. "Follow" he called over his shoulder.

I rose and followed, more than a little confused and nervous. What could the arms master want of me? I'm not an armsman. I had no need for his training.

The practice yard was a morass of mud twenty paces square. It contained several pells: wooden posts as tall as a man, archery targets and racks of wooden spears, swords, and axes. A dozen armsmen were stretching, attacking the pells or sparring with each other. I recognized Ector battling with one of the wooden posts. He wielded a practice sword, not a real one, but even so woodchips danced away from the pell with each assault.

Arms master Mather stood to the side, watching everything, and commenting loudly when a blow was too soft or not targeted well. He was the man who ate at the King's right hand and who had attacked Sigurd yesterday. His dark hair was cropped short to fit under a metal cap, exposing nothing for an opponent to pull during a battle.

His beard was barely a finger-width long, again affording no grip to a foe. He moved with the strength and grace of a wolf.

As we approached he faced us.

"Ready to learn to defend your legs?" he asked Sigurd. "It will give the bruises on your ribs a chance to heal."

Sigurd nodded ruefully. It was obvious he expected the lesson to result in matching bruises on his legs.

Master Mather looked me up and down. "You grabbed at your dagger when I attacked your friend yesterday. What did you plan to do with it?"

I swallowed. I hadn't planned what I'd do, just that I should do something.

"Throw it?" I finally suggested.

"You can throw a dagger?" he asked. He waved at a target ten paces behind him. "Show me your skill."

I have no skill. Not with weapons. My skill is words and music and avoiding needing to use a weapon. I threw my dagger. It slapped against the outer edge of the target and fell to the ground.

Mather grunted, "You can't throw a dagger. Truth now, what did you intend to do."

"I don't know. Just-- You attacked my friend and I needed to do something."

"Likely gotten you both killed." He motioned to one of the runners to fetch my dagger. He accepted it, balanced it in his palm and handed it back to me. "This is an eating tool, not a weapon. Don't bother throwing it, it's not balanced. It's too light for combat, but you could use it in a pinch."

He called to Ector to stop being gentle with the pell and come be useful. Ector stopped in mid-swing and ran to us, panting and sweating in the chill morning air.

The arms master grabbed a wooden dagger from the rack and faced Ector.

"Half-speed," he said, "to show the bard how to use a dagger against a swordsman."

Ector obligingly swung his wooden sword over his head and down at the arms master's shoulder, as Sigurd had been attacked yesterday.

Mather stepped forward, into the blow, and caught the tip of the sword with the base of his dagger and pushed out.

"You can parry a sword with a dagger. Use your leverage on the end of the sword."

He stepped in further. "Once you get inside the sword's reach, it can't cut you." He raised the wooden dagger to Ector's throat. "Slide your weapon under a gorget and you cut the throat."

He tossed the dagger to me. I reached to catch it and missed. The armsmaster cursed softly as I knelt for the weapon.

"Now, you do the moves, step, parry, step, thrust."

I glanced at Ector, who had retreated.

"Not against him," the armsmaster barked. "I don't want you hurting anyone. Do the moves in the air. Imagine an opponent if you can. Do it slowly."

I took a step. "Not so deep."

I waved the wooden dagger. "Higher, further out, keep the tip pointed slightly away from you."

Another step. "Deeper, next time."

I stepped through this several times until Mather was grudgingly satisfied. He scuffed a square two paces across in the mud.

"Practice those moves within this box. Step, parry, step, thrust, turn. Use the full square, repeat until I call halt. After you've rested you'll start again."

I stepped through the movements, humming the pipe notes. I wasn't sure why I was doing this, but at least I could put the time to good use.

I half-listened as Mather explained to Sigurd how to use his axe properly, punctuated by the dull thud of a wooden sword striking Sigurd's thigh. Sigurd was soon practicing parry, step, and swing maneuvers in a block next to mine. Every fourth turn, I'd face him, swinging a heavy wooden axe, sweating heavily as the sun warmed the practice yard.

It's easy to step, lift a play-dagger and step again. At least, it's easy the first three times. Sooner than I expected, it was obvious this was not my normal activity. Within ten minutes, my shoulders burned like wax torches and a river of sweat streamed down my face. I didn't have enough breath to hum my notes. I could barely even think them.

About three years later, the armsmaster called for us to rest.

Sigurd and I dropped where we were standing, which happened to put us side-to-side.

After we panted for a few moments, Sigurd faced me.

"Bard," he gasped, "Did you really draw your dagger when I was attacked?"

I nodded.

"You'd have been killed. Why would you defend me?"

I shrugged, which caused the sweat from my forehead to drip into my eyes where it burned like tiny fires.

"I don't know. I just couldn't let you die alone." I blinked and dabbed at my eyes with my sleeve. My tunic was so sweat dampened that this didn't help.

Sigurd grunted a profanity in a language I didn't think he knew.

"Everyone dies alone. You didn't need to die as well." He pulled a scrap of cloth from his pouch and passed it to me.

I dabbed at my face as my hands shook harder. I couldn't tell if it were because of the exercise or my nerves. I truly didn't know why I'd tried to defend him. I wasn't sure I wanted to know.

I returned his cloth. "It makes a good epic. A hero either dies with his companions or dies saving them."

Sigurd swiped the cloth across his face and looked beyond me into the distance. His eyes lost focus and I knew he was re-living his past. His breathing calmed, while I was still gasping.

"It's not what a hero does." He said quietly. "It's what a brother does. It's what my brother did." He paused and swallowed. Hard. "I had a brother. He was the strongest, bravest, best man I knew. I loved him, admired him and wanted to be a man just like him."

His teeth clenched. "Except he never got to be a man."

Sigurd gazed through me, not at me. He crumpled the cloth and shoved it into his belt. "He got called to a peasant levy. Sent to fight against some kingdom I'd never heard of."

He stared at the ground and dug a furrow in the mud with his finger. "After he left, I snuck away and followed him. I'd be an armsman, just like him. We'd grab glory and find fame together."

His eyes lit up when he spoke of the fame and glory he and his brother would earn, then he looked beyond the pells, into a past he wished didn't exist.

"I caught up with him just before the battle; in a line with a hundred other spearmen. I grabbed a spear and stepped into the line next to him. Told him not to worry, he had a brother guarding his back."

A splinter from the pells lay in the mud by his feet. Sigurd picked it up and pushed it upright by the furrow he'd dug.

"When he saw me, he reached to his neck and told me he'd forgotten his luck charm - back in the camp. Asked me to run fetch it."

Sigurd's voice cracked. He glared at the furrow he'd dug in the mud and the splinter standing next to it. His hand came down flattening the splinter and covering the furrow.

"By the time I got back, the battle was over. The entire line of spearmen had been slaughtered by archers without ever landing a blow. I found my brother's body. Still wearing his luck-charm."

He slammed his fist against the ground, pounding a hole over the furrow. "I couldn't go home. Not without my brother. I wouldn't live in the land where he'd died so uselessly. So, I wandered, selling myself when I could, stealing a meal when I couldn't."

He looked at me again. This time he saw me. His eyes were hard, warning me to stay silent. "It's why I resented you treating me like your younger brother. No man could replace my brother. No man was ever as brave and noble as he was. I never met a man worthy to be my brother."

His eyes softened. Now they pleaded for me to be someone else, someone who had died years ago. "Until now. Brother."

I lowered my eyes to my lap. My hands had been shaking from the exertion. I'd had time to recover, but they still shook.

I'd known from the day we met that Sigurd had a story. I'd known I'd learn it if we spent time together.

I didn't expect to become part of his story.

I swallowed the lump in my throat.

"You'd have done the same for me." I muttered. Those weren't the right words, but I didn't know what the proper words were.

Mather's shadow came between us.

"Let's see what you've learned," he called. I welcomed the interruption. I'd become used to Sigurd as a companion. I even considered him a friend. I wasn't prepared for him to be a brother.

After demonstrating to Mather how little I'd learned, he paired me with a young swordsman who needed to practice attacking while I practiced parrying. Sigurd sparred with

Ector. Their combat echoed across the practice field--an irregular beat of thuds and grunts.

Eventually, it was time for the midday meal. Mather met us as we left the field.

"Not bad," he commented, nodding at Sigurd, "After lunch you'll practice dodge and parry. Those bruises won't heal until you stop getting hit." He frowned at me. "Come back tomorrow morning. I'll see what you can learn."

We made it to the great room and flopped onto a bench. I was starving but wasn't sure I could raise my arm to reach the food. I found the strength I needed. as soon as I smelled the stew,

A bard travels. A man who walks all day builds an appetite and knows how to address a trencher. A man who spends a half-day in mock-battle learns a new level of hunger. I did not address the trenchers, I attacked them like Viking hordes pillaging a nunnery. I was reaching for my third fist-sized loaf when the runner came behind me.

"Master Terrel awaits you. Do you know the way?"

I glanced vaguely up, and he nodded. "Follow," and off he ran. I stumbled behind him, chewing on the bread and wishing I'd grabbed two trenchers.

I was dreading this meeting with Terrel. I'd expected to know both pipes well enough to follow a tune. Instead, I'd barely learned one and not touched the other. I badly wanted him to be impressed by my ability. A man teaches best when he respects his student. I hungered to learn everything he knew.

The way to Terrel's cell was familiar. I could probably find it on my own. The runner motioned at the tapestry of the young man with a harp and continued running.

I paused to catch my breath, called, and slid behind the tapestry.

Terrel set down the harp he had been strumming. "Stand, sing the notes from the first pipe in order."

I sang. He nodded, then requested backwards, and then up and down skipping notes. The sequences with skipped notes matched the songs he'd played, and I started singing the rhythms as well as the tune.

He waved me to stop. "If you want to show off, sing the notes from the second pipe."

I lowered my eyes and shook my head.

"I'm sorry, sir. The armsmaster demanded I spend the morning in the weapon's yard. I never had time to play the second pipe."

He nodded but didn't smile.

"Play it now."

I dug the flute from my wallet. It was slightly smaller than the one I'd played first.

I'd wrapped it in the kerchief Corliss gave me. Terrel reached for the cloth and examined it. "You treat your instruments well. This is an excellent piece of work."

He nodded to the pipe, and I played the notes. They were strange, but also strangely familiar. As Terrel studied me I realized this was a test. I should notice something about the two sets of pipes.

I'd just sung the notes from the first flute. As I listened to myself, I heard the same tones, except that the smaller flute started in the middle of the first flute's range and went higher.

I held the two instruments together, played the lowest notes from the first flute, then the notes from the second.

"The last notes on this flute," I held up the smaller instrument. "are the same as the first notes on this one," I held up the larger flute. "But higher." I hoped I'd solved the puzzle.

He smiled. "The Greeks call them octaves. Compare the two pipes."

I examined them carefully. "The notes that are the same are twice as long on this pipe." I lifted the first flute.

Terrel nodded. "The monks taught you to sing by rote. I'll teach you the theory behind what you've learned."

And so, it started. The monks had taught me simple ciphering, despite my efforts or desires. Terrel found a use for this skill and made me understand why it was useful. The lengths of the pipes, the lengths of the strings on a harp and the placement of frets on a lute were all described by these ciphers.

I was entranced all over again. There was so much to learn. I understood how Terrel had spent twenty years studying and not learned everything there was to know.

However much I cherished my new-found use for ciphering, I found no use for the morning sessions with Armsmaster Mather. If a bard can't talk his way out of a fight, he can always run from it.

After a week of walking in circles swinging a wooden dagger, I explained this to him.

He nodded ruefully. "You're right. You'll never be an

armsman. Running from a fight is your best choice." I smiled. I would have more time to learn the music. "But King Elmar demands I teach you to defend yourself." He glared at the dagger I'd let droop to my side. I raised it back to the defensive position as he continued. "There are fights you can't run from. It's my pride that the man I train doesn't need to run from a fight. He walks away after it's over. His opponent is carried away."

"What if I'm attacked by someone you trained?" I asked, still hoping to escape the weapons yard.

"Then you'd better run." He replied. "But right now, practice the parry, step, attack until you can do it in your sleep. When I'm satisfied with how you do simple movements, I'll show you better moves that might save your life."

That afternoon, I complained to Terrel, and asked if he could intercede and get me more time for music. He studied me thoughtfully.

"How often have you owned more than two coins?" he asked.

"Only once," I admitted.

"And how long before they were stolen?"

"Almost a full day. The innkeeper purloined my purse while I slept." I silently admired my phrasing and resolved to use 'purloined' in a verse.

"You were lucky," he replied. "You could have been knifed or clubbed instead of just tricked."

He picked up the nearest harp and strummed a note thoughtfully. "When you leave the castle, you'll have the musical skills to earn coins by the purseful. You'll need other skills to keep them."

"But" I protested, "when I'm that good I'll be an earl's bard, or maybe even a king's. I'll sing in a household, not a tavern."

Terrel laughed. "You think I only sing for the king's dinner? You'll have to join me on my rounds tonight. Each month I visit every tavern within an hour's walk, spreading the king's news and listening to the peasant's complaints."

My eyes widened at this. I thought being a king's bard was an easy job. Sing during dinner, make up a ditty or two to amuse the court and otherwise relax.

Terrel had more to teach me than music. A king's bard is also the king's eyes, ears, and mouth.

"If you'll be tavern-crawling with me," he continued, "I must teach you a new song. It's a snippet of castle gossip we are to spread."

He plucked a sprightly, simple tune from the harp, a classic mocking song. Once he'd played the melody he sang:

Earl Bella said "My name means war.
I'll drive the Viking from our shore
They won't be raiding any more
Once I bring raids to them.

Earl Bella's plan was brave and bold
To raid a Norseman's native hold
To plunder their ill-gotten gold
And thus reward his king.

173

C. Flynt

He asked the king for shiploads three,
He'd sail these warriors 'cross the sea.
Burn Viking longboats where they be.
And then sail home again.

The Norsemen had a different plan.
They'd fight with every boy and man.
Earl Bella landed, then he ran,
One boat sailed home again.

The Viking longboats were repaired.
The Danish chieftain came prepared.
To leave our kingdom burned and bare.
Til Elmar met with him.

He offered ale for each burned boat,
And bear skins for berserker's coats.
And wine to cool a Northman's throat.
He gave danegeld to them.

King Elmar saved our wives and daughters.
He saved our sons from being slaughtered.
As to why the ale we drink is watered.
Thank Bella and his men!

When he finished I asked, "Is Bella likely to take offense?"

"Very likely. But he won't do anything. His foray into the Daneland was the biggest disaster since Cariadoc lost a war against himself. We're a nation of landsmen who row along a river, not sailors who skim o'er the salt-water swan-road. Some of the army deserted rather than sail, the rest landed too sick to fight. They fired a few Viking long-boats and

174

then they were routed. Too many of the king's Armsmen are now Jarl Gotfred's slaves. When Gotfred sailed up the river to our shores to take his vengeance we were too weak to defend ourselves. So Elmar had to offer enough clothing, wine and ale to satisfy Gotfred's honor."

He plucked the tune again. "We need to make everyone understand that it's Earl Bella's fault that wine and ale are scarce and watered, not King Elmar's."

We ran through the song a couple times, until I'd memorized it to his satisfaction.

I barely tasted my dinner. I was honored by the sign of trust that Terrel would take me with him. I worked out new ornamentations to *Bella's Saga* while I ate and played them to appreciative listeners as they finished their meal.

I was well prepared for this evening with *Bella's Saga*, my Sigurd Sagas, and new verses I'd been saving for a special occasion.

As soon as the meal was finished, the runner brought my cloak and word that Terrel awaited me at the main entrance.

At the first inn, Terrel played three songs, then called for me.

"Good cousins," he declaimed. "Two scalds dwell in the castle this winter. I shall wet my throat while Bard the Lutist entertains you."

Terrel had shared some stories about his life in the east. I'd used them to expand *Sigurd and the Seven Virgins* into *Sigurd and the Nine Virgins*. I had been waiting for a chance to surprise him with the new verses.

I was halfway through the eighth virgin's stanzas when

C. Flynt

he fell off a stool laughing. The other listeners sat with mouths and eyes wide open. Several men blushed and the womenfolk ran off holding aprons in front of their faces.

I considered this to be adequate approval and saved the ninth virgin for another occasion.

We visited two more taverns after that. Terrel played three or four songs, including *Bella's Saga* at each, and then had me sing one or two Sagas of Sigurd.

It was late when we reached the fourth tavern. Terrel suggested I sing first and lead off with the song of Earl Bella.

He held the leather doorway open for me, and I walked into a dim, smoky tavern playing a flourish on my lute and loudly calling, "Greetings. King Elmar sends me with news and tales to amuse."

The patrons cheered and welcomed me then fell silent inviting me to play.

As I started *Bella's Saga* I noticed a mountain of a man sitting nearby, his tangled black hair and beard were as shaggy as a bear's coat. He had drunk heavily. He slumped on a bench with half closed bloodshot eyes and his head nodding almost in time to the music.

That is, his head was nodding until I reached the verse about Bella running away from the battle. I'd barely finished that line when he leaped to his feet, shouting "Knave! Liar! My lord never ran from a battle!"

He pulled a cudgel the size of my forearm from his trousers and swung it like a broadsword at my head.

My life did not pass before my eyes, but my death did. I saw myself lying across a trestle table with my head split

176

wide and my brains dripping onto the floor.

My mind was frozen by the image of my death, but my hands were not. My left hand tightened around the neck of my lute and pulled it behind me, while my right hand grabbed a wine bottle from the table.

As the cudgel plunged toward my head, I parried it with the wine bottle, just like parrying a sword with a dagger in the practice yard.

Luckily, a cudgel is not as heavy as a sword and is easier to parry. The blow missed my head and hit my left shoulder. My arm and hand went numb. My lute slipped from nerveless fingers and hit the stone-paved floor with an unpleasant crunch.

A wine bottle is not as sturdy as a dagger. The glass bottle shattered as I parried the cudgel blow. I finished the step and riposte with the remains of a wine bottle in my hand.

I pressed the jagged edges against my foeman's throat and started to twist when my mind thawed. I was about to kill this stranger.

"Yield or Die!" I shouted up into his face, as blood trickled down his neck where the wine bottle pricked him.

His eyes opened wide. He was suddenly very sober. I saw the image of his death filling his eyes the way the image of my death had filled mine. His cudgel thudded against the floor. "I yield" he whispered.

I wasn't sure what to do next. I'd never been in a serious fight. I'd certainly never won one. Two of my foe's companions rose behind him. Did they intend to drag him back to his seat or pick up the fight where he left off?

Before they made their intentions plain, Terrel stepped into the tavern.

"Good friends," he called. "As the Bard was going to sing, the King drinks his wine watered, but tonight you need not. He has sent me with coin to buy unwatered ale to drink his health."

He tossed a small pouch to the innkeeper, who deftly caught it, jiggled it to judge the weight and began pouring drafts of ale.

"To King Elmar!" called Terrel as the wooden tankards were passed around.

"To the King," came back the echoes as I released the broken wine bottle and retrieved my lute. The back was cracked. Now I wished I'd killed the man after all. This lute had been my sole companion for almost ten years. It deserved better than to be broken in a useless fight in a dingy tavern.

Terrel pushed me out the door. "We'd best leave now, while everyone is pleased with us," he whispered. He glanced down at the crack in my lute. "Give that to me. I'll fix it."

We walked back to the castle in silence. I stumbled to the barracks in a daze and fell onto my pallet without undressing. The brawl happened so quickly I had no chance to talk my way out of it and no opportunity to run. Mather's words echoed in my mind as I saw the cudgel approaching my head again and again.

I fell asleep seeing the cudgel. In my dreams it was a sword, an axe, or a mace. Sometimes my dream self-parried the blow and riposted. Other times I failed to parry the attack and jerked awake as the blow landed.

In the morning I wasn't rested. I felt like I'd been fighting the entire night. My left shoulder was sore and bruised, reminding me how close it had come to being my head that met the cudgel.

Sigurd glanced at my disheveled clothes and saw me favor my left arm. "Too many hours holding a mug of lute?" he laughed and poked at me. The pain shot up my arm and made me wince.

"Sorry," he muttered. "What happened to you?"

I told him the evening's events as we walked to breakfast.

"I should have been there." he said finally. "You needed a brother guarding your back."

I nodded. Perhaps a brother at my back would be worthwhile after all.

"I wish you'd been there," I agreed. "But it happened so fast you couldn't have helped. Terrel and Mather are right, I need to be able to defend myself. I'll never stand in a shield-wall, but I'll certainly stand in a tavern."

He nodded as we addressed ourselves to breakfast. I intended to work up a mammoth hunger by lunchtime.

Mather met me at the entrance to the weapon's yard.

"Raise your left arm," he commanded. He pushed it forward, sideways, and back, watching my eyes as he moved it. I winced a few times. My eyes jerked when he lifted the arm over my head.

"Probably nothing broken," he finally conceded. "You met the fight you couldn't run from last night, but at least you walked away afterward. Any fight you walk away from is good, but there's no honor in letting one of Bella's drunken louts land a blow. At least you didn't let it land where he intended."

I nodded. "I didn't parry fast enough. I need to practice harder."

He smiled grimly. "And it's time to teach you to dodge as well as parry. The next foe you meet might not be so drunk."

I worked my way around the square, just like the other mornings, step, parry, step, attack. Except I stepped faster, parried deeper, and aimed my attacks at the throat of the invisible drunken lout who had broken my lute.

After I'd warmed up doing the moves against an imaginary opponent, Mather helped me don a set of heavily padded armor and called for Ector.

"You'll not be wearing armor in a tavern, but you'll not be fighting a man I've trained, either." he glanced at Ector. "Aim here," he pointed where the neck and shoulder pads joined, "and let him parry. Start at half speed and work up to full attacks. I don't want to see any dainty, lady-like blows by the time we break to eat."

Ector nodded, checked my armor, and stepped away to sword distance. I parried the half-speed blows easily. As he increased the speed and power of his attacks, it got harder, but I blocked most of them. In the end, he was sweating and grunting as heavily as I was.

Sigurd had advanced from only using his axe to wielding his axe with a large round shield the way the Norsemen did. I resolved to ask why he was training with a

Viking shield instead of the Roman style, but my questions would wait until I could breathe.

By lunch time we were both starving. Nobody spoke while eating. Everybody just grabbed the dark bread, bowls of pottage and cups of ale, swallowing as fast as possible.

I finished my last trencher as I walked to Terrel's cell. I hoped he had been able to repair my lute. In truth, any lute is just a lute. But this lute was the one I'd taken from the monastery and used for nearly ten years. I knew its touch and tone and just how to hold it to get every note I wanted.

When I entered Terrel's cell he had my lute in pieces, spread across a bench. He was whittling a curved scrap of wood and frowning at the empty space in the back of the lute's round body.

"I can fix it," he announced. "But I may need to take it completely apart to do it. It may take weeks."

I gasped. I seldom passed a waking hour without playing my lute. It calmed me and helped me focus my thoughts as well as being my livelihood.

Terrel stood and studied the wall of instruments behind him. He took down a lute similar to mine, but with a slightly longer neck and a larger body.

"This is the best lute I own," he said. "You may use it until I repair yours."

I shook my head. I couldn't take one of his precious lutes. They were too valuable.

He sighed and glanced at my lute. "Please, accept it. This is the least I can do after your lute was damaged. Breaking your lute was not part of the plan."

181

I glanced from the lute to his face. He shrugged in embarrassment.

"Plan?" I questioned.

He pressed the lute into my hands, lifted his harp and strummed it lightly. He played his harp the way I played my lute, to focus his thoughts when he had something he needed to say.

"Do you know what King Elmar does when he's gifted with a sword?" he asked.

I shrugged.

"He swings it as hard as he can against the hardest object he has handy. He must know that a blade won't break when it's needed. Better to break a hundred swords here in the castle, than one during a battle."

He picked out a tune I recognized. It was the troll song I'd written for the earl.

"Earl Acton is a good man with a fine eye to a man's potential. He has the patience to nurture and grow a man to be the best he can.

He plucked a couple chords from the harp.

"King Elmar does not have such a luxury. When he needs a man to perform a task, he needs him now. If the man can't succeed, Elmar must find a man who can."

He stopped strumming and stared at me.

"The king needed proof that you had learned to defend yourself, so I took you to an inn where I knew Bella's Armsmen drank. We arrived late enough for them to be drunk. I expected you to be attacked."

He nodded at my lute on the bench. "I didn't expect your

lute to be damaged."

I rubbed my shoulder. The pain still made me wince.

"And if the blow had landed on my head?" I asked.

"I'd be sad. I've come to enjoy you and your music. But the king needs a bard who can defend himself." He shrugged. "If you failed, I'd be teaching another bard soon."

He placed his harp by my dismantled lute, stood, and set a hand on my right shoulder, the one that didn't hurt.

"I don't know what the king will want you and your companion to do, but I know it's important. He doesn't spend an entire season training men to guard the gates or entertain below the salt."

He nodded at the lute in my hands. "Try the tone and see if you like it. I have others if you'd prefer them."

I strummed the lute. It was a fine lute, better than the one I'd stolen from the monastery. It wasn't mine, but it would do. I nodded and our lesson continued.

I'd already received the grandest information. Sigurd and I were being trained for important posts. We wouldn't walk the roads, sleeping in stables and wondering what to steal for our next meal.

I scarcely heard Terrel's words, my thoughts leaped forward to a vague, but glorious future. He finally gave up and set me to playing common ornamentations on the new lute to become familiar with it.

That evening, as usual, I sang below the salt while the Armsmen and peasants swallowed food as fast as possible. Unless I had new songs, few tarried after eating. Sigurd always remained to enjoy my music. Tonight, he was the only listener.

I settled onto a bench next to him and relayed what Terrel had told me. His sleepy eyes opened at the news.

"Perhaps I'll be the next armsmaster and you'll be the king's bard," he mused. "Neither Mather or Terrel are young. They must be almost forty."

I smiled at the thought of a private cell shared with Corliss. I had much to look forward to. Remembering Corliss led my thoughts back to Earl Acton's court and how we'd walked to Elmar's castle.

"The gold!" I blurted. Sigurd raised his eyebrow and waited for me to continue.

"The gold Earl Acton gave us was our first test. He tested our honesty to see if we'd bring the gold to Elmar's court or run away with it."

Sigurd nodded. "Of course." He paused, "Ector must have been carrying the news to Elmar when he met us at the inn where our coins were stolen."

I thought a moment. "How often does Mather guard the king?" I asked.

"Never. He is too busy training new armsmen..." His voice trailed off as he remembered. "Except the day we arrived. It was Mather who attacked me."

I nodded. "Who else would Elmar trust to test a warrior. Ector must have given Redbeard the money to guest us to give the king time to arrange a test. If we hadn't spent the night at Redbeard's inn, we might have gotten to the castle before he was ready."

Sigurd stared blankly through the gray and orange, fire-lit walls as he thought, then spoke softly. "We're constantly being tested. How well can I learn weapon-craft? How quickly do you learn music?"

"Yes," I agreed. "Elmar will keep testing us until either we fail a test, or we prove our worth. We haven't failed yet. If we had, there would be no more tests."

There would be many more tests before King Elmar was satisfied that we were the swords he couldn't break. Once he was certain we were worthy, we would enjoy a fine life at the castle.

Assuming we survived the testing.

I was certain we would survive. I had a brother guarding my back and I swore to guard my brother's back as well.

Chapter Ten

Sigurd and the Solstice Celebration

OCTOBER'S RED AND gold glory faded into November's gray clouds which stormed into December's white blanket of snow.

In early December, Terrel began preparing me for the solstice celebration. We didn't know how many earls, squires and others would arrive for the festivities, but King Elmar was famed for his hospitality.

We practiced with ensembles to play for the dances. We perfected our individual songs for the meals. We prepared skits for the children to perform to amuse their parents and practiced with puppets to amuse the children.

Everyone in the castle helped decorate the yule log. We

joined together to wrap it with garlands of mistletoe and holly and over the next days we carved symbols into the trunk. I taught Sigurd the runes for his name and helped him inscribe them into the log. We joined our name-runes with the sigil for brotherhood.

I'd become used to the idea that Sigurd was more than a road companion and we were destined to travel together and do great deeds. Or perhaps we would simply die during our training. I fully expected to die from exhaustion as we prepared for the holiday.

In the last days before the solstice, the castle filled beyond what it could hold. Our barracks were given to the king's relatives and other lords while the retainers and regular castle staff sought space on the floor of the great hall. It was a merry time, but not suitable for sleeping.

Terrel was present one evening when halfway through *Sigurd and the Nine Virgins* I forgot which virgin Sigurd was visiting and had him coming and going in most unlikely manners. Terrel took pity on my fatigue and invited me to sleep in his cell. I missed the joy and fellowship of the great hall but welcomed the quiet and rest.

The day of the celebration dawned bright and cold. Terrel greeted me with a cup of warm sweet cider.

"The festival starts in earnest today," he told me. "You'll want to tread lightly around the ales and wines if you want to be at your best by the end of the week."

I nodded. I'd learned about the joys and pitfalls of unlimited ale since I met Sigurd. Before then, I'd seldom had the coin or welcome to partake to excess.

Terrel reached behind him and lifted a cloth sack. "It's

the custom for a master to gift his student," he said. "This isn't a new gift, but it's one I think you'll cherish."

I opened the sack and found my lute. As I pulled it from the sack I realized it was not exactly the instrument I'd given him. Fine inlay strips graced the neck; black walnut, rosy cherry, golden maple, and white holly strips ran parallel to the frets. He'd replaced my old string frets with thin leather straps. I tapped one. It had been boiled in wax and hardened like strong armor.

My fingers had longed to caress this neck since it was broken. I let them prance across the strings and played a shepherd's frolicking tune.

Terrel waited for the end of the verse, smiling, and tapping his fingers on his wrist, then he held out his hand. "Now, I'll show you something," he said. He took the lute and slid the frets around. "The inlay marks the different scales of notes: The holly for our shepherd's tunes. The walnut for Greek melodies."

While he moved the frets, I pulled a set of pan pipes from my pouch.

"These are not so lovely as my lute, but I made them for you." I passed him the pipes and accepted my lute. He played the notes and stared at his present for a second. The tones weren't the usual ones. I crafted it carefully for the one man who would understand. This flute had seven tubes instead of the normal five.

Terrel frowned in thought, then grinned. "Both our shepherd's pipes and the Greek pipes together! Splendid!"

He played the Greek warrior dance that captivated me when we first met. My lute's frets were already on the walnut inlay, for the Greek scale. I joined him in the song, triple strumming the lute to match the melody's strange rhythm.

Terrel stopped playing and mimed a battle to my tune. He tapped his wrists and ankles in time to the music while he swayed, leaped, and pantomimed parries and thrusts with his empty hands.

I sang the song as he danced. I'd only learned the meaning of a few of the words, but I knew the sounds by heart. When I paused to take a breath, he raised the flute to his lips while he continued to step and weave. Bursts of trills and leaps of notes flew about my playing and turned the song into a lark's joyful welcome to the morning.

We stopped when we were both out of breath and laughing too hard to continue. A bard can find no joy to match making and sharing music with another master. It was an honor to be accepted in his music and a joy to accept him in mine.

He poured me another cup of sweet cider and took a swig from the jug. "You have an excellent voice," he said. "I'm surprised the monks released such a promising tenor."

I sobered quickly. "I wasn't exactly released," I told him. "I rather released myself."

He raised his eyebrows and squinted at me.

"I was a superb soprano," I stared at a corner of the room, away from Terrel's probing eyes. I had many fond memories and a single shameful one from my years in the monastery. "I was so good I was given special treatment and took it for granted. I reveled in my privileges until I overheard the choirmaster and the abbot discuss whether

190

they should take a chance on my becoming a merely decent tenor or keep me a soprano."

I took a swallow of the cider. "That night, I crept from my master's room. I stole his lute and pouch of coins and headed for the wall, deep into the Danelaw where the monasteries hold less power."

Terrel sobered as I spoke. "I'm not a Christian," he said, "and I don't believe in their sins. I understand your need to leave. I'd have done the same, but you abused your master's trust, and the fates will demand you repay your debt."

I nodded. I'd been remembering my past since Sigurd, and I met. I didn't regret the stolen eggs or departing an inn before I settled what I owed. This was part of the traditional dance of innkeeper and bard. No trust had been given, so there was no betrayal.

Betraying my master's trust and stealing his lute was different, and I knew someday I'd have to atone, whether Terrel believed in sin or not.

He grinned, "But I daresay the fates won't bring you to account today. We should be in the hall making merry as the last guests arrive. Tonight, will be a joyous eve."

The guests arrived in a continuous stream from every keep and village in Elmar's domain. The castle's kitchens were strained to feed everyone, even with the gifts of food and drink brought by the guests.

I was playing my lute near the ale-table as Sigurd entered the great hall carrying a basket of hams balanced on his head. He ducked as he passed through the door. As he straightened, a lad in a worn brown cloak scrambled around Sigurd, spun to face him, and tossed the cloak aside.

The lad was Ermindale, dressed in soft-gray homespun she wore like one of the princess's garments.

She pointed to the hams and laughed "Keep a tight grip. I don't want these hams to be used against my heroes."

With that she gave Sigurd a quick kiss on the cheek, skipped to me and repeated the action. The squire loudly stomped the snow from his boots and she was suddenly quiet and contrite, the exact image of a proper, dutiful daughter.

I bowed in my best courtly manner. I'd just learned to do a proper court bow, instead of doffing my hat and tugging my forelock. The squire strode to us, scowling at the idea that I might be courting his child.

"Good father," she murmured. "Do you recall the two heroes who rescued me when I was lost in the woods. They are now members of the king's household."

His face softened and he smiled when he recognized me. "So," he declaimed, "The gift I gave you was worth more than a gold piece. Just as I promised."

I remembered begging for food like a dog, being attacked by Olaf, the trip with two repentant thieves to Earl Acton's, meeting Corliss, and finally training with the king's bard.

"Yes, squire," I replied, "Guarding your taxes was indeed a great boon."

A bard always speaks the truth. He always speaks the truth his listener wants to hear. It might have even been an actual truth.

"We'll meet again," Ermindale whispered as her father dragged her away to pay their respects to the court.

Moments later she was back.

"Good bard, will you amuse me while I oversee unloading our wagons?"

I followed her into the courtyard and met a new Ermindale.

I'd known Dale, the quiet lad, and Ermindale the dutiful daughter. Now I admired Mistress Ermindale, the ruler of her domain, as she directed the hams to the groaning board, a bull to the slaughter yard, turnips and flour to the kitchen and dozens of other items from various wagons to their proper locations.

I strummed my lute and observed her with great amusement. She soon had everyone available carrying something. She glanced at me and ran her finger along the scar on my neck where Olaf had struck me.

"To think one of our hams did that to you," she murmured. "That pig always caused trouble."

"You heard the tale?" I asked.

She nodded and hummed a snippet of my saga of the Earl and Two Trolls. "Your music is traveling. The tales of Sigurd of the Black Axe and his bard are told throughout the kingdom. You rescue maidens, slay ogres and reform sinners." She grinned. "I don't believe all of the stories, but I'll have a chance to hear them. I'm to spend the winter here as Princess Beornwyn's companion."

I was about to describe my version of our adventures; in case the details had been mislaid by lesser bards but was interrupted by a clatter of hooves and a thud of boots.

I spun and discovered Rishley had saddle trained Midnight more quickly than expected. He vaulted from the coal black steed, stumbled on the cobbles, straightened and grabbed my shoulder in greeting.

"Bard! I'd not expected to find you here. Nor Dale," he paused as he glanced at Ermindale, wearing his old cloak. He choked and bowed deeply. "My pardon, M'lady. I mistook you for a lad, I mean, for a lady I met elsewhere."

Ermindale nodded coolly and politely to him. "I believe we were both at last winter's dance. We may have met then."

Rishley nodded, his eyes focusing on her face, then dropping to the cloak and back to her face.

She straightened. "Is there something amiss with my garments?" she asked.

Rishley shook his head. "Nothing, M'Lady. But please, could you tell me how you got that cloak?"

She shrugged the garment off her shoulder and held it in front of her, displaying how finely she had mended the rips and worn spots. "This cloak? Why, a young man gave it to me. I think he fancied me."

Rishley swallowed again, his face reddened. "It's a bit worn for a lady of your position."

She nodded, "True. But it keeps me warm, and I like it."

She snatched an apple from a basket of fruit and held it out to Rishley's horse.

Rishley blocked her with his arm.

"Careful," he cautioned her. "Midnight is not accustomed to strangers."

He broke off as the horse butted his arm out of the way and accepted the apple from Ermindale. She rubbed the star on his forehead and scratched him behind the ears.

Rishley stared and stuttered. "He never-- I mean, he seems to have taken a liking to you, M'Lady."

"I've always had a way with dumb beasts." She smirked at Rishley, "Will you be dancing this year?" she asked. He nodded, and she continued "Then I shall see you this evening. You may partner me for a dance." She paused and swept the cloak back over her shoulders "If you wish, of course."

She nodded a farewell to us and followed the last of the hams into the great hall.

Rishley watched her sway as she strode away, then turned to me, confusion plain on his face. "That was the Squire's daughter, was it not? I've never spoken to her, but she seems familiar." He shook his head. "It must be the cloak. I never thought the lad would give it away. Not that it earned him any favors."

I nodded and pointed out the stables and suggested a mug of hot cider. Their little play most entertaining. I hoped to see more before the solstice celebrations were over.

I spent the rest of the day trying to teach a group of children to sing together. Terrel assigned this task to me because of my years in the monastery choir. I had hoped to leave children's choirs behind when I left the monastery. This was more of the same agony of dealing with those who either could not sing at all, or had a favorite note they sang loudly, whether it was the right note or not.

By evening, I had selected sets of children to sing together and assigned songs and chants appropriate to their voices. I led them into the hall as they variously marched and meandered behind me, singing of Baldur's death and return, Oestra's upcoming reawakening, the birth of the Christ and other mid-winter songs.

We sang the last notes as the diners finished their first feast. Behind me, heavy feet echoed on the stairs leading up to the King's dais followed by a joyous "Well met, Cousin!"

I waved the children to depart as Earl Acton approached the king's table and Elmar rose to greet him. I'd been so busy with the children that I never saw the Earl's party arrive.

The earl proffered a gaily decorated sword to the king. "My liege," Earl Acton declaimed. "I offer you this, may you never need to wield it."

The king accepted the sword warily. As the Earl stepped back, he raised it over his head and struck the royal table a mighty blow. Wood chips flew and a board cracked. He lifted himself off the floor briefly with the strength of the blow. The sword lodged itself in the table. He needed both hands to wrench it loose.

It came free with a bell-like tone. King Elmar studied the base of the sword closely. "It is not inscribed Ulfberht, but it is a most excellent weapon," he said finally.

"No, not true Ulfberht," Earl Acton replied, "But forged from the same steel by a master smith."

The king smiled, "It is a most worthy gift. You have the finest weapon-smith in the kingdom."

The earl grinned back. "The sword is not my gift, Cousin. The gift is that my king will have the greatest smith, if you will accept him and his family into your service."

196

While he spoke a burly man with shoulder-length blond braids stepped onto the dais with Earl Acton. A hefty blonde woman and the maid I'd seen hand Sigurd his axe trailed a step behind.

The king studied the smith and his family. "You made Sigurd's black handled axe?" he asked.

The man and his daughter nodded.

I'd thought Elmar was smiling before, but his grin now made it look like a frown. He embraced Acton, the smith, his wife, and daughter. He dug into a box by the royal table and gave the earl a thick golden armband, then passed bronze bands to the smith and his family.

The smith and his family retired as the Earl motioned for another gift to be brought. My heart skipped a beat as I recognized the dark-haired, blue-eyed maiden mounting the dais carrying a deep red woolen cloak, heavily embroidered and trimmed with strips of Byzantine silk. To think that Corliss arrived with the Earl's party! I would find a way to escape some of my bardic duties to enjoy time with her.

The king motioned and Princess Beornwyn stepped demurely beside her father. Her soft golden-red hair, the rich color of autumn oak leaves was braided and wrapped about her head. Corliss knelt and held out the garment, which the princess accepted with a smile and then raised for everyone to view. Even I recognized the fine embroidery--a delicate pattern of diamonds within diamonds.

Beornwyn hugged the garment to her chest, then draped it over her shoulders, smiling broader every moment. The red cloak brought out the russet highlights in her hair and made her even more stunning.

Earl Acton cleared his throat. "Your daughter grows lovelier each year, cousin." The king nodded, obviously pleased at the compliment. "She has reached an age where she needs a lady's maid, more than a nurse," the earl continued. "May I offer her a convent trained servant, well-schooled in textile arts and of an age to be a companion as well as caretaker?"

The princess gazed at her father with eyes no man could resist. The king had no intention of denying her Corliss's service. He nodded, took Corliss's hand, and placed his daughter's over it.

The king embraced Acton again, laughing and crying as they pounded each other's backs.

Earl Acton retired, and the rest of the king's earls took turns presenting him with gifts and receiving gifts in return.

Earl Bella gifted the king with fifty armsmen, each carrying a cask of ale. It was a small part of what his venture had cost, but it was a fine gift. Other earls gave the king and princess furs, armor, and jewelry.

Once the royal gifts were presented, Terrel and musicians from the other keeps entered and played a slow, stately tune. The king, the earls, wives and children promenaded around the room, greeting friends and lesser nobles as the armsmen and servants dismantled the trestle tables and pushed them to the walls, making an open space for dancing.

Once the room had been cleared, Terrel struck up a lively tune. The king's and earls' families formed a small circle in the center of the room while the rest of the celebrants joined in a larger circle surrounding them. At Terrel's call, everyone danced, whirling, twirling, and swapping partners as the inner circle stepped deosil and the outer stepped widdershins.

I batted my eyes at Ermindale when she swept through my arms, kissed Corliss chastely on the cheek, and briefly held the princess's soft hand. I flirted for two beats with ladies old enough to be my mother and swung others young enough to be my child.

Everyone was laughing and gasping for air when Terrel finished that tune and sang a song of the season, his strong tenor filling the hall like golden mead. I held Corliss's hand as we joined him on the final verse.

He nodded to me to take my turn with the musicians, and he stepped down to lead the next dance.

We played a lively country tune. The older folks retired to the walls and the younger ones whirled, exchanged partners and demonstrated their nimbleness and skill. At intervals, the men tossed their partner into the air and caught them in an embrace. I noted how the smith's daughter leaped for most of her partners, rather than expect to be lifted by men smaller than she. Sigurd tossed her high while she beamed at him and landed deep in his arms.

Ermindale danced with Rishley more often than she should have. I expected her to be an expert dancer, but she kept making missteps that caused her to trade places with his next partner.

While I played, Corliss stood near the musicians and listened, waiting for my opportunity to dance.

When I saw the dancers flagging, I called a halt and like Terrel, led the assembly in a song of hope for the next season. As the echoes faded I took Corliss's hand to lead the next dance.

And so, the evening and night went. Singing and dancing, with rests for feasting and drinking until the last of the musicians played a lullaby for the last of the revelers and those who had not already retired slept where they were.

Chapter Eleven

Sigurd and the Winter of Discontent

I AWOKE THE next morning tired, but too excited to sleep any longer. Corliss was here! We dwelt in the very same castle. I might see her every day.

When I left Earl Acton's keep I hadn't known if I'd ever see her again. I certainly hadn't expected to see her before spring.

It was the season for gift giving and I should have a gift for her.

I was richer than I'd ever been; eating three meals every day and sleeping 'neath a roof. I even had a fire. But I didn't have coins to buy a gift nor the time or skill to craft one.

I stared at the ceiling considering how to explain how

much I cherished her kerchief.

I shook my head. I'm a bard. What I do is to tell news and sing. I'd tell her how I felt in music. The song would be hers. She'd cherish it forever. Most importantly, it would not cost coins I didn't have.

I know many ballads of love. Like the tales of combat, I carried stock phrases in my head suitable to compose a romantic song in a few moments. Those would not be enough. I had to use the form of the love songs, but not the lyrics she'd heard a thousand times before.

Terrel had already left, so I was alone in his cell. I reached for my lute, crossed my legs, and faced the wall to concentrate on new lyrics.

I strummed a few chords. The form was easy. I closed my eyes, let my mind go blank and sang as the lyrics formed in my mind.

If there were words that lips could form
That gentle ears could hear
I'd find those words, so soft and warm,
And whisper in your ear.
That you would know the love that grows
Within my heart, my dear.

The first verse was good. I needed another. I glanced out Terrel's tiny window into a speck of blue sky and saw an early morning moon flanked by a single bright star.

Again, the words formed in my mind and flowed out my mouth.

If I could call the moon to rise,
And shine at my command.
If I could make the stars fall down,
And glisten in the sand.
The moon would always fill your eyes,
And stars bedeck your hands.

A song needs at least three verses, I strummed and glanced about the room, hoping for more inspiration.

From behind me, Terrel's tenor voice sang softly:

And when your dark hair fades to gold,
And mine may fade away.
I'll cherish you and I will hold
You till my dying day.
But let that parting tarry long,
I'd rather hear you say.
That you will spend this night with me,
And very many days.

I twisted to stare at him.

"You needn't use my verse," he told me. "You want a song for youth, not an older man's longing. The song is lovely. I'm certain your lady will treasure it."

He gathered his harp and the pipes I'd given him yesterday and headed back out.

"But be quick with the last verse or you'll miss your chance to eat. The kitchens are sending food to the great hall as fast as they can, but the guests are descending upon the bounty like locusts on a field."

203

I decided I'd compose the final verse later. The gift could wait, but breakfast wouldn't.

The households took turns cooking to allow everyone to have time to enjoy the festivities. Every village has a dish they make better than anyone else and each was anxious to present their dish to the king and garner his approval.

Earl Acton was in charge of today's breakfast, and he had assigned the task to Squire Bolton who had passed the responsibility to his daughter.

Ermindale was shepherding a board of baked apples to the head table as I entered the great hall. She motioned me to follow her to the kitchen then looked past me and waved again. I glanced over my shoulder to see Sigurd and Rishley.

As the three of us entered the kitchen she spun on her heel, kissed Sigurd and me on the cheek and nodded to Rishley.

"I have special apples for my two heroes," she announced. "You may have the extra one, if you wish," she told Rishley.

She pulled a board with three apples from the oven. The special treats were stuffed with wine-soaked raisins and sweetened with honey.

"I saved these from the breakfast I made for the king and his earls," she said, setting the board in front of us. She grinned at Sigurd, "Small slices, or you'll burn your tongue," she danced back to berate a housecarl who was not coring the apples to her satisfaction.

Rishley ate a small slice from his apple, grinned broadly and rolled his eyes. "Tell me," he glanced at me, then

Sigurd, then back to me. "How did you come to know the Squire's daughter?"

Sigurd coughed, but my years of telling a bard's truth came to my rescue. "We found her in the woods after she ran off and we escorted her home," I told him.

His eyes left me and followed Ermindale as she supervised her staff. "These are the best apples I've tasted since the ones the lad made for us. Do you think she taught him?"

"I believe they learned from the same source," I replied, as Sigurd choked. "Would you marry her for these apples?"

Rishley didn't answer, but I studied his eyes as he watched Ermindale dance about, supervising her kitchen. It was not only her cooking that attracted him.

Sigurd swallowed the last of his apple and glanced at Rishley. "What brings you so far north?" he asked. "The weather is chancy. You never know when the snow might stick." Sigurd carefully avoided my eye as I glared at him.

Rishley spat out a clove. "Me Da, of course. He says to train a horse for a warrior I needs must learn to ride like a warrior. Earl Acton told him three months with armsmaster Mather would be worth a year with anyone else. So, me Da offered two horses to the king for my training. I'll be here until spring, then back home in time to help with the foals."

Ermindale passed by while he spoke and paused to listen.

"You'd best not be giving Midnight to the king," she told him. "He's too fine an animal to be given to someone who won't appreciate him."

Rishley nodded. "I've got other plans for Midnight. I

hope to use him to start my own stable."

Ermindale blushed and raced away to continue haranguing the cooks. The smug smile on Rishley's face made me wonder who was leading whom in their dance.

Earl Bella's chief house-carl started preparing for the mid-day feast and eyed our table. He gently shooed Sigurd, Rishley and I to the great hall.

The daytime was for meeting old friends, forging alliances and informal courtship. We met the smith's daughter, Henga, outside the kitchens as we entered the great hall. She and Sigurd bid me farewell and left to inspect the smithy. Rishley waved and left to confirm that Midnight was properly cared for.

I strolled through the room, playing my lute and singing softly. I sang louder when someone showed an interest. The hall was filled with groups of three or more people, all talking at once and gesturing broadly. This might be the only occasion this year that many of them would meet. Most wore their finest clothes, both to display their affluence and to honor the king's court.

One fellow caught my eye. He wore simple homespun and leather like the lowest of peasants, wore them like linen and fur. His bright, golden hair was cut evenly and short, like a lord's. His close-trimmed beard resembled Mather's. He didn't seem to have any friends in the court, but joined different groups for a few moments, talking seldom and listening a great deal.

I watched him casually, to see which earl's company finally claimed him. I spent most of my effort searching for Corliss, hoping to lure her to a quiet nook and present my song. Alas, she spent the day closeted with the princess and the nooks were always occupied.

Corliss finally appeared with Princess Beornwyn for the evening feast. The princess wore a dress I'd seen before, but the sleeves were now decorated with strips of silk and the collar displayed intricate embroidery of circles and dragons.

The expressions on the earls' wives' faces made it plain how they appreciated Corliss's skill and envied Beornwyn.

The evening banquet and dance was like the previous night, but louder and longer. Tonight, we lit the yule log. The guesting and celebrating would last until the log was fully consumed. It might take a few days, or perhaps a week for the last of the yule log to burn; the memories of the old year and hope for the new leaving the castle on wings of smoke.

Tonight's banquet followed Terrel's and my usual pattern. He entertained the high table, for the king's family and the earls, while I played at the other end of the hall for the armsmen, servants and farmers.

I was content with this. My turn to play for the high table would come in its season.

I was idly strumming my lute as folks ate when Ector called, "Bard, these visitors have never heard *Sigurd's Ride With Death.*"

I demurred, but fists and tankards were pounded on the table until I played. The sudden silence told me my breath wasn't wasted.

Listeners are a fickle lot, so a bard watches as he sings. What thrills them one night will bore them the next, but a slight change of rhythm or tempo can bring the song's wonder back to them.

The listeners tonight fell into two camps. Those whose eyes never left their plates and those whose eyes never left my face. For some, food sustains the body. Others hunger for the music that feeds their souls. A bard never ignores any listener, but I'll confess I sing primarily to those who are most attentive.

The blond-haired peasant from the afternoon caught my eye. He fell into neither camp. While others attended to their plates, or listened to my singing, his eyes never left the head table. His distant smile said he heard music, but it wasn't what I was singing.

I was midway through Sigurd's quest for the healing flower when an armsman entered from outside and shook the snow from his cloak. The door warden pointed him toward the groaning board, but the newcomer scanned the hall and strode to the unknown peasant. As he whispered in the peasant's ear, the peasant's smile faded. The music he enjoyed had gone silent. They left quickly, in the middle of the feasting.

A bard watches and remembers. Tiny details may be needed later to fill a verse or describe an event. The strange behavior of a simple peasant was not worth noting. My efforts were for those who were so enmeshed in my song that they never saw either the peasant or the armsman. They deserved my best efforts, and they received them. By the time Sigurd returned with the potion, everyone was chanting and pounding the table. Terrel stopped playing, and even the king joined in as Sigurd finished his quest.

I had just played for the head table, even if I did it from the far end of the hall.

The feasting lasted for several days. With each dawn I

swore today I would spend time with Corliss and sing her song to her. Instead, each day the princess had new embroidery and needlework on one of her gowns and Corliss joined the dances and retired early.

Eventually, the last of the yule log was pushed into the fire-pit. Everyone had feasted, danced, and flirted themselves to exhaustion. It was a relief when the earls, squires and other guests headed home to their villages and keeps. The great hall was empty with only the king's retainers and armsmen. Now that the celebrations were over, I hoped to find time to spend with Corliss.

Sigurd and I were helping load Squire Bolton's belongings into the small cart he'd be taking home when Mather called to us. "Tomorrow. Bright and early in the practice yard. You'll be slow after all this eating and drinking."

The next morning, Mather met us at the entrance to the practice yard.

He nodded to Sigurd. "You need to learn to defend against two attackers." He addressed me. "Daggers are small. Wielding a short weapon puts you within range of your foe. Defending yourself with a spear is easy to learn and keeps you outside a swordsman's reach."

He demonstrated a set of parries and attacks and had Ector and me take turns attacking Sigurd while he defended himself from a sword blow, a spear thrust, then another sword blow.

When Mather called for us to rest we were more than ready to pause. We sank to our knees and gasped. A spear is much heavier than a dagger, a fact the arms-master had neglected to mention.

209

The ground was cold and frozen, with curls of snow where we hadn't stamped it into the mud. I scooped a handful of snow and rubbed its coolness into my face as Sigurd and Ector did the same.

A bard is prized for his voice and skill with his hands, but his ears are the most important. He needs to be able to hear the string out of tune, or the word out of meter.

I waved Ector and Sigurd to silence when I heard a noise that was out of place. It was too thin and pitched too high for the practice yard. It whined like a hurt puppy, but there would be no litters until spring.

I stood, twisting my head and followed the sound. It led me to a stone-walled storage shed next to the practice yard. The shed had a heavy wooden door, secured with a leather hasp to keep the animals from invading it.

As I pulled the plug from the hasp the door swung wide. Corliss tumbled into the yard, still calling softly for help. Her face was pale as death, and she was too weak to stand.

Ector scooped her up as she fell past me and carried her to the castle. Sigurd pushed the door closed as I latched it and we followed.

Ector carried Corliss to a bench near the great fire and set himself beside her to steady her. I took the other side, offering my warmth and support. We chaffed her hands as Sigurd ran to get help. I'd been dreaming of holding her, but not like this. Her fingers were so cold they almost hurt.

"I-I-I wa-wa-was ju-just ge-ge-getting," Corliss stuttered as she shivered.

Sigurd returned with Ermindale and Beornwyn. The

princess wrapped Corliss in the red woolen cloak that had been her gift. Ermindale handed her a cup of warm wine to sip. Within moments they had whisked her back to the princess's quarters.

Sigurd, Ector, and I returned to the practice yard, but our hearts were distracted from our weapon-craft.

At lunch, Ermindale visited our table.

"It was my fault," she explained. "I offered to bake apples for our breakfast. Beornwyn told Corliss to run get them." She paused and took a breath. "Nobody knew she was in the shed when the door was locked. We were just starting to search for her when Sigurd called to us. She will be fine, but she was chilled near to death. It's fortunate you heard her."

She smiled briefly. "My heroes never miss an opportunity to render aid to a fair maiden, do they?"

She then hurried back to the princess's chambers.

I was less worried during the afternoon when I met with Terrel. He insisted I learn more of the world's music's and how to blend them to tell an old tale in a new way. I balked at learning the meanings of every word in Greek, Gaulish and Danish, but he was adamant.

"You can make pretty songs with mouth noises," he scolded me, "But to create music, you must know nuances of the language, and just what you are saying. You need to understand the subtleties to know when it should be "je t'aime" and when the words must be "Je vous adore" and which words to emphasize for an occasion."

I protested. "Both phrases mean "I love you," what does it matter which gets used in a lyric as long as it scans?"

He sighed and straightened. He'd explained this before and I'd failed to understand. Terrel had incredible patience. He would explain again and again until I understood.

"Je t'aime," he said slowly, "is a familiar form. It's appropriate to use with a close friend or lover. You might say it to Corliss. If you declared your devotion to a king's daughter using that phrase, and he were in a good mood, you'd merely be beheaded."

I looked blank, and he tried again.

"Would you sing *Sigurd and the Virgins* to Ermindale or the princess?" he asked.

I blushed and shook my head, A drunken conversation with a particularly well-traveled armsman had contributed a most unlikely tenth virgin to the song.

"*Sigurd and however many Virgins* is a song of love, is it not? Love in many forms, I daresay." He paused while I digested the idea of my song for Corliss and *Sigurd and the Ten Virgins* being similar in any way. "If you don't understand the nuances of the language, how will you know what song is appropriate to sing when the king is guesting a Gaulish knight and his wife?"

My dislike of being beheaded or angering a Gaulish warlord convinced me I needed to understand the words and phrases of the languages I could sing. Now, along with learning facets of music that I'd never dreamed of, I was learning the spoken languages of places I'd never heard of.

I hadn't managed to see Corliss alone during the solstice celebrations. I'd had no chance to sing her song for her. I hoped to find an opportunity soon, now that the winter was at its peak, and nobody could travel until spring.

212

The next morning, however, Ermindale reported that Corliss had taken a chill and was sick abed. "She'll be fine soon," she assured me. "Beornwyn has summoned the chirurgeon and is caring for her as if Corliss were the princess and she the maidservant."

And so the winter passed, mornings with Mather, learning to thrust and parry with dagger or spear, and sometimes to twirl, kick, feint and dodge. Ector declared I was becoming skilled in single combat, while Mather assured me I'd best avoid any fight I could.

I would have been discouraged, except Mather also told Sigurd that as an armsman he'd be a fine woodcutter.

"Stop swinging like you're chopping wood," he growled after Sigurd nearly split one of the pells in two. "Punch forward, then jerk back so the axe flips around from the wrist. Don't hit with the center of the blade, hit your opponent with the tip."

"But I need to be sure I hit him," Sigurd objected.

"Not like that you don't. Foemen aren't firewood. If you chop a foe like a tree trunk you'll lodge your axe in his bone. His mate will eat your liver while it's stuck. Slice with the tip of the axe-head, and you'll cut armor and muscle. If you miss, you've still got a weapon to defend with. It's not lodged in some worthless carcass."

Mather glared at the pell Sigurd had been chopping. "And we don't have enough pells for you to keep turning them into kindling."

The arms-master finished his circuit, informing Ector that he fought like a girl and Rishley that he'd should stick to driving oxen.

The afternoons with Terrel included lessons in music, ciphering, languages, customs, and more modes of addressing ones betters than I knew existed. I hadn't even realized I had so many betters. I doubted I'd ever meet a Persian sheik, but if I did, I'd learned how deeply to bow.

Ermindale gave me daily reports on Corliss's recovery. She usually found time to speak with Sigurd and me while Rishley was also present. After informing me how Corliss was improving, she would discover an apple in her pocket and ask to be escorted to Midnight to share the treat.

Corliss was sick abed for over a month. When she was finally allowed outside the princess's quarters, she was weak and constantly attended by Ermindale or Beornwyn. I tried to speak with her, but seldom managed more than a few words before she was fatigued and escorted back to bed.

Sigurd's romance proceeded much better. After the evening meal, while he rested and listened to my music, he was frequently visited by the weapon-smith's daughter, Henga. She attended politely to my songs but preferred to speak with him.

After a particularly long day, I decided my voice and fingers needed a rest and I would let Sigurd share the burden of speaking. I asked him to explain why he was learning to use a Viking round shield, instead of the sturdier Roman style. My question gave him a chance to display his knowledge to Henga and gave me a moment to relax.

"It's simple," he said, speaking to me, but smiling at Henga, "The Roman shield is heavy wood and metal, built to absorb a blow without being displaced. You lock shields with your neighbor and present a solid wall to your opponent. It works well for the Romans because they fight as armies and there are enough of them to form a wall or even a square with spears and pikes behind the swordsmen.

"But a hero fights alone. He doesn't have companions for a shield wall." He placed one hand in front of himself, as if holding a shield.

"The Norse shield is ideal for a hero. He can deflect a blow with the edge or hide behind it to conceal his next attack. It's light enough to wave about to distract your opponent, or even use as a second weapon."

He waved his arm to demonstrate this and ended with his arm encircling Henga's neck.

"And you can even use it to drag your opponent into reach," he continued, pulling her toward him. He placed a kiss on her forehead as she nestled into his shoulder.

I'd rested enough and aided my brother's romance as much as it needed. I ambled to the far end of the room to entertain the house-carls cleaning the last of the meal. I did not begrudge him the romance, but I wished I were able to spend as much time with Corliss as he spent with Henga.

The winter faded slowly. The dawn came earlier each day, the snows melted, and the weapons yard became muddier and more treacherous. Mather insisted we practice footwork in the deepest mud and my clothes suffered most grievously.

One morning as the oaks were budding, Mather told Sigurd to spar with him, instead of against Ector.

This was a notable event, and everyone stopped their practice to watch. It was the first time the arms-master had

215

displayed his skill since the day we entered King Elmar's hall.

My friend was obviously nervous, wielding an over-sized wooden axe and bearing a Viking shield. Mather selected a pole-axe and placed a wooden sword into a baldric behind his back. He advanced upon Sigurd with quick strides, swinging the pole-axe in complex waves with no obvious pattern.

Sigurd leaped back to avoid a blow aimed at his chest, then bounded forward to be inside the arc of the pole-axe. This brought Mather within reach of his axe.

As Sigurd moved forward, Mather reversed his grip on the pole-axe, and swung the butt of the pole-arm up in an arc between Sigurd's legs.

Sigurd's previous leap was nothing compared to how he leaped to avoid that crippling blow. He staggered briefly as Mather reversed his grip and swung the poleaxe overhead at Sigurd's left side.

Instead of dodging, Sigurd thrust his shield into the descending axe head with his own weapon concealed behind it. At the last moment, he shifted his shield. Instead of deflecting the poleaxe with the reinforced edge, he let it hit the flat face. He braced the shield with his axe so it wouldn't twist from the force of the blow.

The poleaxe split the light pine shield and lodged itself in the cracked wood. Sigurd twisted his shield, trapping the axe-head. He pulled backwards, to throw Mather off-balance and drag him closer.

Mather, however, did not hold onto his poleaxe. He threw it to the side, still entangled with Sigurd's shield, pulling Sigurd's arm to the left, and leaving his defense open.

Mather yanked the sword from his baldric as Sigurd let go of his shield. The shield and poleaxe flew to the side as watchers dodged.

For a brief moment, both men were defenseless. Sigurd's shield arm was spread wide, and he gripped his axe near the head. Mather's sword was only half drawn, and he was off balance.

As Mather finished drawing his weapon, Sigurd grabbed his axe near the head with both hands, leaped forward and drove the butt of his axe into Mather's stomach.

Mather grunted as he collapsed, swinging his sword at Sigurd's knees. Sigurd was off-balance from the thrust and couldn't avoid the attack. He deliberately fell forward, taking the blow on his thigh, instead of his knee.

The bout had lasted less than thirty seconds, but both men lay on the ground panting. Mather rolled to his stomach, stood painfully, and offered a hand to Sigurd.

"Never underestimate a fallen foe," he said as he pulled Sigurd to his feet. "More practice won't hurt you, but I've taught you what I can. You'll learn your next lessons fighting for your life."

He called the runner, whispered briefly to him, and motioned for me and Sigurd to follow him.

He led us into the castle to the king's private chambers.

We joined Elmar in an alcove where he was speaking with Terrel.

Sigurd and I were not prepared for a royal interview. We were both covered with mud and Sigurd was still panting from his bout.

Elmar studied us with little approval.

"My daughter and Ermindale are close friends with no secrets." he began. "Tell me how you met Ermindale?"

I glanced at Sigurd. He stared above Elmar's head, making it obvious he intended me to tell the tale.

"We met Mistress Ermindale in the woods south of her father's holding."

He nodded. "And did you travel with her?" he asked.

"Yes, your highness. We escorted her from the glade where we found her to her father's abode."

"And that was all the time you spent with her?" he asked most pointedly.

"No, your highness," I replied. "While Sigurd visited her father and received his assurance that she need not marry Rishley, I spoke with her."

"You did not travel south with her to Groom Ryder's holding?" he asked.

"We traveled with a lad named Dale and Rishley, your highness," I replied looking him in the eye as honest men do. Bards learn to do this when they tell an incomplete truth.

He laughed. "You will not lie, but you can't tell the truth, can you? My cousin has an unerring eye for a man's skill."

He addressed Terrel. "Do you think he's ready?"

Terrel nodded. "There is always more to learn, sire, but

he is sufficiently trained."

Elmar looked to Sigurd and me.

"Princess Beornwyn will be old enough to wed this summer." he stated.

"It will be a lucky prince who weds her," I replied. As I've said, a bard tells the truth the listener wants to hear. In this case, I truly believed it. The care she gave Corliss during her illness displayed her character.

He nodded. "I do not trust to luck. There are three neighboring kingdoms with a prince who may wish to wed Beornwyn. Each man is of good repute. Two have visited and presented their most comely faces. I must know the man beneath that facade."

He looked solemnly at me and then Sigurd. "You two will visit their kingdoms and report to me which prince is the best match for my daughter. He must be a worthy ally, a strong king, and a kind, godly man. Since I have no other children, he will inherit my kingdom as well as his own upon my death. I wish to leave a worthy legacy to my grandchildren."

He stood and examined us, scanning us up and down. We wore patched leather, covered with mud, and were dripping wet. We were not what anyone considered proper emissaries to a prospective royal son-in-law.

"You may leave this afternoon. I will expect your return within three months."

I gasped. A single afternoon to prepare for many weeks of travel through three kingdoms? I hadn't had a chance to speak with Corliss, and now, when she was finally able to walk about, I'd be leaving.

I tried to protest as the King nodded to Terrel and Mather, then strode from the room.

Terrel spoke first. "You'll be traveling as you have before, a bard and a mercenary. Sigurd, you'll need to leave your black-handled axe here. It's too distinctive and too many folks have heard the tales of Sigurd Black-axe."

Mather added, "If you can get a post in the castle guard, you should be able to observe the royal family at rest. This will tell you much of their character."

Terrel addressed me, "Bard, you should find the tavern favored by the lesser functionaries. If you sing a song praising the king, they are likely to invite you to the castle to sing the song before the king. It's a way for them to curry favor. That will give you an opportunity to observe the kings and princes."

Mather resumed. "How the court treats two penniless travelers will show their nature. King Elmar rewards service. but has no patience with those whose only skill is begging. He will want a son-in-law with a similar nature."

"Penniless?" I protested. "We came to Elmar with full purses and belts filled with gold. Surely we won't be sent forth penniless?"

Terrel smiled. "What kind of traveling bard has coins in his pouch?" he paused, then answered his own question. "The kind that attracts notice. You'll have a few coins when you leave, but you'll need to return to your egg-thieving days to pass unseen between kingdoms."

Mather interrupted him, focusing on what we should look for, and what the king needed to know. "The king does not want a lecher or a drunken sot for a son-in-law. Only a fool refuses to listen to those who are wiser than he, but a strong king is not led by his counselors like a bull with a ring in his nose."

He continued with a list of traits to observe and tally. I didn't know of a single god or hero who might gain Mather's approval. It was a list no mortal man could satisfy.

After more discussion, Sigurd was taken back to the practice yard to become accustomed to his new axe and Terrel had me memorize couplets that would be useful for getting me invited into court.

As the afternoon sun set, Sigurd and I were ready to depart.

Henga met Sigurd at the gate for a final kiss. Ermindale escorted Corliss to bid me farewell and cautioned her against spending too long in the chill spring air. Corliss whispered a wish for my return and her sorrow at being too sick to spend time with me. I agreed with her, kissed her hand, and let her retire back to the warmth of the princess's chambers.

And then, we departed King Elmar's castle wearing travel-stained clothes and carrying our possessions in shoulder sacks.

A few months ago, we had been heroes, bearing gold and silver, welcomed by innkeepers and cheered by all. Now, we were poor travelers, surviving on what we might earn, beg, or steal.

A few months ago, we were clever, smart and knew the ways of the world. Now, we were better trained in all ways and painfully aware of how little we knew.

A few months ago, we had no goal and no destination

beyond the night's meal. Now, we were embarking upon a quest from a king.

Our tale should be a saga, but I had no idea how to make it believable.

Chapter Twelve

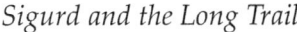

Sigurd and the Long Trail

SIGURD SET HIS usual soldier's pace, striding as if he knew where we were going and what we'd be doing there. I trotted to keep up with him, reviewing what Terrel had told me about the princes, kingdoms, trade routes and dangers.

I was still working the new couplets into verses when dusk fell. We had barely reached the edge of the king's village, on the trail to Earl Bella's castle when I spied a familiar building.

"I think I recognize this tavern. I must have been here with Terrel," I told Sigurd. "We should be able to get a meal and maybe a bed in exchange for songs and news from the castle."

Having claimed familiarity with the inn, I entered first. As I pushed through the doorway into the smoke-filled tavern, I realized why it was familiar. This was where I'd had my lute broken and nearly been killed.

I paused in the doorway, blinking as my eyes adjusted to the dim interior. I jerked as a huge hand grasped my shoulder. Someone thrust his face into mine and studied me with bloodshot eyes. His breath spoke eloquently of his lack of sobriety.

It was Earl Bella's armsman, the one who had attacked me months earlier. This time I was not alone. I had Sigurd with me. But he was on the other side of the door, where he couldn't help. Mather's words about avoiding fights echoed in my mind as I tried to smile.

"I know you!" the near giant shouted, pulling me closer and glaring into my face. "You are the bard who wields a bottle like a dagger!" He stepped back, lifted his beard, and showed his neck. "These scars," he gestured at his neck, "are from this hand!" He grabbed my forearm and lifted it high.

I couldn't move if I'd wanted to. The bear of a man grasped my upper arms and pinned them to my body as he twisted me around to face into the tavern.

His voice was nearly a growl and he declared, "In a fair fight, he bested and spared Beorn. He is Beorn's friend." He twisted me to face him and glanced over my head to the bartender. "Beorn's friend does not pay for ale."

He lifted me to his height. "Sing for Beorn." He laid a finger nearly as thick as my wrist alongside my nose. "But do not insult Beorn's lord, or we must fight again."

I judged the crowd accurately and sang a rousing

drinking song, then *Sigurd and the Virgins* and finally *Sigurd and the Seven Saracens*. Sigurd slipped quietly into the inn while I sang the first song, grabbed a couple of mugs of spiced cider and sat near me.

After the fictional Sigurd had slain the last of the scimitar-wielding sons of the sand, the real Sigurd passed me a cup of cider as a space was cleared in the center of the inn. A broad-axe and arm-length single-edged seax were placed crossways on the floor. Beorn kicked off his boots and danced, stepping around the corners of the weapons, his eyes on the ceiling. Everyone in the room clapped and chanted as he danced heavily, like a bear, almost stepping on the weapons but always missing them.

This was our northern version of the Greek warriors dance Terrel had shown me. It required the dancer know just where his feet and the sharp weapons were without looking.

The tempo the of clapping increased as Beorn stamped and hopped, his arms wide and eyes high, never glancing to see where he was stepping or how close he came to losing a toe.

When the crowd could no longer maintain the clapping rhythm, Beorn did a leap I didn't believe a man so large to be capable of, slapped an ankle with each hand and landed with his feet straddling the axe head. He raised his hands high and clapped as everyone cheered.

One of the younger men jumped to the center and tried to duplicate the dance but stepped on the axe handle within minutes. He retreated back to a bench to the hoots and howls of his companions.

As the jeers died, Sigurd was pulled into the center of

the room to a new round of cheering. He danced more lightly and nimbly than Beorn, twirling, kicking and leaping over the weapons to the rhythm of the clapping. The hours Mather made us spend practicing footwork in the mud were paying off.

He finished his dance by leaping into the air, flipping over to land on his hands, grasping the two weapons and pushing to his feet wielding the axe and dagger. I was impressed at this display of skill and agility. Judging by his face, Sigurd was also surprised he'd managed the feat without losing any fingers.

I finished my ale and sang another drinking song. When it was done, and the ale keg was drained, I sang a couple soft, gentle songs as heads sank to the tabletops. Soon, Sigurd, the innkeeper and I were the only ones awake.

"Beorn has paid for your ale," our host informed us. "You and your companion may sleep by the fire, since no one else is there." He stepped behind a leather door, where I assumed he had a soft pallet and furs. Sigurd and I wrapped ourselves in our cloaks and lay near the fire.

It was not so warm or comfortable as the king's barracks, but I was content. I had learned that I had friends in strange places as well as the brother at my back.

Sleep was not long in claiming me.

The morning reminded me how much more comfortable a pallet is than a stone floor. The only kindness a floor shows a traveler is helping him to rise early. Sigurd and I were on our way before most of the night's revelers had awakened.

It was a perfect day to travel. The sun was bright and

warm, shining through the budding, pale-green leaves. The path was dry and firm, and it was neither too warm nor too cold. Having no taverns to delay our travels, we walked faster, if not happier. With no inns to divert us, we fell to talking.

"Did Mather mention our reward?" I asked Sigurd.

He slapped at an early-season mosquito. "No, I thought Terrel told you."

We both stopped.

"We left the castle with no money and no promise of reward?" We stared at each other. We'd wintered with men of honor. We'd worked and slept with folks who valued their position and duties. We'd even accepted responsibilities. I hadn't understood how much we'd changed until that moment.

Sigurd shrugged. "We can trust Elmar to reward us properly."

I thought of him threatening the Squire over a gold piece and remembered how he lost his brother to an Earl's whim.

But he was right. Elmar was open-handed to those who served him. We'd be well rewarded if we brought him accurate reports of the neighboring princes.

We stopped in a clearing when it was too dark to continue. Sigurd foraged for our dinner while I made a fire. We missed Dale's flair with cooking, but hunger provides flavor when skill is absent.

We met few other travelers this early in the year. Those we met glanced at Sigurd's easy stride and the way he held his axe and gave us a wide berth. Even I saw he no longer carried his axe like a farmer.

Several days later we came to a village. We paused at the edge of the forest and studied it.

"This should be the edge of King Walesyn's lands." Sigurd guessed.

I nodded. "He has one son, Wellach. He visited King Elmar last fall, and was well received, albeit a bit too familiar with wine and ale. An alliance with Walesyn would secure Elmar's southern border and let him move armsmen north, where the Norsemen tend to raid."

I led the way to the village. "We'll need to travel another few days to reach King Walesyn's castle and view the prince, but we may learn some news at an alehouse."

Sigurd nodded. "I could swallow a cup or two of news."

We found a tavern marked with an ale-keg above the door. The doorway was filled with a young man bent double and stumbling into the daylight. Having been escorted from a tavern or two, myself, I recognized how he was being ejected forcibly. The young man stumbled twice and fell at our feet.

He rose to his knees and shouted at the empty doorway.

"A king's son is not treated this way. I'll take my patronage elsewhere!"

A deep voice from within the tavern called back. "With my blessings. Take your patronage as far from here as you will."

The man grabbed Sigurd's leg and pulled himself upright. He was nearly as tall as Sigurd, slightly broader and much drunker.

"Plenty of taverns in this kingdom will welcome my

presence." he announced and lurched down the path between buildings.

Sigurd and I glanced at the retreating form and stepped into the tavern.

The innkeeper glowered at us.

"Well?" he challenged, one hand out of sight and most likely gripping a cudgel.

"Two travelers," I replied briskly. "Willing to trade songs and news for an ale or two."

He studied us carefully, particularly noting Sigurd's axe and boiled leather breastplate.

"I trade coins for ale," he announced. "I'll trade gossip for gossip. You may sing and beg for pennies when there's someone to listen."

It was the kind of welcome I knew well. We were no longer a hero and his bard. We were just two wanderers, worthy of suspicion and probably penniless.

Sigurd dropped a bronze Roman dupondus onto the bar. "We'll test your ale," he announced. "If it's worth the coin, we'll hazard a meal."

"You'll find my ale to be well worth your coin," the innkeeper assured Sigurd as he filled two small tankards. "I've cold roast now, or fresh-cooked fowl in an hour."

We tasted the ale. It was a thinner than I prefer but would do.

"I've had better," Sigurd announced after a hefty sample. "But it might be good enough for a king's son."

The innkeeper scowled. "If you are friends of his, you can take your coins and follow him." he said shortly. His arms tensed as he prepared to throw us out as he'd evicted the prince.

I raised my hands, "We're no friends to the prince. We wouldn't know him to step over, though I think that's what we just did."

He nodded. "It was a sad day when Walesyn kicked him out of the castle. Any other lad would land on his ass and sober up, but Wellach just keeps seeking another tavern that hasn't already had too much of his patronage." He shook his head. "The best thing for the kingdom is if he drinks himself to death before his father passes."

Sigurd glanced at me. "Cold roast and we continue?" he asked. I nodded. We'd learned all we needed to know about Prince Wellach.

The roast arrived moments later on a board with a couple of small trenchers. Our host set the meal down, just out of our reach and announced, "Three bronze pennies."

Sigurd looked at me. He'd bought our ale; it was my turn. I dug a silver sceat from my pouch, leaving only a couple bronze coins.

I held out the coin and closed my hand. "What's the best route to King Christoff's castle?" I asked, before the innkeeper decided to demand a coin for giving us directions.

He grunted. "The easiest way is to follow the trade road west, to Wallech's castle, then north to Christoff's realm. That will take you about three weeks. The fastest way is to follow the river upstream till you reach the trade-road ford. The trail may be flooded in places, but two strong, young men can make that trip in a single week."

I set the coin on the bench top. It vanished quickly and the board was placed before us.

"A bit of free advice," the host continued. "The river trail is not patrolled. It's likely safe this early in the season but sleeping by your axe is best."

We nodded and addressed ourselves to the trencher and meat. The bread was gritty and the roast tough, but after several days of rabbit and squirrel it tasted as grand as anything we ate at King Elmar's court.

Rabbit was what we ate that night, a half-day's walk up-river. The trail was not "flooded in a few places." In a few places it was soft, sticky mud. The rest of the trail was completely under water. We forced our way through the undergrowth near the river rather than floundering along the flooded riverbank.

After several nights of sleeping in damp cloaks and eating half-raw rabbit we found a trail following the river on high ground. Sigurd stepped into the path and paused, staring at his feet. I followed his example, studying the ground as if I understood what I saw. It was a game trail, covered with hoof prints.

"Deer?" I asked Sigurd, pointing at the cloven prints. He shook his head.

"Boar," he replied. "A sounder. At least one sow, maybe three, a litter, and it looks like a boar as well." He glanced back into the brush and then at me. "We may as well take the trail. It will get us away from them fastest."

I nodded. Boars are vicious and smart and inclined to attack without warning. When men go boar-hunting they take trained dogs and large parties. Two men with no dogs to aid them might kill a boar, but they'd acquire nasty wounds that would likely fester.

We stepped quickly along the trail. As we crested the next hill, we saw a caravan with several men and mules.

I smiled at Sigurd. "We should be safe if we travel with them. Maybe they'll want to hire a guard, or I can earn us a few coins with songs and news."

As we approached, the traders gathered between us and the mules, forming a battle line. This was no surprise. They needed to protect their goods and we might be bandits.

A burly red-haired, red-bearded young man strode to the front. I stepped forward to greet him and noticed how the ends of the battle line were moving to encircle Sigurd and me, rather than staying back to protect the mules.

"Greetings," I called, tapping Sigurd's waist and shifting my hand left and right to bring his attention to the movements. "My friend, Sigurd and I welcome the opportunity to travel with you for a few days. We offer song. news and a ready axe for defense."

The leader grinned. "Well met, youngling. Ragnar the Redhand will accept your fealty. You may go Viking with us. I graciously grant you each with one-half a share of the plunder. Ragnar is known for finding rich plunder."

I stopped short. I studied the mules behind him. They weren't carrying trade goods. They bore shields, spears, and axes. These weren't traders, they were a Norse war party on their way to pillage a small keep or monastery.

A bard needs a nimble tongue in situations like this.

"Noble Ragnar, blood-handed and feared, we thank you for the offer to join your famous band and share the glorious bounty." His smile got broader. A man who names himself Redhand is a man who thrives on praise. "However, Sigurd and I are oath-sworn and not free to join your glorious band."

The smile vanished like the sun slipping behind a cloud.

"Ragnar the Open-Handed is not accustomed to refusal," he growled. "If you do not wish to join my party as equals, you may join as slaves."

The band of warriors surrounded us as we spoke. Sigurd had used the moments while I exchanged words with Ragnar to loosen his shield and prepare his axe for fighting.

"There are twelve of you," Sigurd spoke slowly. "You can capture us, but I assure you there will be fewer than nine of you standing when that's done. Twelve is a small band for raiding, but nine is smaller."

Ragnar snorted. "Were you a fabled warrior, like Sigurd of the black axe, your argument might have merit. But I declare you boast, and Ragnar will lose no men taking you for slaves."

Sigurd tapped the edge of his shield gently with the flat of his axe. "Black handle or plain oak. I swear by Odin that my axe thirsts and it will take three men or more to slake that thirst."

Ragnar studied Sigurd, assessing his obvious familiarity with the axe and shield.

"Ragnar the Generous understands barter." He wasn't quite frowning, but not smiling either. "Oaths to men are not like oaths sworn before gods. They can be broken easily. Ragnar will offer you a full share apiece to break your bond and swear fealty to him. Fourteen warriors," he glanced at me, "Thirteen warriors and a bard are a better band than twelve mighty foemen."

Sigurd didn't relax, but his voice was gentler. "Will Ragnar throw the choice to the gods? We can lead you to wild boars. Let the first kill decide if we shall join your band. If your men blood the first boar, we will join your raiding party, but if the gods favor Bard and me, we will go our own ways."

Ragnar grinned and nodded. A hunt, a contest, a chance to prove his skill, and a feast afterward. What more could a Norseman want?

He called to his men, "A hunt and a contest! An extra share of the gold from the monastery to the first man to blood a boar!"

Sigurd asked for a few moments to prepare and told me to build a fire while he made a boar spear. I lit a fire and hoped Sigurd would be safe during the hunt. I wondered how he intended to score the first blood. I expected to write a fine saga of this adventure.

Sigurd returned with a tree nearly half again as tall as I. He trimmed off the branches and threw them onto my fire until the trunk formed a spear with a foot-long limb as thick as my wrist jutting out an arms-length from the tip.

He rotated the sharpened tip of the spear in the blaze to fire-harden it.

"You'll carry this," he whispered. I stared at him with wide eyes. It hadn't occurred to me that I'd be involved in the boar hunt.

"Me?" I whispered back. "You know I'm not warrior trained!"

"You jabbed a spear at me in the practice yard enough times. This is the same. You jab at the boar and distract him while I circle and use my axe. With luck, we won't go a-Viking this summer, and we might see Henga and Corliss again. I can't fight a boar alone. If we get a chance, I'd rather escape in the confusion, but it's best to be prepared to fight a boar."

Put that way, I had little choice. I preferred the idea of having a brother protecting my back to me protecting his, but the obligation went both ways.

Sigurd and I led the way back down the path with the Vikings fanning out behind us like a flock of geese; a flock of smelly, bearded, well-armed geese.

Fifty paces later, there was a scuffle and high-pitched squeal to our right. One of the Vikings shouted joyfully and hoisted a suckling boar on the tip of his spear.

"First Blood!" roared Ragnar, but his call was drowned out by a scream from our left. A full-grown sow was responding to the suckling's cry, racing to avenge her young. One of Ragnar's men was on the ground holding his thigh and another was falling as the sow charged at Sigurd and me. Her head held high and mouth wide open, I gazed at the long, yellow teeth and hoped she was not as skilled as Sigurd at dodging a spear.

I barely had time to lower the spear as Sigurd stepped beside me. The sow attacked me face on. I braced myself and drove the spear down her throat. Her frenzy forced me backwards several steps as she surged up the shaft to ravage me, the spear-tip jutting out the side of her neck. The branch Sigurd left in place was all that prevented her from devouring my fingers.

235

Sigurd stepped forward as she pushed me back and smashed his axe into her forehead, cleaving the skull. This slowed the beast, and he had time to bring his axe over his head and down once more on her neck. That blow separated head from body and splintered the spear.

Ragnar strode forward. "A good blow," he said, studying the sundered boar. "But Ragnar claims first blood."

Sigurd stared him in the eye. "Ragnar, Babe Slayer would be best served to concede defeat graciously. The contest was who should slay the first boar, not an unlucky piglet. The gods granted you a suckling but granted us a full-grown boar. I'd not dispute the gods."

Ragnar glanced nervously upwards. The Norse gods take a dim view of oath-breaking.

"Well argued, " he admitted. "Ragnar the Reasonable will grant you leave to part ways." He glanced at Sigurd's bloody axe. "But it would be great joy to plunder with you beside me."

Sigurd relaxed. We were free to go. Probably. Trusting a Norseman is not a way to grow old.

"May we take a small portion of the spoils of the hunt as our share?" I asked.

Ragnar laughed. "You bargain like a Byzantine: always a bit more. I will grant you as much of the piglet as you can cleave in a single blow."

The suckling was lying on the ground. Sigurd strode to it and swung his axe underhanded. He caught the piglet on the hammer end of the axe and flung it into the air. As it fell, he swung his axe upward, catching it in mid fall just before the hind legs. The two halves of the piglet spun into the air and Sigurd caught its back end with his left hand.

"We will take these," he announced. "and thank Ragnar the Generous for his open handedness." He sauntered up the trail in the direction we'd been traveling.

We strode away from Ragnar and his men displaying our backs, to show we were brave. But we walked quietly, listening, because we were not foolish.

Ragnar was true to his word, and we left unmolested. He had injured men to care for and a boar to butcher. He fared less well in the contest than he had hoped, but his men would feast tonight and tell a tale of how they had tricked wayfarers into slaying a boar for their meal.

As the hubbub faded, Sigurd whispered. "Are we still in sight of them?" he asked.

I glanced over my shoulder. "No," I replied. "Shall we walk faster?"

Sigurd was already trotting ahead of me. I sprinted to catch up.

"The Norsemen were headed to a monastery," he said, taking deep breaths. "A monastery will have walls. I say a wall is a good thing to put between us and Ragnar."

My heart paused a beat and I stumbled. This would be the first time I'd been in a place of worship since I stole away from the monastery where I'd been raised. I didn't know if I feared it would be familiar and comforting or strange and unsettling.

Despite my misgivings about the religious order, I agreed with Sigurd about the wall.

We crested three hills before we came to the monastery.

The monks were tilling a field outside a wooden barricade. Several wood and stone buildings stood behind the wall.

As we came over the hill, the monks dashed for sanctuary. They were closing man-tall wooden gates as we approached. If we had been a war-party, we'd have breached the wall before the gate was latched.

"Pilgrims, " I gasped, struggling with Latin I'd not used for years. "We come in peace with news and a warning."

A gray bearded abbot pushed to the front of the monks. My use of Latin had convinced him we weren't Vikings.

"Speak, my son," he greeted me. "What warning do you bring?"

"Danish raiders," I replied. "three hills back, intent on sacking the monastery. They'll likely arrive tomorrow."

He stepped away to let us enter. "How many?" he asked.

"Twelve," I replied.

"Ten," corrected Sigurd, wiping the blood from his axe.

He was learning to speak truth like a bard. I'd forgotten the two men who had fallen to the sow, but if the monks wanted to believe he had slain two of the raiders, so much the better.

After we were admitted the abbot had the gate closed and latched. He ordered his brethren to collect arms and armor and be ready to fight by morning.

We contributed the piglet legs to the kitchen and were rewarded with a fine meal and a mug of strong, dark ale. After the meal, the monks retreated to pray. The abbot invited us to join them in the chapel.

Sigurd shook his head. "I honor your Christ," he said,

"but he is not my faith. I'll not profane his shrine with an unbeliever."

The abbot gazed at me. I stood slowly and followed him to the chapel.

I sank to my knees and didn't pray. While the monks prayed and chanted, I reviewed my life since I'd left the monastery: the eggs I'd stolen, the cheer and solace I'd given with my music, the landlords I'd cheated, and the deeds Sigurd and I had done.

I believed more of my actions were good than ill, but I was not in a state of grace. The theft of coins and lute from the monastery was an act I could not bring myself to confess.

Dawn brought a red, brooding sun and Ragnar's war party. The Norsemen crested the hill just after dawn. They expected to find the monks working the fields and hoped to slaughter them before they retreated behind their walls.

Instead, they met the abbot, flanked by Sigurd and another burly cleric, standing with a dozen monks, all armed and armored.

Ragnar strode forward. He had eleven warriors with him, one obviously limping with a cloth bandage on his thigh. He examined the line of monks, assessing their arms, armor, and ability to use them.

"Ho, Sigurd, Ragnar's Bane," he greeted us. He glared at the abbot. "Will you ransom your monastery, or must we slaughter?"

The abbot laughed at him. "I count you outnumbered," he replied.

Ragnar grinned back, confident. "A Norseman is worth

two Celts," he countered. "That's why Vortigern invited Northmen to Anglia."

"Do you see a Celt facing you?" the abbot replied. "Hengist led my father's father here, and here we stay."

Ragnar's smile faltered. The monks were not slender Romans or short Celts, but big, burly Saxons.

The abbot pushed his argument one step further. "A flight of the gray goose will carry a man to his reward, be it Heaven or Valhalla."

The shadows around us shifted as several peasants with longbows showed themselves on a palisade behind the wall.

Ragnar grimaced, shrugged, and grinned engagingly. "Gold from plunder is best, but any gold is good gold. Will you bargain with Ragnar the Ever Prepared? We wintered in Byzantium and brought trade goods when we departed."

This about-face was expected. The Norse were known to plunder whenever possible, but if they couldn't win an easy battle, they traded. A leader gained more stature from a successful trade than from an unsuccessful raid. As long as he found ways to profit and reward his men, they would follow him.

In short order a cloth was laid on the grass before the gate and the abbot, Sigurd and I viewed bundles of silk, pouches of spices, small bits of jewelry and exquisite little daggers. As we eyed the trade goods, the monks and Norsemen glared at each other and made sure nobody took advantage of the distractions.

The Abbot pointed to a bundle of silks I did not believe he wanted. "I will offer a half-penny for that."

Ragnar shouted back "A ha'penny? For silks from far Cathay? For a bronze coin, I will let you view one thread. Briefly."

"My pardon," the abbot replied. "I mistook them for kitchen rags. Two sceats, and you may keep the rotting twine that binds them."

And so, the bargaining went. In the end, the abbot received three packets of spices from the orient and gave Ragnar a gold Denarius and a cask of dark ale.

Then the Norsemen brought out the remains of the boar and the abbot broached a keg of ale to seal the day's dealings. The monks and Norsemen ate together and toasted their new trading partners. I sang of Sigurd and then a tale of Thor, Odin, and Loki contesting with a giant. Where Loki played clever tricks to win the games, I replaced his name with Ragnar. I finished the song with a new verse.

Ragnar Redhand,	ever ready,
Lose a wager,	find a feast,
When outnumbered,	trades for treasure,
Laughs at what the	fates foretell
Seize success from	all adventures.
Fights the Fates and	makes them yield.

Ragnar roared with laughter and boasted how in a contest with the giants he would find a way to emerge victorious. He tossed me a hand-sized bundle of silks. "In case it takes more than your clever tongue to win a maid's favor," he called, and laughed at his jest.

I thanked him and sang drinking songs as the fire burned late into the evening.

Sigurd and I retired with the monks to sleep behind walls, leaving the Norsemen with the half-full ale-cask and the rest of the boar.

Once safe within the monastery, the abbot called us to sing the evening prayers. Sigurd waited in the courtyard while I accompanied the monks into the chapel and sang vespers for the first time since I'd left the monastery as a child. I heard the words differently now, as an adult, than I had then. The echoes and memories were both comforting and disturbing.

Outside the wall, different songs echoed through the night. When we awoke in the morning, Ragnar was gone and with him the ale cask. All they left was the boar's bones.

The abbot escorted us as we left the monastery. When I told him we were heading to King Christoff's castle he smiled. "Give my greetings to Brother Matthew when you arrive. Let him know we'll visit him once the fields are planted." He glanced at the clouds in the northwest. Storms were raging in the hills. "You may find the water too high at the trade-route ford. If you walk a half-day upstream, there's a smaller ford that might be passable."

He studied me. "You are a member of the flock but are not comfortable within the monastery walls. I won't ask or pry, but I will offer you short sermon and a prediction. Our Father does not waste or misuse his tools. You are on the path you are meant to travel. Someday this path will lead back to your faith."

He pressed a wooden cross on a leather strap into my hand. "You need not hide your faith," he told me. "You may wear this below your tunic if you aren't ready to acknowledge it yet. But you wear your faith, whether you bear the cross or not."

With that, he left us. The only path I was certain I should travel was the one leading back to King Elmar and Corliss. So far as my faith was concerned, it could contest with Ragnar's fates, and I'd see which won.

Chapter Thirteen

Sigurd and the Prince's Requiem

THE ABBOT MAY have been mistaken about my returning to the faith. but he was correct about the river. It was already high from the melting snow and the storm in the hills only made it higher.

When we reached the trade road the river was almost overflowing its banks and the ford was impassable.

The road leading to the ford was dry enough for us to sit for a meal. We were happy to rest, watching the river surge in frothy white and brown billows while we paid proper attention to the bread, cheese, and ale the grateful monks insisted we take.

"The river is dropping," I observed, shortly after

finishing the last of the ale. "If we spend the night here we might be able to ford it in the morning."

Sigurd examined the roiling river.

"It might drop enough to ford tomorrow, but it will still be high and tricky. If the abbot is right about the ford upstream being easier, we'll have a better chance there. If we can't cross today, we'll be able to cross in the morning. We may as well walk upstream now."

I didn't like the idea of plodding upstream and then back, but I agreed. Walking would be better than waiting for the river to drop enough to ford here.

After a half day of slogging along the muddy trail, we discovered the second ford was not passable yet, but the storm waters were definitely passing. We expected to cross in the morning. I made a fire while Sigurd hunted, and we had plenty of rabbit for our dinner.

In the morning, the river had dropped enough for us to try the ford. We wrapped our clothes into bundles and tied them to our shoulders. It was unpleasant to strip in the cold morning air, but the thought of wearing cold, wet clothes after fording the river was even more chilling.

I held my lute above my head with one hand and linked the other arm with Sigurd's. We walked slowly and carefully across the ford. In the center, where the water was hip-deep and the current strong, we took one half-a-step at a time while the other braced. It was painstakingly slow, but we needed an anchor in case we lost footing.

Once we passed the deepest section, we raced out of the river as quickly as we could. We were both chilled through and shivering. Only a convent's welcome is colder than the spring runoff from a snow-covered mountain.

"Chopping firewood would warm you," I suggested to Sigurd.

"A brisk walk will warm both of us," he replied, pulling his tunic over his head.

He was determined not to chop wood, so we fought our way through the underbrush until we found the trade road and finished our trek to King Christoff's lands.

We reached a tavern about noon. We didn't need to discuss whether or not to stop. Our clothes were mostly dry, but the chill was still in my bones. Hot wine and a fire called to me.

The tavern keeper jerked in surprise as we entered. His head spun so quickly his light-brown beard swayed. He wiped his hands on a pale knitted vest he wore over his homespun tunic.

"Is the ford passable already?" he gasped.

We shook our heads. "The river is still too high," Sigurd told him.

"The upstream ford is passable if you are a pair of fools," I added. "Do you have warm wine and a fire for two travelers with news from Elmar's and Walesyn's lands?"

"The wine isn't warmed, but you're welcome to the fire. Are the tales of Wellach drinking the kingdom dry true?"

I nodded and related what we'd learned from the surly innkeeper.

This news, followed by the saga of *Sigurd and the Three Thieves*, gained us a dish of stew and a cup of ale. I told of Elmar's solstice celebrations while we ate, and we left the innkeeper satisfied that he'd have tales to enthrall his listeners this evening.

As twilight fell, Sigurd spotted smoke rising over the next hill. As the stars began to appear we trotted to an inn at the outskirts of King Christoff's village

We decided to follow Terrel's and Mather's plan-- entering separately to each gain entrance to the court. Sigurd would try to befriend a guardsman and I'd come in a few minutes later and hope to get invited to the castle.

When I pushed through the door, Sigurd was arm- wrestling with a heavyset man. Sigurd and his opponent were both straining, sinews standing out on their arms and teeth clenched. Sigurd's arm was being slowly pushed back while four men behind him counted loudly. His opponent was also shaking with the effort, his black-bearded cheeks bouncing as he gritted his teeth with each push.

When the count reached ten, Sigurd relaxed and let his arm be pinned. His opponent grinned at him. "Not bad," he said. "There's few men who last a count of five, let alone ten. With a bit more strength, you might be a blacksmith."

Sigurd rubbed his upper arm and grinned back. "I might be farmer, too, but I'd rather be a guardsman. It's not such hard work, and they always have too many coins." He turned to the men who had been counting and held out his hand. Each placed a bronze coin in it and congratulated him.

My friend passed three of the coins to the innkeeper, buying a cup of ale for each of them and settled back to exchange lies. He tossed the final coin to me calling, "Ho, Bard, moisten your throat and sing something for my friends and me."

I sang the *Earl and the Trolls*. When I finished, one of Sigurd's new companions tossed me a bronze penny.

"Did you travel from south of the river?" he asked.

I nodded and took a sip of ale.

"Do you know the one about the horse, where Sigurd picks flowers with his teeth?"

I nearly choked on my ale as his friends cheered and called for the song.

As I sang "Pound, Pound, Pound," the guardsmen pounded the bench top with their cups. I finally understood why the song was so popular, and it had nothing to do with the effort I'd put into the shifts in meter and rhyme pattern.

Men enjoy pounding on tables and the song gave them plenty of opportunity for pounding.

As I finished the last verse, a young man entered the tavern and the guardsmen fell silent. I glanced at the newcomer and saw nothing of note, aside that he was better dressed and groomed than the others. His mouse-brown hair was cut short, in a warrior's style, though he did not carry himself like an armsman.

The newcomer smiled at the guardsmen and the innkeeper. He dropped a silver coin on the bar and said "Ale, my good man. One for everyone, that they may toast our king."

This was worth a cheer and a toast. I guessed the newcomer to be a member of the castle and began the song Terrel and I had composed extolling Prince Ackley as their future king.

The tavern fell silent. A bard loves silence when he sings.

249

It means the listeners are paying attention, and they want to hear the song. It's the highest praise a bard can receive.

This was not that kind of silence. The guardsmen gazed into their cups, not at me. The young noble turned his face away from me and the innkeeper stared into the fire.

I stopped in mid-verse. "Is something amiss?" I asked.

The guardsman who had requested *Sigurd's Ride with Death* spoke. "You're from south of the river, so you can't know. Prince Ackley took a chill while hunting and died of fever just after the solstice."

The noble studied me. "From the south?" he asked as I nodded. "Do you have word from the abbot?"

I smiled. "He sends greetings to Brother Matthew and--" again I stopped. The same silence had fallen.

The noble explained. "Brother Matthew sat with our prince throughout his illness. He caught the fever and died a week later. They lie unburied for lack of anyone to deliver the mass and blessing. Did the abbot say when he will send a new priest? All are anxious to have them set to rest."

I shook my head. "The abbot sent greetings but didn't mention sending a new priest. He doesn't know of Brother Matthew's death."

The young man studied at me closely. The cross the abbot had given me had slipped from beneath my tunic while I played my lute. He stared at me and spoke softly.

"You sang in a Latin form and bear the cross. Are you church trained?"

I couldn't deny it. I nodded, with a sinking feeling in my stomach that I would regret this.

He smiled and lifted his hands hopefully.

"Do you know the masses? Can you sing the burial rites? It would mean so much to the queen. We fear for her sanity, her only son lying unblessed and..." his voice cracked as he fell silent.

The guardsmen and the blacksmith stared at me. One of the guards mouthed a prayer. It was obvious the prince had been well loved. They needed the burial to close the book of his life and go on with their own lives. If the guardsmen felt this strongly, I could only imagine the mother's grief.

"I'm not a father," I whispered, "not even a brother. But I've sung the death rites."

The noble embraced me. "Thank you, sir," he cried. "We will have the graves blessed when the abbot sends a priest, but at least my cousin can be buried."

I was hurried from the tavern to the castle. The noble had the King and Queen summoned from their beds and before I could explain further they arranged for the burial to happen in the morning. The prince had already lain in state and the coffin had been stored outside for longer than anyone liked now that the days were warmer.

I was given Father Matthew's cell for the night. I could have slept on a fine tick mattress over tight cords, except I could not sleep at all. I lay on my back staring into the blackness, remembering the masses I'd attended, how I'd felt when I first sang at one, how the brothers swayed as they prayed, the life I'd shared and how and why I'd left the monastery.

I could not sing the mass. I never learned any parts except the ones I sang. Even if I recalled the words, I was not ordained. For me to deliver the mass would be a sin. Terrel might disagree, but to the Church, and to me, that would be worse sin than violating my master's trust.

The abbot's face formed in the blackness. Perhaps I dreamed him telling me that leaving the family in grief and uncertainty would also be a sin. I could not deny them solace when it was in my power to ease their suffering.

My eyes burned. Whenever I blinked another face appeared with another demand that I not forswear my faith. I thought I'd left that faith behind so many years ago, but it had found me.

I was still staring into the blackness when I realized I could see the stones in the ceiling, and it was no longer night. I gazed at Brother Matthew's robes and briefly considered donning them. I shook my head. Wearing the garment, I wasn't entitled to would be a mockery. I might not wish to live within the church, but I wasn't willing to mock it.

Footsteps echoed in the hallway outside my cell. A moment later a young man peeked around the doorway.

"The altar is ready for you," he said softly.

I nodded and followed him to the chapel. I entered through the apse, opposite the main doorway, and stepped onto the dais. The church had gray stone walls as tall as a man, and smoke-darkened oak timbers rising above to a crown twice as tall as a man. It was lit with tapers and torches along the walls. The beam of early morning sunlight fell on the pale wooden cross behind me, making it shine like gold. The king, queen, and a few dozen others in dark mourning robes knelt in the nave. The caskets were on trestles between the dais and the nave, closed in deference to the warm days.

I was uncomfortable, standing where a priest should stand. I had no words to speak. I could not sing the final mass. I closed my eyes, seeing my old monastery, and opened my mouth. Words I'd never expected to hear again flowed into the chapel, filling the space, and echoing back to me.

> Requiem aeternam dona eis, Domine
> et lux perpetua luceat eis.

I could not sing the mass, but I could sing the prayers and hymns. I could not give the Prince true last rites, but I could pray for his peaceful passage beyond this world. This would soothe his soul and provide closure for his family until a Father arrived to lay him properly to rest.

I opened my eyes and sang to the assembly, instead of to my past.

> Eternal rest grant unto them, O Lord
> and let perpetual light shine upon them.

The king knelt and stared at the floor in front of him as the queen and a young lady sobbed. I finished to silence until the last echoes faded away.

Then the king, the cousin I'd met the night before and four other men in mourning robes lifted the Prince's casket. Six men wearing heavy wooden crosses picked up Brother Matthew's casket. I continued singing as we treaded slowly to the graves. This time I did not sing the church prayers,

253

but the north country dirge.

> This ae nighte, this ae nighte,
> Every nighte and alle,
> Fire and fleet and candle-lighte,
> And Christe receive thy saule.

The path to the grave was lined with peasants, guardsmen, and minor nobles, all with their heads bowed, tears coursing their cheeks. As we passed they chanted the dirge with me.

As we reached the gravesite, I sang a final prayer. I never met the prince and knew nothing of him. Except what I saw in the faces around the grave. They showed he was loved and lamented. My throat tightened and I nearly choked. I closed my eyes to control myself and shifted to a higher key to hide how tight my throat was. I would not disrupt this ceremony by stopping or having my voice break.

The first shovelful of dirt hit the coffin and then the second. I opened my eyes as the men of the household took turns filling the grave and crossing themselves. After I finished the prayer, a noble escorted the queen back to the castle. Another tugged the king's robe and nodded to follow her. The king shook his head and continued shoveling dirt into the grave, the tears still running down his cheeks.

I scooped a handful of dirt and tossed it into the grave, crossing myself. The king smiled briefly at me, nodded, and continued burying his son.

I left him there and found Sigurd on the path. We

walked in silence to the castle. All we could do had been done. It was time to continue north to examine the last prince.

As we walked around the castle, the postern door creaked open and the Queen ran to us. She pressed a small pouch into my hands, murmured a thanks and raced back into the castle with her kerchief covering her face.

A royal crest and the letter "A" were embroidered on the pouch. It must have been the prince's. Inside it were two gold pieces.

I stared at Sigurd. "I can't," I choked. "Not for this."

He shrugged, "You can't refuse, You can't reject their gift any more than you could refuse their need."

I nodded absently. I would donate the gold pieces to the next church we encountered.

Sigurd and I walked on in silence. My mind was still spinning through my years at the monastery, the abbot's prediction, and the tears on a king's cheeks. The sorrow the prince's death caused made me believe he would have made a fitting husband for Beornwyn.

I lamented him perishing before we met him.

The first inn we passed smelled of breakfast. I'd had none, but it didn't matter. My feet followed the path north until Sigurd veered to the door and pulled me beside him.

The innkeeper greeted us by crossing himself. "Good bard," he said, "It was a fine ceremony. Will you and your friend accept a meal from me in thanks for your service to my king?"

I was speechless. I didn't want more payment for the

service I was unqualified to sing, but the only coins I had were the gold ones I'd sworn to give to a church.

Sigurd pushed me onto a bench. "We will be happy to accept a meal," he replied. "My friend needs to eat."

The eggs, bread and warm ale brought me out of my thoughts and into the tavern. Our host was telling of how the prince had first eaten here, sitting on a guardsman's lap to reach the tabletop. Today's burial had brought the pain of the prince's death back to those who knew him. They were bringing his memory to the surface one last time. Soon his life would just be another story told to children and travelers.

We let him finish the tale, thanked him for the meal and were on our way.

For several days I was recognized as the one who sang the requiem for Prince Ackley and each innkeeper insisted on giving us food and drink.

As we left the last tavern in Christoff's land, our stomachs comfortably filled and our ears even fuller, I asked Sigurd, "How does the news of what we did at the castle travels so much faster than we do?"

He pondered this for a few steps. "Perhaps the news doesn't stop for ale," he replied, rubbing his stomach, and belching contentedly.

I had to agree. We were spending more time in taverns than we had in the first weeks of our travels. We'd need to pick up our pace to complete our journey in the three months King Elmar granted us.

Chapter Fourteen

Sigurd and the Plights of Princes

AFTER THE NIGHTS spent in taverns being regaled by tales of the prince, we welcomed our first meals in the barren stretch between kingdoms. The quiet dinner of half-cooked rabbit was most welcome.

It only took two days for the novelty of rabbit to wear off. By then I'd pushed my memories of the dead prince and the abbot's prediction out of my mind. Instead, I pondered how much we needed to learn of Prince Cuthbert and how soon I could return to Corliss. Judging from our conversations, Sigurd had similar thoughts of Henga.

The first sign of a village is the tavern. If a man can grow grain, he can brew beer and ale.

This stone and wood inn was quiet, with a slight shadow of smoke coming from the chimney.

"Do you think we'll get a free meal?" Sigurd asked.

I shook my head. "We've outrun the news from Christoff's lands. We haven't stopped for ale in over six days."

"The inn looks empty," He observed. "With no guardsmen to cozen out of a few coins, there's no need to enter separately."

I nodded and we strode to the inn, anxious for news and ale. I pushed aside the wooden door and we entered together. The innkeeper lazed on a bench with his feet by the fire. He had the hard face and soft belly of a man who had seen many hard years and was now enjoying a softer life.

He lifted his head and raised his eyes as we entered. When he saw we weren't locals he pulled his feet back from the fire and stood.

"Welcome," he boomed. "Welcome to my inn. You're the first travelers I've seen since the snowfall."

"We've come from the south," I replied. "Would you trade a meal for news from King Walesyn's, Christoff's and Elmar's lands?"

His eyes widened. as he made space for us by the fire. "You've traveled far for this early in the year. What brings you north so soon? We could still see snow, you know."

I abandoned the clever ruses Terrel, and Mather had worked out for us. We had not used them in the first two kingdoms. The sooner I learned about Prince Cuthbert, the sooner Sigurd and I would be heading back to King

Elmar's.

"We've come to see if Prince Cuthbert would make a suitable husband for King Elmar's daughter."

The innkeeper stopped in his tracks and turned to face us.

"Prince Cuthbert?" he asked. "Cuthbert Fairhair or Cuthbert the Black?"

This time I stopped. Two princes? Nobody warned us about two princes.

"Two?" I croaked. "In one kingdom?"

The innkeeper laughed. "You're far from home. Everyone nearby knows the tale. When King Beldon had been wed for ten years with no heir, a priest convinced him to pray to St. Cuthbert for assistance. Not being a man to ask favors for nothing, Beldon promised to name a son for the saint and raise him in the faith. He even took a mistress to make the saint's job easier."

Our host paused to set two fist-sized mugs of foaming ale in front of us. "In a few months the king's mistress announced she was with child, and the king rejoiced. A month or so later, the queen was also with child.

"King Beldon didn't know which son was the gift from St. Cuthbert, so he named them both Cuthbert and raised them as brothers."

I shook my head. "I'm surprised there is no saga of this. It's a tale well worth telling."

The innkeeper nodded. "Cuthbert the Black is proud to be a king's son, but not so proud of being a by-blow. He deals harshly with those who remind him how he came from the wrong side of the blanket."

"A nasty conundrum. The elder son is a bastard, and the second son is true, which is heir to the kingdom? Has King Beldon made a choice?"

The innkeeper's face fell. "He has not. And likely will not. He was struck ill during the solstice celebrations and has been unable to speak, walk, or raise his right arm since. I hear talk of gathering the earls to an Althing to declare which of the princes should rule if he dies without indicating his wish."

I had a sinking feeling in my stomach. Would I be requested to sing another requiem soon?

"Is there a priest present to perform the rites?" I asked, fearing the answer.

"Of course!" boomed the innkeeper. "Do you think we're all pagans and druids here? There are as many Christians as anything else in this kingdom. Not that Beldon was a Christian, mind you. He followed the old ways. The promise of raising his sons in the faith was likely why the priest gave a dispensation to take a mistress."

By now it was dark, and villagers came to patronize the tavern. When they saw travelers, they asked questions: are the fords passable? did we pass any traders who might buy wool? did we see any of their relatives along our way?

Each of these questions came with two pints of ale, one for the asker and one for Sigurd or me. My tongue was developing a mind of its own when the innkeeper pushed plates of stew and bread in front of us.

After eating, my tongue behaved again. I sang the song of the *Earl and the Trolls*, several drinking songs and selected portions of *Sigurd and the Ten Virgins*.

Three days and five taverns later, we reached the outskirts of King Beldon's village. My cunning questions revealed that Cuthbert the Black was smart and unforgiving. His servants obeyed him out of fear. Cuthbert Fairhair's men liked him but were less fervid about following his orders. Cuthbert Fairhair was the better liked of the two princes but was considered less clever than his brother.

Cuthbert the Black would probably be the heir to the throne, and his brother would become a landless earl assisting him.

Sigurd and I discussed this as we approached Beldon's court.

"An alliance with a king is preferable to one with a landless earl," I suggested.

"True," Sigurd replied. "But Beornwyn deserves better than a cruel husband."

I agreed. From what we'd learned, Cuthbert Fairhair would be the better husband, but Cuthbert the Black the stronger king.

"Perhaps the Althing will vote in favor of the heredity instead of the order of birth."

We were a day's walk from King Beldon's court when the death-bells tolled. By the time we reached the castle, the king lay in state with a long line of peasants, lesser nobles and guardsmen paying their respects.

Sigurd and I joined the line. After we viewed the corpse we planned to mingle with the crowd and observe the princes.

The line moved slowly as we listened to prayers, toasts, and good wishes. Eventually, we reached the head of the line. The dead king lay atop a table, clothed in a white robe, draped with mistletoe and holly. Several gray haired men wearing similar robes stood behind the table chanting softly. A young man arrayed in a black tunic and gold chain waited just past them to greet mourners and accept condolences. I noted his gold-blond hair and decided he must be Cuthbert Fairhair.

He looked slightly familiar, but I'd never seen this prince before. The way he moved tickled a memory I couldn't quite reach. He moved like a man accustomed to command. Like a king, or an earl... or the peasant I'd seen studying the royal table during the solstice celebrations.

The guest's behavior at Elmar's feast fell into place like verses in a song. He had been passing as a peasant to observe Beornwyn and King Elmar when he'd gotten word of his father falling ill.

I thought better of him, both for studying the royal family before he announced himself and for abandoning his quest when told of his father's illness.

While I pondered his behavior the line edged forward, and I neared the prince. My instructions from the king and Terrel were to remain hidden and observe him, not to make my presence known.

A bard follows the world's tune, but he composes his own words. This is in a bard's blood. He can do nothing else.

I doffed my cap and said, "King Elmar of the East sends his condolences."

Promised Rewards

The prince jerked his head, examined me, and then studied my companion.

"The bard from Elmar's castle? Sigurd of the Black Axe?" he asked. He caught himself, glanced about the great hall and whispered, "Return tonight, please, just after moonrise. To the postern gate and tell no one." He pulled a token from his pocket and pressed it into my hand as a we passed by him.

We each accepted a small cup of ale from a servant, toasted the dead king, exchanged a few words with the mourners and left.

Sigurd spoke first as we walked away. "Bards have a strange way of keeping secrets."

"Not strange," I replied. "And not secret. I'll wager we learn all we need to know about our prince straight from his mouth tonight. He's invited us back to discuss how to aid him in becoming king."

We spent the rest of the afternoon visiting inns and taverns near the castle to learn of the princes and the royal court. I sang mournful ballads of love, honor, and death. You would think no two lovers ever lived to wed to hear me sing that day.

The songs earned us a handful of bronze and silver coins and more news of the two princes. It confirmed what we had heard. Cuthbert the Black was a crafty, clever and ambitious man who would lead a kingdom efficiently, and probably expand it at the expense of his neighbors. He rewarded those who did his bidding and was known to be unyielding at getting what he wanted.

Cuthbert Fairhair would be a kinder, more forgiving

king. Also generous to those who served him, but less single-minded about taking what he wanted.

As a warrior searching for pillage and a possible earldom, I'd prefer the ambitions of Cuthbert the Black. As a bard, enjoying the comfort of well-stocked alehouses, I supported Cuthbert Fairhair.

Moonrise found us at the castle wall's rear gate. Displaying the royal token gained us quick passage. The postern door opened as we approached, and Cuthbert Fairhair motioned us into a narrow, dimly lit corridor. He wore the same black mourning clothes he'd worn earlier in the day.

"Do you truly come from King Elmar of Eastmarch?" he asked as we entered.

I nodded. We were from Elmar, even if not sent as emissaries. Sigurd remained silent. He saw I was composing our lay as the tune unfolded.

The prince smiled for the first time since we'd arrived. "This may shift the balance," he said. The smile faded and he spoke slowly. "My father died without declaring his heir. My brother left to gather the earls of the realm leaving me to greet the mourners. He is likely telling them he will be the better king and promising rewards if they support him.

"If I present the Althing with an alliance with King Elmar, it may outweigh my brother's offers and make me king."

He broke off as a trumpet sounded outside the walls.

"That's my brother's call," the prince said softly. "He must have ridden day and night to gather the earls so quickly. I'll have to greet them, but we have a few moments before the gate is raised."

He stared at the ceiling for three beats, then back at us, "Do not speak of this meeting. You must join me at the Althing when I urge the earls to choose me for king."

I nodded. A moment later Sigurd nodded also, trusting I knew what I was doing. I won't claim I did, but the melody and rhythm of the events fit my words. I had no right to promise King Elmar's aid to anyone, but Cuthbert Fairhair was the better husband for the lady who nursed her maid back to health. I wished him to be king.

He glanced at Sigurd's weapon. "That is not your black axe," he noted. "Do you have the famous axe with you? It will be more effecti-"

A bell within the castle clanged twice then stopped abruptly.

"That's the alarm bell," Cuthbert mused. "They must be summoning me. I'd best leave you now."

He broke off as the door at the far end of the corridor opened and an armsman stepped into our hallway, closed the door, and leaned against it.

"Your lordship," he gasped. "Flee. Your brother is slaughtering your guards and servants in their beds."

The alarm bell clamored once more, an urgency in its peal.

Cuthbert stepped towards the guardsman. "I must go, I must speak with him and stop this madness."

"Too late, milord," gasped the armsman. His legs folded and he slid to the floor, leaving a deep red smear on the door behind him.

265

The alarm bell fell ominously silent as the thud of heavy boots echoed in the rooms adjacent to us and shouts of "Find him!" reverberated in the hall.

"My people," Cuthbert cried. "I must--"

Sigurd took a step towards the door we'd come in through. "This is a bad place to be trapped," he whispered. "We'd best escape while we can."

"But I must talk to my brother," the prince protested. "He must stop this--"

A voice from the next room shouted. "Find him. One hundred gold to the man who kills Fairhair."

Sigurd grabbed the prince's arm and pulled. I pushed him and he stepped with us rather than fall over.

"You can't aid them now," Sigurd told him. "Those who escaped are safe. The rest are dead. Better to live."

I pushed the prince through the door. Sigurd glanced left and right and nodded at the outer wall. We pulled our companion across a courtyard, paused in the shadows, and gazed back. Torches moved from window to window, but we saw no signs of fighting. The surprise had been complete.

"You need to hide," I told him. "Your brother isn't taking the chance of you influencing the earls. He wants you dead." I glanced at his mourning garb, rich, black, and distinctive. "You need peasant's clothes like you wore at Elmar's solstice festival. Do you have leather and wool handy?" I asked.

He took a step towards the castle.

"Not there!" I grabbed one arm as Sigurd grasped the

other. "Are there servant's quarters out here where you can get clothing?"

He nodded dumbly, barely visible in the moonlight.

It was obvious to Sigurd and me that Cuthbert the Black was intent on killing his rival for the throne. Cuthbert Fairhair was confused and not understanding, much as I'd been after singing the requiem for Prince Ackley. Like me, he was easily led while he was confused, but I worried how he'd behave once he gathered his wits.

He led us to a thatch-roofed cottage near the wall. A white-haired serf with eyes wide and round in the light of a single candle peered around the door. Sigurd pushed past him, scanning the room for foes. He demanded clothes to fit the prince as I shoved Cuthbert into the hovel and slammed the door behind us.

The man stared at Sigurd and the prince. Behind him an equally white-haired woman wrung her hands.

I spoke softly. "His men are slain, and he must hide until it's safe. Do you have common clothes he may wear?"

The man pulled a tunic and pair of leggings from a sack hanging on the wall. "Our Gerard's clothes will fit you. Please, my lord, let the lad go with you. He'll serve you well, he will."

Cuthbert took the clothes and paused, staring at them. A tear leaked down his cheek as he lowered his hands and regarded the man and woman. "He has," Cuthbert spoke softly. "Better than ever I deserved."

The woman moaned. The prince dropped the clothes and hugged her. "Good mother, but for his warning, I'd be slain," he sobbed. "But it cost-- it cost him--"

267

I interrupted. "Your highness, Please. We must flee. Dress quickly."

I turned to the man and his wife.

"Prince Cuthbert Fairhair will return as the rightful king," I told them. "'Til then, you'd best hide and warn others who favor him to hide as well."

I spoke as though I foresaw the future. In truth, I knew how this saga should end. I just didn't know what was in the verses between now and that happy ending.

The man pulled to his wife away from Fairhair. "Let him dress," he told her. "We'll hide at my cousin's farmstead." He stuffed clothing and food into the sack that had held his son's clothes.

As soon as the prince had changed from black mourning clothes to soft gray wool and leather Sigurd quenched the candle, plunging the room into darkness.

As we stepped out of the hovel, men fanned out from the main gate, searching the grounds inside the wall as well as the castle's interior. Sigurd pointed at the man-sized gate we'd entered by. I nodded and we crept towards it, holding to shadows whenever possible.

Two watchmen stood guard at the rear gate. Sigurd and I had spoken briefly with them when we showed them the prince's token. They were friendly then. I hoped they were still friendly.

As we approached, they watched the activity in the castle, unsure what they should do. When they recognized the prince they stood erect.

"Your highness," said the taller man, "What is happening? Is there an attack? The bell rang, but--"

I interrupted him. "Cuthbert the Bastard brought armsmen to slay his brother and massacre his followers. We must get Fairhair away until he can return safely. Open the door, quickly."

"I think not," the shorter guardsman replied. "Better you stay here until the new king arrives." He reached for the sword at his hip.

The taller guardsman stepped behind him, grabbed his sword hand and yanked it high. He wrapped an arm around his companion's throat, holding him.

"Flee, your highness," he grunted, as the shorter man struggled.

Sigurd stepped forward and thrust the butt of his axe into the shorter guard's solar plexus. The breath left him in a whoosh, and he collapsed as his companion released him.

"You'd best run also," Sigurd told the guard. "You'll have no friends here after this."

The gatekeeper nodded. The two of them unbarred the door. The guard ducked into the narrow tunnel through the wall, motioning for the two old peasants to follow him.

The prince spoke. "He may be right," he nodded at the unconscious guard. "If I speak to my brother we will work out the succession and stop the killing."

He still couldn't believe his own brother wanted him dead.

Sigurd and I had no problem believing this. Perhaps we leaped to conclusions. A bloody massacre makes a grand saga, but it might be too dramatic for reality.

If we were wrong, we'd have our prince in a safe place

when he didn't need to be saved and we'd be embarrassed. If we were right, and we didn't take him to a safe place, he'd be dead.

A man can recover from being embarrassed. I've done it many times. Few men recover from being dead.

If we left him in his current state, he'd surely be slain by morning, and King Elmar would have an aggressive, unscrupulous neighbor to his west. Arguing with him was likely to get us all killed.

I winked at Sigurd, standing behind Cuthbert. Then I dropped my eyes to the armsman on the ground and back at the prince. Sigurd read my thoughts and tapped the Fairhair on the shoulder. As Cuthbert faced him, Sigurd rapped him on the forehead with the handle of his axe, as he'd done to the bull when we first met. A grown bull pauses in its tracks when Sigurd strikes it. The prince collapsed so quickly I barely caught his shoulders before he touched the ground.

Sigurd grabbed his feet, and we scurried through the tunnel.

The guardsman stood waiting as we exited. The two peasants had vanished into the darkness.

"My prince?" he gasped, his face gleaming pale in the moonlight.

"He swooned," I explained, "His brother's attack on top of his father's death has overwhelmed him. We'll carry him to safety. Find everyone who's been his friend and tell them to hide. Your prince will be back soon."

Sigurd studied the woods and fields around us. "Where do we go now?" he asked, glancing first at me and then the guard.

The guard pointed at two paths. "That leads to Elmar's lands, and that towards Christoff's. Christoff's castle is closer. Ackley and Fairhair are friends. He will find welcome there."

I nodded at the path to Elmar's lands. "That one will be less patrolled. The bastard will expect him to go where he has friends."

Sigurd and I lifted the prince and trotted along the trail to Elmar's kingdom.

We lumbered down the path in the dim moonlight, tripping on occasion, and stumbling more often. We never dropped Cuthbert, but I fear he scraped along the trail frequently. A peasant's sturdy leather jerkin has certain advantages. I hoped we were eluding anyone Cuthbert the Black sent after us.

Fairhair awoke after we left earshot of the castle. We released him and he sat, shaking his head, and looking about, dazed.

"What happened?" he asked. "Where am I?"

"You swooned, your highness," I told him gravely. "Sigurd and I carried you to safety."

Cuthbert stood and swayed, grabbing Sigurd's arm.

"I must return to the castle," he said. "I'll talk with my brother. Together, we can end the bloodshed."

"This way," I told him, pointing toward Elmar's domain. I looped one of his arms over my shoulder as Sigurd took the other and we strode off, dragging him with us. He stumbled in the darkness with us half-supporting him.

barely able to keep to his feet. Perhaps Sigurd had hit him too hard.

By dawn, we were footsore and trudging slowly, the prince getting heavier with each step. I wondered if he'd ever recover enough to walk on his own when we stopped to catch our breath. We led Cuthbert to a clearing beside the trail and collapsed. We had barely stopped gasping when hooves pounded behind us.

Cuthbert chose this moment to recover enough to stand.

"That may be news from the castle," he took a step towards the path.

Sigurd and I each grabbed an arm and pulled him back into the undergrowth.

"It probably is news from the castle. And a reward for your head," I hissed, as we pulled him into a crouch.

Two riders bearing black and red pennons on their lances galloped past us.

After they passed I turned to Cuthbert.

"Your men?" I asked.

He shook his head. "My colors are red and gold. Those are my brother's men."

"Then we must avoid them until we know it is safe for you to be found."

Cuthbert protested and tried to convince us to escort him back to the castle to speak with his brother.

Sigurd lifted his hand and listened. We heard nothing, and he nodded to me. "He was much quieter, and we were much safer while he slept." He rubbed his fist in one hand.

Cuthbert glared at me. "I forbid it," he said forcefully. He was a young man raised to privilege and accustomed to command.

I pulled myself as tall as I could. I was several inches shorter than he, not raised to privilege and had never commanded anyone in my life, let alone a prince and heir to a kingdom.

I stared at him with narrowed eyes. I preferred him to his brother, but he was making it difficult to save his life. If he were to be saved, Sigurd and I were the only ones who might manage it.

I deepened my voice, borrowing the tone and cadence King Elmar used when overruling his counselors. "Your highness, we intend to save your life," I told him. "We shall do this with your help, or with you unconscious, whichever is easiest."

He glared at me and tried to assert his authority, but my gaze was sterner than his and Sigurd kept tapping the handle of his axe. He dropped his eyes.

"Am I your prisoner?" he asked.

"No, your highness, a companion, a guest perhaps. You need wise counsel. Wiser than we can provide. You'll find it in Elmar's court. Wise counsel, safety, and a time to grieve."

He protested once more but fell silent when Sigurd rapped his axe handle against his shield suggestively.

We didn't encounter anyone along the trail. As animals sense the coming of a storm and find shelter, peasants sense upheavals in the courts and hide.

By noon, we were tired and hungry. We grinned at each other when we spotted a rough-cut log building with a

273

wooden ale barrel by the door marking it as an inn.

The prince stood tall and tried to lead. "I shall announce myself and demand food and drink for us."

Sigurd grabbed him before he took a single step. "Bard?" he asked.

I nodded. "I'll go in and see if it's safe for you, sir." It was strange, being a lackey to a man I led. Fairhair frowned, then nodded reluctantly.

I approached the inn calling for the innkeeper. Opening the door let a shaft of light into the tavern. It fell upon a heavyset man wearing an apron over a leather tunic facing away from me, doing something with his hands. As the light crossed his shadow he growled, "Another beating won't change anything. I haven't seen him."

Then he shouted, "But I'll not be beaten like a dog again!" He spun with a weapon in his hand. Not the usual cudgel innkeepers keep handy, but an actual battle mace flew at my head.

The part of me trained by Mather noted how he swung like a wood chopper, not a skilled armsman. The rest of me declared that being struck by this mace would be fatal, regardless of skill. I pulled myself backwards on the door frame and fell inelegantly on my ass. The mace flew over my head and struck the door above me with a crash of splinters.

The innkeeper paused. "A bard?" he asked. "I thought--- my pardon." He reached to help me rise, and we both noticed one of his fingers bent backwards. I ignored his hand and pulled myself erect.

"That may be most un-welcome welcome I've ever

274

received," I said, smiling. "I'm just a traveler, hoping for food and drink, willing to trade news, songs and perhaps a few coins. I assure you I do not beat innkeepers."

My host grimaced. He spoke carefully around bloody gums where teeth had been. "It's not the welcome I normally give, but my patrons don't usually take my own cudgel to me. I tell you; I had no love for Bastard the Black before, and I've got less now, but I'd give him my grandmother rather than face another such beating."

"You have news from the castle?" I asked.

"Aye. Cuthbert the Black has announced himself king, declared Fairhair outlaw and offered one hundred gold pieces for his head. I'd not be him for all the gold in this kingdom. I wish him luck and Godspeed out of it."

I put a pile of coins on the counter. "I'll be walking for several days. Do you have a small cask of ale and some meat to carry with me?"

He stooped to lift a quarter-firkin cask from behind the bar, grimaced and dropped it. "Damn," he muttered, and peered at me. "You can keep your brass if you'll help me splint my finger. I just can't do it one-handed."

Minutes later, we'd tended to his finger so it could heal and didn't hurt as badly. I tore up an old cloak and wrapped his chest where they'd broken three ribs. When this was done he thanked me and told me to help myself to food and drink. I slid the quarter-firkin cask of ale, a wooden cup, a half fowl, bread, and cheese into a sack and bid the tavern-keeper farewell.

As I left the inn, I waved my hand in a wide arc and proceeded along the trail. I paused as soon as I was out of sight of the inn. A few moments later, Sigurd and Cuthbert forced their way through the underbrush to join me.

Our unwilling companion spoke first. "This is unacceptable. I am a prince, not some outlaw to be skulking through bushes."

"Your lordship, yesterday you were a prince. Today King Cuthbert the Black has declared you outlaw and placed a bounty on your head. He prefers it be delivered without your body attached to it."

"King Cuthbert!" he spat. "He's not king until the earls meet and declare him king. We are but princes today."

I shook my head. "He's announced himself king. If he can acquire your head, none will contest his declaration. We must get you away from his riders. They are showing no mercy in their search for you."

Sigurd, ever practical, pointed back into the underbrush. "We passed a clearing about ten paces back. It's hidden from the road. Do you have food in that sack?"

I nodded and we pushed our way out of sight of the trail. As we ate, I described what had occurred at the inn. Despite my bardic training, I told it as it happened. This tale needed no embellishment.

Cuthbert kept muttering, "He can't." and "He wouldn't." He finally fell silent and listened, his face blank.

Eventually, he sighed. "You're right. As long as I live, I'm a threat to his crown. I can't say which of us the earls would favor, but the chance exists that they might support me."

Sigurd frowned. "If you hadn't been meeting us, he'd have trapped you in your rooms and killed you. That would solve the riddle of who should be king."

"If I return, I can rally the earls who favor me," Cuthbert mused, "or would I be better served to gather support outside my kingdom?"

"You won't live a day if you show yourself," I told him. "Men who hate your brother are willing to sacrifice you to avoid beatings. How quickly would you be betrayed by someone anxious for his favor?"

He nodded. "I must gather support from outside my kingdom. I'll hope for a better outcome than Vortigern's. I can approach Christoff or Elmar. I am known to King Christoff. He is my best choice for an ally."

I told him of Ackley's death and how distraught it left King Christoff and his wife. He'd find little support in the mourning kingdom.

"King Elmar may not know you, but he has a reason to favor you over your brother. Your brother will be a dangerous neighbor. Elmar prefers an ally to a threat on his border."

Cuthbert nodded to my argument. We had finally convinced him to go to Elmar's court with us.

If we could avoid his brother's men--and everyone else-- we might even get there.

Chapter Fifteen

Sigurd and the Homeward Trek

SIGURD DRAINED THE last of the ale and studied the sky. It was a clear day, slightly before noon.

"We'd best travel after dark," he stated, "to avoid running into Black Cuthbert's men. We should sleep now and be rested for the evening."

I agreed. Sharing a meal and deciding on a plan made everyone more comfortable and inclined to relax. Walking all night, half-carrying a prince, walking another half-day while listening for pursuit and finally drinking our share of the ale all contributed to our desire to rest.

"We should keep a watch," I replied, glancing at the Prince and knowing Sigurd would catch my meaning. "I'll take the first nap."

Sigurd glared at me but agreed. I trudged to the far edge of the clearing and was asleep by the time I had my cloak wrapped around me.

It was easy to slumber on the damp, rocky ground when I was totally exhausted. It was impossible to sleep once I was merely tired. I woke after a couple of hours, not rested, but unable to sleep.

Sigurd and I traded places. Our whispers woke the Prince, and he joined me sitting at the edge of the clearing. He was silent, staring at the dirt by his feet. He sifted a few rocks between his fingers and peered at me.

"I owe you and Sigurd my life," he murmured.

I protested and he raised his hand. "I'm not the wit or schemer my brother is, but I'm no dolt," he paused and scooped another handful of rocks. "Despite how I've behaved today."

I held my protest as he continued, shaking his head, "You two saw more deeply than I. I can only claim I was addled by my father's death and brother's betrayal."

He dropped the rocks and rubbed his forehead. "And perhaps the result of a blow. I'll not accuse anyone of striking me. Such an act would require I strike back at friends who saved my life. I must have hit my head when I fell."

I smirked and nodded in agreement. He would have hit his head if I hadn't caught him, and we might have bumped his head while we dragged him away from the castle.

He scooped the gravel and once more filtered it through his fingers, watching as the smaller pebbles dribbled out first, then the larger ones. He gazed into my eyes. "I wish for you and Sigurd to escort me to King Elmar's court, present my plight, and beg for his assistance."

This was a formal request from a near-king. I accepted it. The easiest task to accept is the one you've already half-completed.

He swirled a finger in the dirt, "I'll follow your rede to slink about as a peasant. But I was raised as a prince. Playing the peasant does not come easily. If I fail to act properly, you must remind me."

I nodded ruefully. Telling a prince how to behave would be much harder than carrying him all night.

He scooped another handful of pebbles and sifted them through his fingers. What had been a formless collection of dirt was now ordered sets of debris, the larger stones surrounded by masses of smaller ones.

He studied my face and asked, "How did King Elmar hear of my father's death so quickly to send condolences?"

I wondered when he'd ask that question. It was easily a two week walk between the kingdoms.

"We were sent after your father fell ill, but before he died," I answered. It was a bard's truth, but a truth all the same.

He stared at the dirt, sifted another handful of stones, and glanced at me. "Do you know why I was at the solstice celebration?" he asked.

"To observe Beornwyn," I replied. "Would you have declared yourself if you hadn't had to return home so abruptly?"

281

He smiled. "She's lovely and people speak well of her. I had hoped to present my father with a promise of a bride and an alliance as a solstice gift."

I told him of Beornwyn caring for Corliss. His eyes glowed, and then dropped.

"She'll wed a king," he said softly, "Not a landless prince."

"Then we must make you a king, your highness," I replied, smiling. "With Sigurd of the Black Axe and his famous bard aiding you, how can you fail?"

I strummed my lute softly. While he paused to dream, sifting the dirt through his fingers, I had been composing a lay.

> Beneath a rock, the adder sleeps,
> Dispensing death when bidden.
> Beneath a smile, Black Cuthbert keeps
> His plans and secrets hidden.
>
> You'll never trust an adder,
> Nor hold it in your hand.
> You'd best not trust the bastard
> As ruler of your land.

He chuckled at this bit of doggerel. "He'd have you hung for that."

I grinned, "But the innkeeper we just left would sing my song when none of your brother's men were around to beat him."

Sigurd rolled out of his cloak, sat up, and yawned.

"That's the first new verse you've made since we left the monastery," he said. "It's good to see you back to normal. How many dragons will I kill while contesting with the Northmen?"

"I think the dragon will kill the Northmen, and the noble spear-carrier will spit the dragon, while Sigurd cowers behind him."

I strummed a merry tune and sang softly.

Great Sigurd waits his chance to kill,
While others race to fight.
The dragon swiftly eats his fill,
Till he's too gorged for flight.

The noble spearman swiftly pins
The dragon to the ground.
As Sigurd leans upon his axe,
While gazing all around.

Sigurd frowned in mock dismay. "Not so well formed as my other sagas, but it will have to do."

He gathered the leftover meal into the sack and shouldered it.

"Almost dark, " he said. "We should be walking. Quietly."

The prince stood. "I'll not be a burden to you, I'm able carry the food and I'm weapon trained. I have no sword, but if you fashion me a staff, I can fight if needed."

The idea had merit. His life would be safer with two armsmen than with just one. Sigurd quickly chopped a

283

sapling and stripped the branches. Within minutes we were back on the trail walking softly and listening.

Treading quietly and not talking gives a man time for contemplation. Sigurd was right--this was the first time since we left the monastery that I'd composed a new song.

I'd been fashioning doggerel and sagas from the time I learned to sing. My verses gained me favors and approval from the monks, if not from the abbot.

The recent nights at the monastery, then singing the requiem for Prince Ackley had left me realizing that there was no meaning to my songs or to my life. I spent the years before I met Sigurd wandering in the desert, searching for the reason God had given me the gift of song and the purpose for this gift.

Now I had a purpose. The care and devotion Princess Bcornwyn had shown while nursing Corliss to health deserved a reward. The church taught me that God takes no direct actions. He relies on his vessels to implement His will. I had been chosen to be the instrument of His will. I was to bring a reward, in the form of a suitable husband and kingdom, to Beornwyn.

I was so pleased with my understanding of why I was here and what I must do that I almost whistled a cheerful ditty. I swallowed the thought when Sigurd raised his hand. Ahead was a dim light and shouting. I couldn't make out the words.

We should have hidden. We were fugitives avoiding capture, but, Sigurd is a hero, Cuthbert is a prince, and I am a fool. We treaded quietly toward the glow.

The light spread from the open doorway of a rough-hewn timber inn into a small courtyard illuminating three men: an innkeeper and two armsmen. One armsman held the innkeeper while the other struck his chest and stomach with a truncheon. The light from the doorway glittered on their metal caps and scraps of chain mail stitched to leather armor.

Before I realized he was moving, Cuthbert stepped into the clearing and shouted, "Hold and explain yourselves!"

The armsmen noticed him and yelled, "Fairhair!" They dropped the innkeeper and sidled towards the prince, drawing swords as they approached.

Sigurd swore quietly and readied his axe and shield. "Guard my back," he whispered as he stepped in front of the prince.

The armsmen paused when Sigurd showed himself.

"We've no fight with you," the leading one said. "Stand aside and we'll split the reward."

The other laughed, "Or try to protect him and we won't need to share."

Sigurd held his shield before him, hiding his axe from their view.

"Sigurd Black-Axe protects the prince. Leave now and he will let you live," he growled at them.

The two armsmen paused and glanced at each other.

"A fool's boast," said the first as they split to attack Sigurd from left and right.

They weren't trained by Mather, but the way they moved showed they knew how to use their weapons. The tavern-fighting techniques I'd learned would be useless against them.

Other tricks however might help. I called "Sinister," hoping Sigurd remembered the Latin I'd taught him, and heaved an egg-sized rock at the armsman on his left.

The armsmen ignored my call. They'd already judged me to be no threat. The rock bouncing off his iron cap didn't hurt him, but it distracted him for an instant.

He glanced at me to see what I was doing and loosened his stance slightly. Sigurd was already moving, hooking his axe-head over the sword, and pulling it aside.

The light, linden-wood Norse shield is made for swift movements, either for defense or as a second weapon. Sigurd stepped close to the armsman, raised his shield abruptly and caught his foe under the chin. His foe's head flew backwards with a sharp crack as he collapsed.

Sigurd spun as the other armsman advanced, swinging his sword at Sigurd's unprotected back. He was one step too far away, and one second too slow. Cuthbert was already lunging at him as he stepped. Cuthbert's staff caught the armsman below the heart with a dull thud and the crack of breaking bones. His foe fell backwards, kicked, gasped, and fell silent.

Sigurd stood and panted, glancing back and forth at the two armsmen. Neither of them was a threat. The first lay on his back with his head at the wrong angle. The second armsman stopped breathing after the single gasp.

The innkeeper stood now, supported by a sturdy woman and a pretty young girl. He held his stomach and gasped, "Thank-ee, strangers." The woman and girl led him to a bench where he collapsed, groaning. The woman walked warily toward us.

"That one," she pointed to the one with a broken neck, "held my man. That one," she prodded the other with her foot, "beat him. I'll mourn neither of them." She spat on each man's face and strode back to the inn, helping her husband totter inside. The young girl tarried a moment to smile briefly at us and followed them.

I pulled off the helmets and addressed Cuthbert. "Do you know these men?"

He shook his head. "They aren't from the castle, nor any of the nearby earls."

Sigurd pointed at the mismatched armor and sigils. "Sell-Swords," he said shortly. "Cuthbert Black must have hired men with no ties to the castle to slay Fairhair's men. His own men would refuse to slay comrades in their beds."

"What do we do with the corpses?" I asked.

"We can't just leave them," the prince replied. "It would be trouble for these folks if the bodies were found near here."

Sigurd pointed to the deep blue tattoos on their arms. "They aren't Christians," he said. "You needn't sing a prayer. Strip them and dig a grave. They'll have a shovel or two in the tavern."

I collected daggers, swords, buckles and bits of armor, piling them to the side while Sigurd and Cuthbert strode into the inn. They came out moments later with a pick and a shovel. Sigurd broke ground with the pick while Cuthbert shoveled, separating the earth and stones.

After stripping the bodies of anything useful, I squeezed into the inn's tiny front room to beg another shovel.

The innkeeper's wife was wrapping a cloth around her husband's chest and stomach, ignoring his gasps and groans. I asked if they had another shovel. She nodded to the pretty maiden who ducked into the back and returned with a short-handled spade.

The innkeeper grunted as his wife wrapped another cloth about his ribs. "I thank ye for burying them. I'd be helping you dig if I--Agh, gentle, woman!--could."

I agreed. He was in no condition to wield a pick or shovel.

"We've food, drink and beds for you," his wife said over her shoulder. "That and thanks are the best we can offer."

"That's more than we ask or expect," I replied. "We accept and thank you."

I carried the shovel to the graves. With Sigurd breaking the soil and Cuthbert and me emptying the holes the task went quickly. Once the holes were waist deep, we dragged the bodies into them. I placed bronze coins I'd taken from their pouches over their eyes. I had no reason to wish them well, but I didn't want their spirits following us for lack of the ferry-man's fee. We shoveled dirt over them and piled stones atop the graves.

By now, we were each gasping and sweating in the warm spring night. I'd have been happy to leave the graves as they were. I'd had my fill of funerals with Prince Ackley.

Harald's and Shawn's words echoed in my mind: killing a man takes a toll on you, and it goes easier when you honor your foe. These dastards didn't merit any favors, but this wasn't for them, it was for us.

Cuthbert, Sigurd, and I joined in the death-rites. Sigurd

intoned a North-man's chant affirming they died in battle and should be welcomed to Valhalla. Cuthbert and I joined the refrain declaring this as truth.

With our duty done, we returned to the inn, Sigurd carrying the pick and shovels while Cuthbert and I gathered the armsmen's belongings.

As we entered, the older woman called and the pretty girl came out with a tray bearing three cups, a jug of ale, meat, bread, and cheeses.

"Please, your lordships, be welcome," she said, placing the food in front of Sigurd.

I distributed the cups, and we toasted our host who grimaced back and spoke haltingly.

"They wanted me to say when I'd seen Cuthbert Fairhair. Wouldn't believe I hadn't. They swore he'd passed here." He stared at Cuthbert. "You be Fairhair, be you not?"

Cuthbert had not yet eaten or drunk. "I am," he replied, staring at the man's bandaged chest. "I am aggrieved that you should suffer such. My father did not countenance the beating of freemen, nor do I."

The innkeeper grunted. "They said they be Cuthbert Black's men and traveled as King's Law. Be it so?"

Cuthbert Fairhair shook his head. "My brother claims the crown, but he'll not wear it long." He glanced at Sigurd and me. "Sigurd of the Black Axe and his bard have pledged to right this wrong."

The innkeeper raised his eyebrows, and his daughter's eyes grew larger. They looked at Sigurd, and then at his oak-handled axe. "Be that the black axe?" he asked.

289

Sigurd shook his head, his mouth being full of meat and cheese. He swallowed. "My famous black axe is in keeping for me at King Elmar's court. I return to retrieve it."

I took a hint, and having eaten while Sigurd and Cuthbert spoke, strummed my lute, and sang.

> Good King Elmar, needing heroes,
> Needing men of wit and might,
> Welcomes Bard and welcomes Sigurd,
> Feasts them well for many nights.
>
> Sends them forth with spring's first thawing,
> Sends them far from fief and land.
> "Find a prince that is most worthy,
> A prince fit for my daughter's hand."

My companions paused in their eating to listen. Walking silently for a few hours had given me time to compose a lay they'd not heard.

Sigurd spent fifteen verses hunting with new-found companions when a monster came upon them. It killed each man it met until it reached Sigurd, who slew the beast. Then came the monster's mother, larger, more fearsome and bent on vengeance. Sigurd, of course, slew her as well.

I doubted Ragnar would recognize his contest with us, but Sigurd smiled at how our boar hunt had grown to him slaying two horrific monsters.

The innkeeper nodded in time to the lay, his wife glared, unbelieving, and the young girl gazed at me, Sigurd, and the prince. Their inn had never been graced by such heroes.

Promised Rewards

I stopped singing when Sigurd finished slaying the monsters. I had composed more verses but needed to eat. I glanced at our foemen's belongings, and then to Sigurd. He nodded, and I faced our host.

"Would you have use for these?" I asked. "We do not wish to carry them."

He studied the pile. "The small metal bits I can use. I'll sell the caps to a smithy, but I've no use for weapons or shields." He studied the prince. "Mayhap a sword would suit you better than a staff."

I scanned the armor, then Cuthbert. "You can't learn to act like a peasant, but you might pass unrecognized as a simple armsman."

He hefted the two swords, then swung one against the floor. It cracked and fell in pieces at his feet. "Better now than when I need it," he muttered, glancing at me. I grinned, knowing where he'd learned his trick of testing weapons.

The second sword didn't shatter. He selected the better of the scabbards, hung it over his shoulder and sorted through the rest of the armor.

The innkeeper pushed himself to his feet. "My pardon, good gentles," he said with some effort. "I must be laying down." He nodded to the pretty maid, "Geothe will tend to ye. There be three rooms in the loft."

Goethe smiled at us, blue eyes wide and golden curls peeking out from beneath her snood.

I shrugged. "Sigurd? We planned to travel tonight."

He grimaced as the prince spoke, "Perhaps a night's rest and an early start. We'll go faster in daylight."

291

Sigurd glanced out the tavern door. Clouds had rolled in while we attended to the corpses. Walking an unknown path with no moonlight would be slow travelling. He'd rested no more than I had this afternoon. Neither of us wished to pass up an actual bed for the promise of a few hours barely resting on rocks.

We nodded to each other without needing to speak.

Goethe brought us another tankard of ale and joint of meat and sat silently watching us as we ate. I tried to coax her into speaking, but she just giggled and blushed.

After we finished the second pitcher of ale, the day's excitement and lack of rest caught up to us. I sang *Blazon* but paused to yawn after the second line.

Goethe noticed my yawn and pointed out the ladder to the loft.

True to our host's description, the loft held three cells, each with a fur covered cot, walls that nearly reached the ceiling, and rawhide flap doors.

I was struggling with my boots when Goethe pushed aside the leather and stepped inside. She smiled and reached for my boot. It came off easily with help. In the next cell, Sigurd's boots hit the floor and the straw tick mattress rustled as he stretched out.

Goethe started to unlace my tunic, with a smile that was half-shy and half-enticing. This help surprised and confused, but it did need to be removed before I slept. Sigurd was already snoring gently, and I hoped to be asleep before he reached his full volume.

When she reached for the lacing on my leggings I stopped her.

She glanced into my eyes as I stared into hers. So large and blue. Her red, full lips red still held a half-smile.

"You saved me Da's life," she whispered. "I'd be honored to thank you."

I shook my head. All the years I'd dreamed of this, but now, with a beautiful landlord's daughter asking to share my bed, all I saw was that her eyes were not quite as blue as Corliss's.

I kissed her forehead gently. "I thank you for you offer," I whispered back, "But I'm sworn to another." She smiled ruefully and backed out of my cell, blowing me a brief kiss.

A moment later I heard whispers from Sigurd's cell, but no change in his snores. Light footsteps padded down the ladder. I was sorry for her. Two stalwart heroes she might have bedded, but one wished she were someone else and the other was too tired to be aroused.

I barely finished my thought before I fell asleep and woke to Sigurd jostling my shoulder. "Can you put on your boots without aid?" he asked archly.

I glared at him. "As well as I ever could," I replied. "What woke you?"

He tapped his ear. There was activity in the common area. I slipped on my tunic and boots and crept to the edge of the loft.

Goethe was preparing the fire for cooking. She glanced up, saw me, blushed, and scooted into the family's quarters.

The innkeeper stepped carefully into the common room a moment later. "Breakfast, m'lords?" he asked. Sigurd and I nodded as the prince called, "I'll be down shortly."

293

Breakfast was bread, cheese, and warmed mead. Between two swallows, Sigurd glanced at me, eyes wide in shock and said, "Horses!"

I wondered what horses he meant, then remembered. The armsmen we'd slain had been riding when we'd first seen them.

The innkeeper took a ragged breath. "The horses be stabled afore the beating. They be there yet."

Prince Cuthbert waved at Sigurd. "Do you ride?" he asked.

Sigurd shook his head. Mather had trained him in foot-combat, not horse-combat. I shook my head as well. My experiences with Midnight had not endeared horses to me.

Cuthbert took a swallow of mead. "I ride, of course," he said thoughtfully, "But I'll not ride while you walk."

He faced the innkeeper. "It would go ill with you if the horses were found here. We'll lead them away and set them loose."

The innkeeper opened his mouth as if to say something, closed it, took a breath, and decided to speak after all.

"I be knowing a man who trades in horses," he said. "He'd have these in Wessex in a sennite and none the wiser from whence they came. I can give ye a few silver for them, though I've got but few to give."

Cuthbert glanced at me and Sigurd. "I'll not take coin from the man who suffered a beating on my behalf," he said. "If your friend pays for the horses, take the money as thanks for your service."

The innkeeper ducked his head and pulled his forelock.

"Thank-ee, milord. 'Tis most gracious. I'm wishing you a long reign."

Cuthbert acknowledged him and stood. Sigurd and I swallowed the last of our mead and followed his example. We left without seeing any more of our landlord's lovely daughter.

We walked in silence for an hour or so, listening for hoof-beats. As the mid-morning sun got warm Sigurd addressed Cuthbert. "My thanks for guarding my back."

"You are welcome," the prince replied. "But my defense was unneeded. You were ready before he started his stroke, but by then, I was committed to my thrust."

He nodded at me. "Well called, Bard. When you shouted I knew Sigurd would attack left, and I should engage his mate." He waved at us. "You are well attuned to each other."

I agreed. I thought to describe our winter with Mather but decided to leave our training a mystery.

We passed from King Beldon's lands into the wilds no one claimed. The trail was little used, and taverns were far apart.

Once we were certain we were beyond the reach of his brother, Cuthbert relaxed and proved to be an excellent travel companion. He made good use of Sigurd's axe while Sigurd gathered rabbits and the occasional pheasant. I tended to the cooking with little flair but few complaints.

On the second night between taverns, I tuned my lute after we finished eating and sang the full saga of Sigurd's travels from Elmar's castle, including his besting five mounted warriors and resisting the lewd advances from a dryad.

295

C. Flynt

Sigurd strode both night and day
Through dark and solemn woods.
Until he could not lift his feet
And slumbered where he stood.

Then came a lass with apple cheeks,
Red cherry lips like few he'd seen.
A comely form and welcome smile,
Her long, free locks were palest green.

She said "Come join me in my wood,
Come live with me and be my man.
I promise you'll be treated good.
I'll give you joy if any can."

"But I must warn you if you stay
And share my bed within the trees,
You'll be with me for all your days,
For none I bed may ever leave."

She wrapped her arms about his chest,
And gently gave him kisses three.
"Oh, come with me and take thy rest
And live with me within my tree."

She laid his head upon her lap.
A pillow soft and warm,
"Tis here that you shall take your nap,
And you'll be sheltered from the storm."

Said Sigurd "When wood's grain makes flour,

When dogwood barks and begs and pants.
I'll be with you within the hour
And bring to you my best romance."

With sunrise, Sigurd woke alone,
Within that wood so green and fair.
His head was resting on a stone.
And silvery laughter filled the air.

He felt soft breezes on his cheek,
And like a whisper heard them say
"Oh, leave me now, if that's you're will,
But when you come again, you'll stay."

Cuthbert laughed at those verses. "A most willing lass," he jested, "but too well rounded to be a sylph."

He sobered quickly. "She never approached my bed. Either she prefers heroes to landless princes, or she was too embarrassed at being rebuffed by two lusty young men. She'd have fared no better with me. Until I'm told otherwise, I hold myself betrothed to Princess Beornwyn."

A few days later, we reached the outskirts of Elmar's lands and taverns were a day's walk or less apart. The first tavern we encountered was a rustic building of peat and untrimmed logs. The doorway was a deer hide with the fur facing out.

Within the tavern it was dark, warm, and smoky. Our host was a burly man with a shock of black hair. His broken nose and the scars on his face and hands spoke of a good many fights he must have won to still be standing.

He leaned on a stout cudgel and announced. "Welcome,

friends. I allow none armed within my inn." He pointed to the corner. "Swords and axes will be safe there."

Sigurd and Cuthbert glanced at each other. The prince shrugged and removed his belt and scabbard, leaning the sword against the wall. Sigurd followed suit.

We placed ourselves on the bench nearest our weapons.

The host grinned, revealing several missing teeth. "Will you be paying with song, work or coin?" he asked. "I love a new lay, have plenty of wood to split, and don't mind coins, either."

Cuthbert stood. "I've no fear of firewood," he announced. "Sigurd, may I use your axe?"

The innkeeper laughed. "Another Sigurd? Well, you're brawnier than the last one, even if your axe isn't as black." He turned to me. "And you'll be wanting to sing the song about the horse, won't you?"

My mouth hung open. I swear that I pride myself on being the master of all situations, but this was beyond my comprehension. I'd never been in this inn. How did he know of me and my songs?

Cuthbert laughed, "A victim of your own prowess and fame. I wonder how many farmer's sons have named themselves Sigurd and enlisted a bard to sing their exploits?"

The innkeeper laughed as well. "The last bard knew twenty verses of the horse song and sang of *Sigurd and the Five Virgins*. Do you know more of Sigurd's sagas?"

I picked up my lute. I had my honor to defend. Others might claim to be Bard the Lutist, but I'd make it plain that I was the best Bard the Lutist.

I sang every verse to *Sigurd's Ride With Death*, pausing to sip ale when Cuthbert returned, and Sigurd took his turn at chopping wood. The innkeeper sat with eyes closed, nodding, and smiling as I sang. He was as rough looking a hulk as I'd ever seen, but he appreciated music like few I'd met.

After a bowl of stew, I sang *Sigurd and the Eleven Virgins*, for our host and several patrons who had arrived while we ate. The escapades of the eleventh virgin, the well, and the bucket left everyone gasping and choking with laughter and embarrassment.

I felt justified in declaring myself the best Bard the Lutist.

None of the travelers knew Beldon had died, or how Cuthbert the Black had claimed the crown. We delivered the news of Beldon's passing but did not feel the need to spread word of Cuthbert's attempt to take the throne. I sang my song comparing Cuthbert the Bastard to a poisonous snake and all agreed it would be best if Fairhair acquired the kingdom.

One shaggy haired man wearing patches of ring-mail on hard leather squinted at Sigurd and me. "Do you know if the Cuthberts will contest for the crown?" he asked. "I've a sword to sell and I'll be happy to swing it for the Fairhair."

Cuthbert opened his mouth, but I cut him off. "No man knows what the future will bring," I told him. "But I'd not be surprised if a man who stays in this area may find a chance to use his sword to good purpose."

He nodded and returned his attention to his mug of ale.

The innkeeper let folks talk, then asked, "Do you know

the song of the Earl and Trolls?"

"I do," I replied. "I wrote it for Earl Acton."

He laughed. "You and at least three others. Still, you sing the tales better than most."

I bristled but set about to prove I sang my songs better than all not most.

It was very late when our host announced we'd more than earned our lodging. He brought out a stack of pelts and we wrapped them about ourselves and curled up on the floor before the fire.

I fell asleep thinking of the song I'd not sung that evening. I wasn't going to sing the song I wrote for Corliss until she heard it.

In the morning our host requested another song to pay for breakfast. He closed his eyes, nodded, and smiled as I sang a druidic morning hymn to Brigit, the Goddess of sun and poetry.

> Thou Brigit of the kine,
> Thou Brigit of the mantles,
> Thou Brigit of the morning light,
> Drive away the chill of night,
> From all thy fields and cantles.

When I finished singing he stood and smiled more broadly. He dished up bowls gruel and mead for us and spoke.

"A bit of advice, You're an excellent bard--better than most. He glanced at Sigurd, "And you seem to be more than a common warrior. Do not fashion yourself as Sigurd and his bard but go make your own names for yourselves."

Cuthbert was in the midst of quaffing his mead. He choked and coughed so hard he needed to go outside to catch his breath.

I thanked the innkeeper for his words, and we continued on our way.

Once the inn was behind us Cuthbert apologized. "I should not laugh at you being told to be yourselves, rather than copying yourselves. I truly understand being compared to yourself and found wanting. I've spent my entire life as *the other Cuthbert*."

"You will be King Cuthbert soon," I replied. "To distinguish you from Prince Cuthbert. I fear Sigurd and I must live our lives in our own shadows."

He grinned at the joke. "At least you are building large shadows to live within."

Chapter Sixteen

Sigurd and the Councils of Kings

THE NEXT DAYS passed swiftly. When we talked, Sigurd spoke of Henga, I spoke of Corliss, and Cuthbert spoke of Beornwyn. We did not speak of Cuthbert the Black and what might be happening in his kingdom. Those discussions would wait until we reached Elmar's court.

Each day got warmer as we walked out of the mountains and into the valleys. We finally reached a tavern I recognized one midday. It was one of the taverns Terrel and I visited. We were mere hours away from Elmar's castle.

The innkeeper reclined on a bench in front of tavern, enjoying the warm spring sunshine. He stood as we passed by and called, "Bard! Sigurd! Welcome back. Come, share an ale with me. Do you have news? Or new sagas?"

We gladly followed him into his inn. He set three mugs of ale in front us. "Anyone who travels with my friends need not pay," he told Cuthbert.

He addressed me and Sigurd. "Will you spend the night, or are you eager to visit the castle?"

"The castle," I replied as Sigurd nodded with ale foam above his lips.

"Then I'd rather have news than song," our host declared. "I can repeat the news later, but I can't sing your tunes."

I laughed and told him news of Walesyn and Christoff. I neglected to mention the happenings in King Beldon's lands. Elmar should hear that news first.

An hour passed before we continued our journey.

Cuthbert observed, "I'm not against free ale, but if we stop at every tavern where you are known, we may never reach the castle."

I nodded my agreement, but it was hard to pass by people I called friend with a brief hello. Sigurd exchanged greetings with armsmen, smiths and merchants as often as I greeted innkeepers.

We were not heroes here. We were too well known. But we were respected and appreciated. It was comfortable to see faces I recognized, see them smile at me and to exchange kind words.

I was struck with the realization that this was what it meant to be home. Sigurd's shoulders relaxed and even his gait was less guarded.

We were returning home, for the first time in our lives.

Promised Rewards

Despite Cuthbert's misgivings, we arrived at the castle in the late afternoon. King Elmar was holding court as we entered the great hall. We paused to let our eyes adjust to the dim interior as the herald announced, "Bard, Sigurd and an unknown armsman."

King Elmar stood and motioned us forward. He called the runner, who must have grown a full hand taller while we were gone. "Fetch Mather and Terrel" he commanded the runner and then called, "Wine and cheese in my chamber."

He led us into the small room where we'd been three months earlier. Within moments a tray with wine, cheese, bread, and cold meats was brought. By the time we had filled cups and toasted the king, Mather and Terrel arrived.

King Elmar wiped his mouth and studied us. "My cousin said you deliver more than expected. I sent off two men, and three return. Tell me what you have learned."

I had practiced this telling. "We traveled to Walesyn's land first. Prince Wellach knows the inside of a wine bottle over-well. His father has thrown him from his home, and he lives in taverns when he's not being ejected from them as well."

Elmar nodded. "I suspected as much from the time he visited us."

"Prince Ackley." I took a sip of wine. "Would be an excellent husband for Beornwyn, save that he died during the winter."

Elmar lowered his eyes. "Christoff's wife is a cousin to mine. I must send condolences. What of Beldon's domain? Is his son suitable, or must I look to Brittany or Wessex?"

305

"King Beldon died before we reached his castle," I replied.

Elmar sighed. "Alas. He saw a good many seasons. His rest is well deserved."

"His son," I continued, "declared himself king, and baptized his reign in blood."

Elmar sat straight. "Explain yourself," he commanded.

"King Beldon bore two Prince Cuthberts. The elder, Cuthbert the Black is an acknowledged bastard. He claimed the throne. The other, Cuthbert Fairhair, younger but legitimate, escaped the slaughter."

Elmar glanced at Cuthbert, but since we'd not named him, he did not acknowledge him.

"Tell me of the two Cuthberts," he ordered Sigurd, ignoring me.

Sigurd glanced at me for support. I shrugged. Elmar did not want a bard's truth.

"Cuthbert the Black is known for his cunning. He is shrewd and ruthless; open handed to those who do his bidding, vengeful to any who thwart him. With promise of reward and fear of punishment, his followers will do what he demands." He paused for breath. "Cuthbert Fairhair is well loved. He is not so clever or driven as the bastard. Though a trained warrior, he seeks accordance rather than battle. His followers will die for him unasked."

Elmar considered. "Cuthbert the Black is king, and Cuthbert Fairhair is in exile. Is this so?"

We nodded. Elmar looked at Cuthbert. "You are from King Beldon's land?" he asked. Cuthbert nodded. "Which

306

do you prefer for king?"

Cuthbert swallowed. "I favor Fairhair, your majesty. I believe he will maintain peace with his neighbors and build bonds of trust and friendship."

Elmar spoke to me last. "What do you add to this saga?" he asked, "and do try to avoid your bard's truth, but tell me what you actually saw and heard."

I repeated the tales I'd learned and described the events I'd seen. I finished my tale saying, "I'd not sleep well beneath Cuthbert the Bastard's roof, nor would I send someone I cherished to him."

Elmar nodded. Mather and Terrel had been silent, but Terrel now spoke.

"You'll have composed a lay or two in your travels. What would you sing of Beldon's sons?"

I sang the two verses comparing Cuthbert the Black to an adder.

Terrel smiled. "I see you did not learn subtlety on the trails. And Fairhair, have you anything to say of him?"

> Brave and gallant, honor bound,
> By turns both cautious and bold.
> A head that's fit to wear a crown.
> By nature, crowned with gold.

Elmar looked at each of us in turn. "I know your counsel. I fear I must now be introduced to your companion." He turned his attention to the prince. "Your name?" he demanded.

"Cuthbert, son of Beldon, known as Fairhair, your majesty."

Elmar glared at Sigurd and then at me. "I should have listened to my cousin. He warned me you'd deliver more than asked, both good and ill." He addressed Cuthbert. "I cannot acknowledge you within my court. It would mean a war with your brother, leaving my lands open to raids from the Danes."

The prince's face fell. His shoulders drooped and he stared at the floor for several beats. He squared his shoulders, raised his head, and stood. "I'll not cause discomfort by my presence," he declared. "Nor will I beg for what you cannot offer. I have weapons and skill and shall find my way in the world."

He took a step towards the door when Elmar commanded "Hold."

This was the voice I'd tried to duplicate when I failed to convince Cuthbert to join us. The actual king's voice was more effective. The prince stopped and glanced at Elmar, a question on his face, though his feet faced the exit.

"I said I could not acknowledge you. I did not say I would not aid you."

He glared at Sigurd and me. "You brought him here that I might help him regain his throne." It was a statement, not a question, but we both nodded. "Did you tell him the price of my aid?"

Cuthbert interrupted my reply. "That is not a price," he said. "It is a prize. A prize richer than any I might ask."

Elmar nodded. "You shall eat below the salt tonight. Sit near the fire. After the meal, listen to Bard and wait for a peasant maid and her two friends to join you. If she will accept your suit, you will be a king and a husband." He nodded to the three of us. "You may retire to prepare yourselves for dinner." He glanced to Terrel and Mather. "You will attend me."

We left his private chamber heading for the barracks. Once there we found fresh clothing, bathed, and tried to remove the evidence of our travels. I finished barely in time to visit the kitchens for a quick meal. I accompanied the servers into the great hall. As the food was served, I took my place at the far end of the hall, below the salt, to entertain the armsmen and peasants.

When the meal was done, King Elmar, Beornwyn and their retinue retired. I moved to the side of the hall furthest from the fire and continued singing. My saga of Sigurd's travels drew the crowd away from the fire.

After five verses Ermindale and Corliss led a lady in peasant's wool with a hood pulled around her face to the fire. She sat next to Cuthbert, while Corliss and Ermindale sat discreetly on the next bench.

Sigurd's adventures during our travels lasted long enough for Cuthbert and Beornwyn to become acquainted. When the princess stood, her companions also rose. Ermindale waved gaily as they left the great room, and Corliss smiled at me. My task was complete. I could rest. I would spend part of each day with Corliss. The silk strips Ragnar gave me would please her. I hoped her song would please her more.

Moments after Beornwyn and Corliss left, the runner returned. He stood patiently while I finished a verse and announced, "The king awaits your pleasure."

Kings need not await anyone's pleasure, least of all a bard's. I followed the runner at a quick step, wondering why the king would wish my company at this late hour. I had a stomach curdling thought that Beornwyn had rejected Cuthbert's suit and Elmar was wroth with me for bringing a problem to his court.

The runner escorted me to the king's private nook. Terrel, Mather and Ector broke off speaking as I entered. The platter of wine and cheese was bare.

King Elmar motioned me to stand before him. "My daughter has accepted Cuthbert Fairhair's suit. For that I thank you." He paused. "A prince without a kingdom is a most vexing problem. For that, I shall reward you as you deserve." He rose and left the room.

I glanced about in confusion. Mather and Ector refused to meet my eyes.

Terrel stood. "Your skills will be put to use this fortnight," he said. "You'll need to travel quickly and keep your wits about you."

I nodded, with no idea what he meant.

Ector took pity on me and spoke.

"King Elmar cannot go to war with King Cuthbert," he explained. "But neither will he aid him should his people revolt. Nor will he forbid any of his own earls from taking advantage of the turmoil to send raiders into Cuthbert's domain. Mather and I will gather such men as may wish to raid those lands. You and Sigurd must raise an army from the earls to support Fairhair."

I nodded. It sounded simple when he said it, but I still had no idea what I was to do.

Terrel spoke again, toying with an empty cup. "You must rouse the earls to revolt. As you and I spread King Elmar's news about his kingdom, you must spread dissent and discord and hope of revolt throughout Cuthbert's land."

He raised the cup to his lips, found it empty and glared at it. "You have a start with your verses about Cuthbert the Adder and Fairhair's God-given crown of gold, but we need more sagas, and we have but a few hours in which to compose them."

He set down the cup and gazed at it sadly, then motioned me to follow him.

He explained as he led me to his cell in the tower, "In your sagas, Sigurd fights bandits and monsters. We'll need a song or two in which he comes unbidden to aid men who need his help. They will start as songs about those who are beset. Sigurd will then enter and right the wrongs. We'll rework your tale of Sigurd with the monster and its mother so that he is not among the revelers when the monster first attacks but comes later to save them. We'll also need to expand your descriptions of the Cuthberts into full ballads and add some subtlety."

I nodded once more. At last, something I understood. I must write sagas. I can do that in my sleep, which I'd not had in a while.

I mentioned this to Terrell. He frowned. "You misunderstand King Elmar's request," he said. "You leave before sunrise and must be prepared. You must hot-foot it throughout Beldon's domain letting everyone know Sigurd is coming to undo a wrong. You'll be praising Fairhair and discrediting the dark Cuthbert. Sigurd will follow you to gather the earls' armies to meet at Beldon's castle in two weeks."

I gasped. Travel without Sigurd? That was my life six months ago, but now it was unthinkable. Who would I jest with? Who would guard my back?

Terrel reached for his harp and plucked the tune to my saga of Sigurd and the monster. "We must work quickly to compose the lays you'll need."

Hours later, we had three new songs and I'd memorized the important parts. I was ready to collapse when Ector coughed outside Terrel's tapestry-covered doorway. He pulled aside the cloth and entered.

"My apology," he explained. "The scribe is writing down Cuthbert's tales and a map, but this tale seems useful.

"When Fairhair was fourteen, he, Cuthbert the Black and their cousin Hallam hunted a stag. In mid-chase, the cousin's mare stepped in a hole and fractured her leg. Hallam was thrown and broke his arm. Cuthbert the Black held to the chase and brought down the stag. Fairhair stopped to slay Hallam's mount, then carried his cousin home."

Terrel smiled. "Perfect. A tale showing their nature, without snakes or God-given golden crowns." He grinned at me as Ector left. "We must construct this saga next. It will be the best. It might even have some subtlety."

We bent our heads together to compose another song. I realized I'd soon depart, with no chance to sleep. I resolved to find a shady tree and a nap before I'd walked an hour.

By dawn the tips of my fingers hurt clear to my elbows. I was enjoying fond memories of nights spent wrapped in a damp cloak sleeping upon sharp rocks when Ector returned.

"We're ready to leave," he said. "The horses are saddled and waiting."

"Horse?" I gasped. "I can't ride--"

"You'll learn," Ector interrupted me. "There's not time for you to walk to Cuthbert's borders." He grimaced ruefully, "We'll travel like Sigurd in his *Ride With Death*."

I protested to no avail. I hoped to see Corliss, at least briefly, now that she was healthy, but I would be leaving before most of the castle was awake. I pulled the silks Ragnar gave me from my pouch and handed them to Terrel. "Will you gift these to Corliss for me?" I asked. He frowned, then nodded.

Mere minutes later, I clutched the high pommel of a saddle, while Ector led my horse into the fading darkness. My mount was determined to bounce both me and my lute into pieces.

"Stick to the saddle," Ector called. "You hurt the horse when you bounce like that."

I held my reply. A youth of his gentle upbringing would not understand the words I found appropriate to describe riding. After about a thousand hours, I either learned to bounce with the beast, or became too numb to notice when I wasn't properly connecting with the saddle.

I'll grant we traveled faster on horseback than I walked. We left Elmar's fields and farms behind by nightfall and were in the wild woods by full dark.

When it was too dark to ride, Ector guided us into a clearing to let the horses crop until the moon rose. Then we returned to the trail. The moon was high when I spotted the

313

rustic inn where I'd been told about the other Bards and Sigurds.

I called to Ector, "There's an inn just off the trail. The ale was fine. Could we stop and rest a bit?"

He shook his head, "I am ordered to get you to Cuthbert's lands as quickly as possible, then return to gather such armsmen as can be spared. Elmar can't call a levy during planting season. The army will be smaller than I'd like. We'll need as many armsmen you can gather."

"There's an armsman who wished to fight for Fairhair waiting at the inn," I told him.

He changed direction so quickly I nearly fell off.

Ector examined at the tavern's rough walls and rougher doorway. "You do find friends in the most unlikely places," he said, sliding easily from his mount and raising his arms to help me return to earth.

"I need no help dismounting," I told him. "I'm no fainting maiden."

He laughed at me. "Nor horseman either. Slide off and I'll catch you."

My leg didn't want to lift over the saddle, but I managed to pry it up and slide over the side of the beast. True to his word, Ector caught me. As he expected, my legs failed to support me. The pain exceeded any I'd ever known, and I was certain nothing below my armpits would ever function again.

"Step," he said softly. "It will hurt, but it will pass more quickly." He took a step backwards and I had to step with him or fall.

314

After twenty steps I was able to support myself and Ector led me to the doorway.

"Now, show me your armsman," he said, raising the deerskin to let me enter.

The innkeeper was busy stirring a pot of stew over the fire. He glanced at me, smiled, and called. "Ho, Bard, most welcome." He blinked as Ector stepped beside me. "You have a new Sigurd? The other looked the part better."

Ector raised an eyebrow at me. I shrugged. I'd explain this later if I explained it at all.

The shaggy-haired warrior we'd met on our last visit looked up from a bowl of stew. "Is there to be a sally against the Bastard?" he asked. "I've chopped as much wood as I ever wish to see. I'd rather swing a sword."

My companion sat next to him and spoke in low tones. I sat near our host and accepted a bowl of stew and a cup of ale.

"Eat now," he told me. "You'll sing the better for it."

I nodded. This was the first meal I'd had since we left the castle.

"Do you sing?" I asked our host.

He shook his head. "Nary a note you'd care to hear. But I can chant any saga I've heard twice." He tapped his finger against his oft-broken nose and began *Egil's Saga*.

I let him display his knowledge as I slopped stew with chunks of trencher. Once I'd finished both the stew and ale, I lifted my hand, and he stopped reciting.

"You may like this saga," I told him. "It speaks of the two Prince Cuthberts." I tapped my lute for a rhythm and chanted the song of the stag hunt, emphasizing the cadence, instead of the tune. He listened with eyes closed, mouthing the words after I said them.

When I finished, he said "Again." I repeated the saga, and this time he chanted most of the words with me. When he faltered, I repeated the verse.

When I finished he nodded, "That's a fine saga. Not so grand as the tales of the Aesir, but well formed. It marks the difference between a ruler and a leader."

I nodded without speaking. I'd hoped the burly innkeeper might learn the gist of the saga, not that he'd fully memorize it in two hearings. I never expected him to see through the events to the song's message. I resolved to not judge a man by his appearance.

Ector stood as we finished the saga. "Meet here, in a week, with your friends," he said to the armsman, dropping a small pouch which clanked as it hit the table. The warrior spat on his hand and held it out. Ector spat on his and sealed the bargain.

The horses were cropping in the clearing by the tavern. They trotted to Ector when he whistled. He had to help me onto my horse. My legs screamed fire and ice as we trotted down the trail. Luckily, they became numb before we'd gone far.

I didn't know I could sleep while riding until Ector reined in his steed and the bouncing stopped. We were in a clearing next to the trail. The horses were eagerly cropping before I unwrapped my fingers from the pommel.

"This is where we part," he announced.

He stumbled as he dismounted. Our time in the saddle

had been nearly as difficult for him as for me. He took a several staggering steps away from the horses and back. When he reached to help me off my steed I didn't protest. By now, I'd learned to ride well enough, but had much less practice getting off the horse than I wished.

He supported me as we walked a halting promenade, step, pause, step again.

After a few passes around the clearing, I took my steps without halting.

Ector checked the sun as it rose toward its zenith. "I must be back to Elmar's lands to gather men-at-arms, and you have taverns to visit," he said, pulling horses away from the grass and back to the trail. "You should be a half day's walk from the first tavern. You have the map?"

I patted my tunic, feeling the parchment and nodded. He mounted his tired steed and waved. "I shall expect a fine saga of this ride when we next meet. I'll wager it will be more exciting and less wearisome by then."

I waved back and hobbled down the trail as his hoof-beats retreated.

I was to entertain at twenty taverns--a thought that should have filled me with joy. But only ten days for these visits. I'd have to move quickly.

I increased my pace as soon as I was able. The pins, needles and cramps slowly left my legs when I allowed them to walk instead of ride. They were accustomed to walking and understood it.

I was soon striding at Sigurd's soldier-pace, not my customary bardic meander. Another glance at the sun told me this would not be sufficient. I ran until I was out of breath, walked until I stopped gasping, and then more running. If Pheidippides could run from Marathon to Athens, I could run and walk to a mug of ale.

When I saw my first farmstead, I stopped running. I wanted to arrive at the tavern ready to sing, not gasping. This inn was in Earl Barden's lands, who had been Fairhair's name-giver. I expected a warm welcome for my praise of the prince.

The tavern's door was open wide to the spring warmth. I pulled my lute to my chest, strummed a jaunty tune, and stepped inside.

"Good morrow, good host," I called. "Is there bit of ale for a thirsty bard? I bring news and song and a most dry throat."

He scooped a cup of ale from an open cask. "A bit of cheer would be welcome," he said, setting the ale in front of me.

I did it no little honor. It wasn't strong but soothed my raw throat nicely. I strummed the lute and sang.

> When autumn's sun is golden warm,
> 'Tis time to flush the stag.
> To ride before the winter's storm,
> And chase the deer's white flag.
>
> So said Cuthbert, dark as night,
> To Cuthbert, bright as day —

The innkeeper's cudgel slammed into the table in front of me, knocking over my empty cup.

"I'll have none of that!" he roared. "Not here. Not now."

I stared at him; my eyes wide. He had been friendly a moment ago but was not friendly now.

"Good host?" I begged, "What offends you?"

"No songs of the princes," he said. "Sing an old saga, a Christian hymn, or even one of the Sigurd lays, but not of Fairhair."

"So close to Barden's keep, I expected Cuthbert to be well thought of."

He glared at me with narrowed eyes. "'Tis not Barden's keep today, nor for the past week."

My mouth fell open as he continued, "Cuthbert the Black came guesting a week agone. Ate the earl's meat, drank his wine, and slept on his best furs. Then rose in the night and slew the household." His voice was low and tight, anger and outrage barely held in check.

"It's Earl Gower's land now, and he will hear nothing ill of the king nor anything good of the exile. Some think otherwise. I'll have no fights in my tavern, so there will be no songs to fuel that fire."

I gasped. I was more upset by the guesting customs being violated than the massacre. Killing one's enemies and rewarding one's friends is a time-honored tradition among the kings and earls. But to eat a man's meat and then attack him was against the most sacred rules of the Christians, Druids and Norsemen.

"Slew the entire household?" I whispered.

My host nodded grimly, "So far as anyone knows. Some say it was Thane Gower, Brandon's most trusted servant, who passed out the knives. Be it as it may be, he's Earl Gower now, and I won't have fights in here."

I was speechless.

With danger from ill weather and beasts, denying a traveler food and shelter is akin to slaying him. The Celtic laws state travelers are to be given food, drink, and a place to sleep. The Norse have Odin's rules describing the rights and responsibilities of host and guest. The Christians make the sharing of bread and wine a sacrament. The very act of sharing food creates a bond of good will. To break that bond wasn't merely a sin. It was an affront to all the gods and all humanity.

I nodded slowly. "I'll sing the tales of Sigurd, to please your guests." I assured him. "I'll not provoke a fight in your inn."

But I swore I would provoke a battle at Cuthbert the Bastard's castle. This unspeakable act must be avenged.

I was already composing a saga of the Black Prince and Earl Barden.

It would not be subtle.

Chapter Seventeen

Sigurd and the Field of Combat

THE INN FELL silent as I lowered my cup. The ale was tasty; my throat had been dry. Now it was time to depart from the drinking songs and sagas I'd sung when I first arrived.

With nineteen taverns behind me, I had honed my performance to a sharp edge. A rousing drinking song, to gain everyone's approval. Next was *Sigurd's Ride With Death*, to introduce the sagas of Sigurd of the Black Axe and give everyone a chance to pound the tables. Once they knew Sigurd, I sang *Sigurd at the Feasting*, to show him coming when needed and defeating evil. I had the crowd engrossed. It was time to sing the song of Cuthbert the Bastard defying the guesting customs.

I wasn't certain I left people angry enough for Sigurd to raise a host against Cuthbert, but I knew I left the Bastard no friends where I passed.

I tapped my lute to the tempo of my heartbeat as I chanted the first of Odin's Guesting laws:

> A guest arrives when the sun is high,
> To let his host prepare
> The food and drink and bedding
> That host and guest will share.

This is a stanza everyone knew. Many patrons hoisted a glass in honor to the verse. Anyone who had traveled more than a day's journey had guested at least once.

I strummed one of the Greek chords Terrel had taught me. Chords not used by the Church or the Celts. A strange pattern disturbs the ear and makes the listener uncomfortable. I didn't want them happy for the next verses.

I sang,

> Black Cuthbert came to Barden's gate,
> The clouds were red in the setting sun
> He called out "Bring the food and drink,
> For me and for my men.

> Thane Gower opened wide the gate,
> To let Black Cuthbert in.
> To Barden he said, "We should feast
> This man who'll soon be king."

Earl Barden slew the fatted calf,
He offered drink so fine.
Black Cuthbert took the choicest seat
And swilled the blood red wine.

I stopped and tapped the lute again, chanting the next of Odin's Guesting laws. Slowly and carefully, to make the words echo in everyone's ears.

The host has earned the best of meat
And let him eat his fill.
The guest should take the second best,
That he may praise it well.

I returned to the unsettling melody.

Black Cuthbert took the finest hen,
And the choicest cut of meat.
He passed the platters to his men
Before the earl could eat.

He never offered thanks or praise,
For comfort, drink or meal.
The meat was tough, the wine was sour,
The bread was dirt 'neath his heel.

Earl Barden, that most gentle host,
Did offer sweets and more.
Black Cuthbert took a single bite,

And spat them on the floor.

Each set of verses began with a stanza of Odin's guesting rules, followed by the Bastard violating and abusing them.

Finally, after quoting the last of Odin's rules, I completed the story of betrayal.

Within the night, Black Cuthbert rose,
Like a fox among the hens.
And Gower passed assassin's knives
To arm the craven men.

Like shadows in a moonless night,
They crept about the keep,
Each knife was sheathed in a brave man's heart
As he did lie asleep.

When morning came and shadows fled,
There were no hymns to greet the sun,
Earl Barden lay in a sea of red,
This most foul deed was done.

The blood ran deep throughout the hold,
Unleashed by dagger's foins.
Thus Gower gained the land he rules,
And thirty silver coins.

The song stopped abruptly with the gift of Barden's lands to Gower, the man who had been a trusted adviser and friend.

It didn't stop to silence. Nor were there cheers and calls for another song. The tavern echoed with the growl of a storm in the treetops: deep, moaning and boding ill.

The innkeeper was not happy. A bard is supposed to amuse the patrons and cajole them to buying more food and drink, not arouse their anger.

I slid from my stool. "I'd best be leaving," I said softly.

The innkeeper glared at me with half closed, frowning eyes. "Yes, you'd better. You needn't return."

I strode from the inn and paused to let my sight adjust to the moonlight. Before I'd taken ten steps a voice called behind me.

"Ho, bard, a moment."

I tensed. Twice I'd been attacked by the Bastard's supporters after singing my song. Once I'd been defended by Fairhair's friends, and once I defended myself. Even Mather might have approved. I walked away after his comrades carried my attacker back to the tavern.

I glanced back. The caller wasn't armed and wasn't running to attack me. The moonlight glinted on his blond hair and beard, reminding me briefly of Sigurd.

"You sang of Sigurd coming when he is needed." I nodded as he continued, "If he comes here, he'll find help."

I grinned at him. "Sharpen your axe," I told him. "You'll see him soon."

I strode down the trail. I had no more taverns to visit. I could take my time on the road to Cuthbert's castle. If I'd done my job well and Sigurd accomplished his task and Ector and Mather and Terrel all succeeded, a mighty army would await me there. If any of us faltered I'd find too few men and we'd be slaughtered.

This left me of two minds about hurrying to the meeting place. I wanted to see the army and know my saga had a happy ending, but I feared an encounter with Cuthbert the Black's men desiring my head on a pole.

I patted my pouch. I still had most of the coins Elmar had provided for this task. I could easily declare my bargain fulfilled, take this purse and head to places where nobody knew of Cuthbert or Elmar. Months ago, my fondest dream was a pleasant walk with a full pouch of coins.

That dream had become a couplet without rhyme, lifeless and worthless.

The moon was bright. Once I adjusted to the night, I could have trotted and arrived sooner, but I had no hurry. Sigurd needed a day to reach this last tavern and another day to bring the armsmen to the castle.

Would Sigurd catch up with me before I reached the battleground? I smiled at the thought. My smile told me that no matter how many dark thoughts I held, I'd fare my way to the castle to jest with Sigurd and guard his back.

The Northmen say it truly: Bare is the brotherless back.

Thinking of Sigurd and Elmar led my thoughts to Corliss. I hummed her song as I walked and pictured how her eyes would soften as I sang it. If we succeeded and Cuthbert gained his throne, she would dwell in his castle with Beornwyn. Cuthbert might need a bard, in which case, I might be there as well.

Dreams of spending our days working and living

together occupied me until moonset. Walking unknown trails with no moon is a task for desperate men. I wasn't desperate. I searched for a place to sleep and spied a crofter's hut. More importantly, I noticed a barn where I'd find a roof to shelter me and hay to sleep on.

When I'd first left the monastery, I'd been a boy in a world of men. I learned how to avoid being seen when I didn't want to be seen. Those skills came back to me. I slipped into the barn without waking the animals, rolled my cloak around me and was asleep within seconds.

I woke with the first graying on the horizon. It wasn't dawn yet, but I discerned the trail well enough to tread along it. I was gone before the farmer knew he'd had a guest.

I chided myself. I might have asked for a meal and perhaps learned the news, but until Cuthbert Fairhair was on the throne I was safest being unseen outside a tavern. I was a will-o-the-wisp that appeared long enough to sing my songs and raise an army. I faded into the night when my work was done.

Would it be hubris for me to write the *Saga Of The Ghostly Bard* or must I hope for a scald skillful enough to do my tale justice?

I had just finished the fortieth verse of the *Ghostly Bard*, in case no sufficiently skilled bard chose to write my saga, when the beat of horse's hooves interrupted my song's rhythm. I couldn't count them but must have been over a dozen.

I leaped into the bushes beside the trail and ducked low. I pulled leaves in front of my face and peered between them as the horses trotted into view.

The man riding the lead horse had blond hair streaming beneath his iron cap. I recognized him as the one who assured me Sigurd would find help in the last village I'd visited. He had red and gold ribbons on his spear. Behind him, Rishley rode Midnight and led a less spirited steed with Sigurd clinging to the pommel.

I stood and waved. Midnight reared and Rishley struggled to keep his seat. He dropped the lead to Sigurd's mount, which promptly stepped to the side of the path to devour a clump of clover.

The lead armsman kneed his steed toward me, lowering his spear, when Rishley called, "Friend Bard!" The armsman paused, studied me briefly, nodded approval and raised his spear.

Sigurd slid from his saddle and grabbed the pommel to support himself.

"Well met!" he called and took a staggering step. We embraced and pounded each other's backs, then stepped apart and examined one another.

He had deep shadows beneath his eyes. His cheeks were sunken and gaunt as he studied my face.

"Are you ill?" he asked.

I shrugged. "A bit tired. Nothing a good night's sleep and a battle won't cure."

He laughed. "I can't offer you any sleep, but I believe we will have a fine battle."

Midnight stomped his feet, and the rest of the horses crowded him, anxious to either be allowed to crop or to continue on their way.

The leader raised his hand. "A brief pause," he called. "Tend to the horses first."

The horses were most willing to rest, as were the riders. We were several hours of hard riding from the tavern.

Sigurd had cheese and mead in his saddle pack. He was sharing this with me when Rishley approached with bread and meat.

"A merry chase you've led us," he greeted me. "We've been a day or less behind you for the last week and just now reached you."

Sigurd nodded, chewing on a chunk of cheese. "I don't know what sagas you and Terrel composed, but the taverns have been buzzing like kicked-over beehives." He swallowed. "But not as happily."

Rishley nodded. "The problem has been winnowing down those willing to fight to just those able to fight." He glanced behind him, and I counted nearly twice as many men as horses.

"We take turns riding and running. The only way to reach the castle with the other groups. This village has the least time to get there."

The armsman who had been leading approached us. "We need to be riding again if we're to arrive before the battle is over."

Sigurd blinked at his mount. "I'll let you ride," he offered graciously. "I can run for a while."

I considered the saddle and remembered how my backside had relished life since I stopped riding and demurred. "I can see you've had more practice than I. You should ride, but I'll let you carry my lute and travel sack, to make my running lighter."

We might have continued this discussion, but the armsman tapped my shoulder and called, "Runners, start moving. We'll pass you soon, then wait ahead to change riders."

I noted how most of the horses were led. These men rode as well as I. Many of them preferred to run.

I preferred to run for the first quarter hour or so. These men did not walk and run, the way a man can go for hours. They ran hard, knowing they'd soon be riding. They could catch their breath on horseback.

By the time we reached the cropping horses, the next set of runners were out of sight. Rishley boosted me into a saddle, and we were off at a canter, two or three horses being led by each rider.

We left the trail at sunset. The lead armsman pointed ahead. "About an hour's ride to the castle," he said. "We'll rest here tonight, so all the armsmen arrive at dawn." He grinned at Sigurd. "A most clever plan."

Sigurd nodded as if he'd worked it out. I recognized Elmar's and Mather's cunning in the plot. Small groups of armed men coming from different directions, converging on Cuthbert the Black's castle at once giving him no warning and no time to gather more forces.

These men treated Sigurd, Rishley, and I like guests. They collected firewood and slipped into the woods with slings, leaving us to relax. After my trek through their kingdom, I felt I'd earned it.

We didn't have a banquet, but we ate well. I sang of Earl Acton and the Trolls, *Sigurd's Ride with Death*, and other uplifting songs. I did not sing of the Bastard's abuse of guesting. These men were ready to fight. I did not need to inflame them further.

Sigurd roused me before dawn. We breakfasted on warm ale and cold meat and were striding along the trail as the sun crept over the horizon.

We came upon Cuthbert Fairhair and a host of armsmen on a field before the castle's outer gates. We'd already heard the challenging trumpets.

"Well met, Bard, Sigurd," he called. He noted the men we brought. "And well met to you, also."

Mather stood behind him. "Gather your weapons and join the shield wall to the left. Horsemen, to the center," he called.

A trumpet sounded from the village. The gates opened and men streamed out. They marched onto the field, spreading into a shield wall flanking a dozen mounted armsmen with archers and sling men behind.

Dark Cuthbert had more men than I'd expected. His shield-wall, bristling with spears, filled the field. Our force was laughable in comparison.

Sweat pooled between my shoulders. Cuthbert motioned to Elmar's runner, who bore his red and gold banner, then to Sigurd and me. He strode into the field with the standard-bearer beside him, leading two of us. The runner appeared both proud and scared, striding on Cuthbert's left, leaving the prince's sword hand free in case the discussions went badly.

From the far side of the field, a black and red banner emerged as Cuthbert the Black, his standard-bearer, and two armsmen strode to meet us.

Cuthbert Fairhair proceeded at a ceremonial pace, slowly and deliberately. I couldn't see his face, but he gave no indication he was concerned by our forces being outnumbered. Was he unable to see we must lose the battle? If he wished to die for his throne, he was welcome to. I had other desires, though I feared I wouldn't live to see them.

I considered running. This was my last chance to scamper from the field like a rabbit and hide in the woods until the battle was over.

I glanced at Sigurd, his face stern, his eyes assessing the armies. He wouldn't run. He'd die beside Cuthbert if he had to.

I shuddered. My gut wrenched with the realization that I'd rather die guarding Sigurd's back then live knowing I'd abandoned him to die alone.

I'd lived my life as a tavern ditty, full of merry romps and a jolly finish. Now I saw my life as a tragic saga, ending with a noble death.

This realization did not cheer me, but I straightened my back, determined to make my saga worthy of the telling.

It took me forever to reach this understanding, but, we were only halfway to the meet-point, with an eternity left to travel.

I barely had time to blink before the eight foemen met in the center of the field. The two Cuthberts in the lead with their standard-bearers and attendants flanking them. I didn't recognize the earls attending Cuthbert the Black, but both appeared well trained in the use of arms, arrogant and certain of themselves. Their swords were sheathed, but they held their hands clenched. Did they anticipate a fist fight?

The earl on Cuthbert the Black's right bore the symbol I'd seen when I sang in the first tavern. That marked him as Earl Gower. His history of perfidy and his confident arrogance worried me. I resolved to keep a close eye on him.

Cuthbert Fairhair spoke first. "I contest your ascent to the throne of our father," he declaimed formally. "I call for you to lay down your weapons, summon an Althing, and follow the rede of the earls."

Cuthbert the Black smirked at him. "Really, brother. Are you still so naive and untutored? Unlike you, I can count our forces. There are three of my men to every two of yours. Give me your head, and I will spare those so foolish as to follow you." The way he glared at Sigurd and me, I doubted we'd be spared.

My stomach clenched and sweat dripped down my back. Cuthbert the Black was accurate. He had more men, and even I saw they were trained armsmen. The men we fielded were mostly peasant levy, with a scattering of trained soldiers to hold them together.

It was my worst fear come true. We would be routed on the field, then run down and slaughtered as we fled. Sigurd shifted his axe from hand to hand. He was also nervous.

Fairhair raised his left hand slowly and made a motion as if training a dog to lie down. The standard-bearer dipped his banner. It wasn't the proper gesture of surrender, but it appeared to be one. Cuthbert the Black's forces raised a triumphant cheer.

I shed a tear and my shoulders sagged. I'd come to value

Cuthbert. I hated to see the effort Sigurd and I had put into this meeting come to nothing. However, once he surrendered his head, I might keep mine. In truth, I preferred my head to his.

Our standard-bearer raised his banner and waved it. A trumpet sounded behind us, followed by the thunder of horses and a soldier's marching chant.

New armies emerged from the woods on both sides of the field, flanking Cuthbert the Black's forces. A squad of mounted armsmen galloped into the gap between those men and the gate. The Bastard's men were now surrounded with no route for retreat.

I relaxed and stood tall. I should have known Mather would not commit his men unless he was certain they could win the day. He brought the same cunning to the field that he displayed in personal combat.

A young lad bearing Earl Barden's banner led the army on my left, surrounded by men who looked ready to die defending him. Those men must have saved him when the Bastard slaughtered the rest of his family. They held their weapons ready, eager to meet Gower's forces and make them repay the spilled blood.

It was time for Cuthbert the Black's attendants to worry. The earl to his left glanced about nervously, but Gower remained calm and arrogant, staring down his nose at us.

Fairhair spoke. "I count quite well, brother. I count six to three and a more favorable placement. I retract my request for an Althing. You and your earls may give me your swords. I will let you leave the kingdom."

Cuthbert the Black barely glanced at the new armies.

The earl to his left shifted his feet, while Gower glared at Fairhair.

"My liege," said the nervous earl. "Perhaps discretion would be advisable."

Cuthbert the Black waved him silent and frowned at Fairhair.

"Good brother," he acknowledged. "You make a most cogent argument. I fear I must cede your point." He reached to his belt for the hilt of his sword.

His hand was hidden behind his cloak as he fumbled to surrender his weapon. He shouted "Now!" and lunged forward, a slender dagger in his hand striking at Fairhair's throat as Gower threw a handful of dirt into Fairhair's face.

Cuthbert Black's hand and dagger were level with his belt, thrusting upward in an attack I recognized. It was the first maneuver Mather taught me. When you slide your dagger under your opponent's gorget and into his throat the battle is over.

I cursed myself now that I understood Gower's clenched fists. They were prepared for Fairhair refusing to surrender and had planned this attack. With Cuthbert Fairhair blinded and distracted by the dirt, he was unable to defend himself from his brother's dagger. All Mather's cunning and armies wouldn't matter if Fairhair was slain.

I needed to do something, block the blow, kick at the Bastard, anything to stop him, but the events happened faster than I could move. All I could do was gasp as the dagger flew towards Fairhair's throat.

I barely saw the second flash of steel as Sigurd's black-handled axe dived between the Bastard and Fairhair. It cleaved the air like a hawk stooping on its prey as Dark Cuthbert drove his dagger upward.

The bastard's wrist cracked like a log being split into tinder. The dagger fell to the ground between the two men, still clutched in a severed hand. Cuthbert the Bastard sank to his knees, grasping his wrist as his blood spurted.

The two earls paused; swords half drawn. Surprise and confusion evident on their faces. Sigurd's intervention had disrupted their plans.

Fairhair shook his head, dislodging the dirt, and spat, "Your swords, cousins. Swear fealty and you may remain. Attend him and you may join him in exile."

The earl who had suggested discretion finished drawing his sword, using only his fingertips. He dropped to one knee and laid his weapon at Fairhair's feet.

"I was misled," he said. "I swear fealty to the rightful king."

Earl Gower left his sword in its sheath and knelt beside the Bastard, pulling a cloth from his breast, and tying the stump.

He spat at Fairhair's feet. "I serve your better," he swore.

Fairhair wiped the last of the dirt from his face. All saw him standing while Cuthbert the Black and his men knelt. He raised his left hand with the palm up and the standard-bearer lifted his banner high, swinging it back and forth. The trumpets behind us blared victory as Cuthbert the Black's men laid down their arms.

I listened to cheers from all sides and gazed in wonder.

The sun gleamed bright and golden through the trees at

the edge of the field. It was barely two hours past dawn. I felt as if the battle had lasted a full day, when in fact it never started. My heart finally believed I would see another day and acclaim Cuthbert as king.

Cuthbert the Black was pale, but the blood no longer spurted from his wrist. He tried to stand but fell back to his knees.

Fairhair spoke to Gower. "Your swords," he said, "I will have you escorted north, beyond my lands. If you are ever seen in my kingdom again, I'll have your lives." He smiled grimly. "I believe one hundred gold pieces is the standard price for an exile's head."

Sigurd held his axe ready as Gower dropped his weapon to the ground and pulled Cuthbert the Black's sword from its scabbard. Fairhair gestured and a mounted armsman approached from the right, leading two shaggy ponies.

"I'll ride my own horse," declared Gower.

"You own no horse," Fairhair replied. "I loan you this pony to speed you from my sight. I advise you to use it to good advantage."

Earl Gower glared at Fairhair, as if he could get his way by simply asserting it. "I said--," he stated.

Fairhair stepped forward, nose to nose, glaring back. "You say nothing. You spoke once. It was treason. You have no voice in my kingdom."

Gower held Cuthbert's glare, accustomed to bullying him.

Fairhair growled, "I offer you your life. Leave before I rescind that gift."

Gower dropped his eyes. Cuthbert was a king now, not the younger brother of an acknowledged prince.

Fairhair stepped back as Gower aided Cuthbert the Black to the ponies and helped him mount. The two left with no further words.

The other earl was still kneeling.

"My liege?" he asked.

Fairhair stared at him. "The bulk of your lands are forfeit. You may keep your household and the adjacent fields. You may take up your sword, but only in defense of your king. Do not try my temper."

The earl nodded and lifted his weapon, sheathing it while still kneeling. He rose and trudged towards Cuthbert the Black's men.

Fairhair's men had already passed among the Bastard's supporters and escorted the leaders to us. Each in turn set his sword at Fairhair's feet, swore fealty, and regained the right to bear his weapon. A good many forfeited a portion of their lands.

The sun rolled slowly across the sky. I wished I were elsewhere, out of the sun, but I was present as Cuthbert Fairhair's bard. It was my duty to view the events, remember and report them. I repeated the names of the earls as they surrendered their swords. Each surrender required a verse in the *Saga Of Cuthbert Fairhair*.

With the last of the earls' swords offered and returned, Cuthbert, his loyal followers, Ector, Mather, and of course, Sigurd and I made a grand entrance into the village and paraded to the castle. Cheering men, women and children lined the roadway. Spring flowers fell among us like autumn leaves. Every time Cuthbert nodded to someone, the crowd shouted, "Hurrah!". When Sigurd waved his black-handled axe the cheers were even louder.

I strutted and preened, but a bard is not a prince, king, or hero. I prefer it that way. I'd feast just as well this evening, without carrying a heavy sword or axe.

The feasting was grand. I sang above the salt for the new king and his earls. Sigurd and Mather sat at Cuthbert's right hand. Ector and Rishley sat to his left. I sang every lay Terrel, and I had composed for Cuthbert Fairhair and his brother.

They greeted the songs praising Fairhair with cheers and toasts while the ones decrying the Bastard were met with hoots and derision. Cuthbert the Black may have been accepted as king when he had followers with swords behind him but without them he was unloved.

King Cuthbert donned his crown for the feast. I doubted he'd wear it often. It looked heavy and uncomfortable. His eyes roved about the hall, assessing his subjects. I saw sadness and anger when he noticed a space where a friend should have been. A friend the Bastard had slain.

The next days were much like Elmar's solstice celebration. People milled about the castle during the day, forming new alliances, assembling new staffs, and comparing new lands.

The evening was for feasting and toasting the new king.

Cuthbert held court each afternoon, accepting more oaths of fealty as riders informed the distant earls of their new king, proven by right of arms, bringing an alliance with a neighboring kingdom and soon to be wed.

Many earls acknowledged Cuthbert as lawful king within a few days. With their support he had enough loyal armsmen to quell any dispute. It was time for King Elmar's men to return home.

Mather, Sigurd, and I discussed this outside the castle.

"Must we ride?" Sigurd asked again.

Mather spat on the ground, disgusted. "It's the fastest way home, and it's how the bulk of the men will travel. There wasn't time to bring many unmounted," he paused and stiffened.

"Harald," he called. I saw Harald, former sergeant, former bandit of the wild-wood and sometimes described as a reformed troll striding away from us.

He turned at Mather's call and glanced to his side. He had no way to avoid meeting Mather, who broke into a run.

Mather pulled a dagger from his belt as he ran. Harald had been a deserter from the king's army, a crime carrying the death sentence. Earl Acton bought his pardon but apparently Mather refused to accept it.

I cried out as Sigurd took a step forward. Mather lunged at Harald. Harald parried the blow with his left forearm, knocking the hand wide to his left. He punched at Mather's throat with his right hand. Mather caught the fist with his forearm and drove it to the side and past his face.

By now, both men had stepped inside each other's reach. Mather's dagger was behind Harald's back, with Harald's hand holding it to the outside. Harald's fist was beyond Mather's head, with Mather's arm blocking it from another punch.

Then Mather's dagger was on the ground as they

pounded each other on the back.

"You haven't forgotten anything," Mather said.

"You're still as fast as ever, my friend," Harald replied.

"Cuthbert needs a sergeant," Mather told him. "If Acton can spare you, it puts you farther from Elmar. Not a bad thing."

Harald nodded. "The earl has good men. He never needed me. Might Shawn join me?"

"We'll talk with Cuthbert after dinner. Your service may be a wedding gift."

Mather was still smiling when he returned to us. "Good man," he said, "and two men we won't need horses for." He glared at us. "I've got enough mounts so you can each ride."

I wasn't happy about riding, but it would get me to Corliss sooner.

The evening banquet honored the men who had helped Cuthbert regain his throne and were now returning home. It was grander than the previous night's with many rounds of toasts and too many speeches.

After the formal dining, King Cuthbert had a groaning board set with hams, fowl, wine, and ale. He invited all to eat and drink their fill for as late into the night as they wished.

He strolled once about the hall, shaking hands and thanking the armsmen. Then he retired behind the tapestry to his quarters.

Sigurd and I observed the throng. When we visited this room for King Beldon's viewing it had been filled with people, but quiet and somber. Tonight's crowd was smaller, but it was bright and noisy. Everyone was jubilant and talking. I was commenting on this to Sigurd when a runner approached us.

"Please, good heroes, the king requests your presence." He bowed away from us, obviously in awe of the great Sigurd and his famous bard.

We followed him beyond the king's table into the hallway behind the throne. Like Elmar, Cuthbert had a nook for private meetings with his advisers.

He stood when we entered and held out his arms. "Good friends," he called. "I've been remiss for not rewarding, or even thanking you for your deeds."

I smiled and shrugged. Elmar promised to reward us. I hadn't expected anything from Cuthbert.

"Without you, I'd have been slain when my brother took the throne. Your guidance and aid are the only reason I'm standing here, instead of lying in a grave."

Sigurd murmured a vague reply.

"I cannot reward you as you deserve," Cuthbert continued. "There is not enough gold in this land for that." He turned away from us to face the table. When he faced us again, he held two leather pouches. "This is but a part of what I owe you," he said, passing the gifts to us. They were quite heavy.

"There is a place in my castle whenever you wish it," he said. "I offer you food, drink and beds for as long as you desire them. I cannot make you earls and grant you land, but you need not toil unless you wish to."

I tried to speak and failed. I'd dreamed of being a king's bard, but never considered a life as a king's guest.

"Finally, I declare that I owe you a service. When a time comes that you are in need, summon me, and I will do all in my power to aid you." With that, Cuthbert embraced each of us.

By now, I had traveled so far beyond speechless I feared I'd never find my voice again. We managed to thank him and returned to the great hall. Neither of us was ready to speak but we felt the need for a cup of ale.

Sigurd studied me, over the rim of his cup. "Does this mean I won't need to be a hero any longer?" he asked. "Who will provide you with adventures for your sagas?"

"Mayhap we'll quest for a few weeks a year. Save a maiden or two, slay a few dragons and then come home to rest."

We silently toasted the idea of spending most of our time resting.

"Do you think Corliss and Henga will accept part-time heroes?" I asked.

He smiled and we retired to our pallets. The next day would be the first of several long days of riding.

By noon the next day, Sigurd and I were on horses being led back to Elmar's castle. I wondered how he would reward us for finding him a son-in-law and gaining him an alliance. I doubted he'd match the gifts Cuthbert had given us.

I hoped he would not give us horses.

Chapter Eighteen

Sigurd and the Last Stanza

THERE ARE MANY songs of joyful jaunts beneath the blue skies and green leaves. Pleasant promenades, spirits soaring with the trilling birds, nourished from nature's bounty and thirst quenched by quaffing from clear, burbling brooks.

There are no songs of the trip back to Elmar's castle. We rode hard, ate little and drank after the horses.

We arrived at the castle well after dark. Ector and Rishley helped Sigurd and me off our mounts. They led the horses away to be cared for, leaving Sigurd and me to care for ourselves. We joined arms and helped each other stagger to the barracks and our pallets.

New men slept on our pallets, but we found empty

spaces and collapsed without removing our boots. My legs twitched and cramped for most of the night. I was so exhausted I barely noticed.

By morning my legs had become re-attached to my hips and I could walk almost normally. I woke when the other men rose to attend their day's chores. I stared at the ceiling and realized I had no duties. I'd done everything King Elmar had asked and quite a bit more. I could finally relax.

My eyes had almost closed when the runner approached.

"The king summons Sigurd and his bard," he announced, and ran off.

Arising reminded me of several days of riding. My legs did not buckle, but my bones had been replaced with strips of soft leather. Sigurd's careful steps told me he felt the same.

King Elmar was not at his table, but a guardsman escorted us to his private cell. Ector and Mather were with him when we entered.

"King Cuthbert has sent a formal request for my daughter's hand in marriage," he said slowly. "You stood beside him when he became King and have had time to observe him. You favored Prince Cuthbert. Do you also favor King Cuthbert?"

I nodded. "He grew quickly into his new role. He is firm, but fair."

Sigurd added, "He punished those who rose against him, but seldom harshly. He exiled Cuthbert the Black and his unrepentant supporter, rather than having their heads."

Elmar nodded. "A kind king, if not a wise one.

Beornwyn may need to take him to task."

He stared blankly beyond the wall. "I need to plan a wedding. I've always known it would happen, but never considered how to do it." He paused, his eyes focusing on the wall, instead of beyond it. "I must discuss this with Terrel," he stated, then looked back to the four of us. "You may leave."

We walked quietly back to the great room. Ector needed to see to the horses and Mather headed back to the practice yard, leaving Sigurd and me alone in the empty hall.

It was strange.

Sigurd shifted his weight from foot to foot and gazed at the barren hall. We had nothing to do and no place to go. After months of constant training, journeys, and quests, we were lost.

After several beats Sigurd glanced at the doorway and said, "I wonder if Henga is busy."

I spread my hands. "You can find out easily enough, At least she's not cloistered in the princess's private domain."

He nodded. "I guess I can."

He ambled out the door with a gait that was half-hurrying and half-delaying. I wondered at his reticence. If I could speak to Corliss I'd not be of two minds.

Ermindale called, "Friend bard, might we cajole you into entertaining two maidens while we do needlework?"

Ermindale carried a long gown, while Corliss held strips of silk and sewing tools. As I watched them proceed to the bench near the firepit I understood Sigurd's confusion. It had been nearly six months since I'd spoken more than

347

three words with Corliss. I was anxious to speak with her and had no idea what to say.

Ermindale made this easier. "Come, good bard. I'm told that my heroes have been having adventures without me. I wish to hear all about them."

I sang of our meeting Ragnar and hunting the boars. I might have expanded my part in slaying the dragon slightly, but only by seven or eight verses.

When I finished, Ermindale lifted a sleeve of the gown and examined it critically. "This will be lovely, but I will have a simpler gown when I wed Rishley." She glanced at me and giggled. "Don't tell him. He doesn't know he'll ask yet."

She studied what she had done and stood. "I need to talk to Beornwyn about this," she told us. "I'll be back in a half hour."

I was now alone in the great hall with Corliss. We hadn't done more than glance at each other. I plucked my lute gently. "Would you hear more?" I asked.

She nodded shyly. I moved to sit on the floor in front of her. I sang the song I'd written for her so long ago.

If there were words that lips could form
That gentle ears could hear
I'd find those words, so soft and warm,
And whisper in your ear.
That you would know the love that grows
Within my heart, my dear.

She continued sewing while I sang, her eyes never

348

leaving the heart she was embroidering on a lap-sized piece of silk.

I finished the song and paused. "Did you like it?" I asked.

She nodded.

"I wrote it for you," I whispered. She looked up from her needlework, her eyes wide.

"King Cuthbert has offered me a position in his castle," I hurried on. "I can be there. I mean, I'd like to be there. To be there with you."

I'm a bard. Words are my toys and my tools. Why were they hiding from me now?

I stumbled into a phrase I didn't expect to hear myself say. "I wish to wed you."

"Oh, Bard," she said, as her hand twitched, pulling the thread, and breaking the outline of the heart.

"I'm... I'm most honored. Truly I am." She stared at the heart in her lap. She tried to repair it but tangled it worse.

"But Ector--He--He's been kind to me while you and Sigurd were gone. He's to be the captain of the Queen's guard after she weds Cuthbert. I accepted his pledge. We are to be wed the week before the royal wedding."

I gasped. "But-- I thought--we--" Again, I cursed the words I couldn't find. All the words I found were wrong.

She set aside the silk--the heart was broken beyond repair--and placed her hands on my shoulders.

"My poor bard," she said. "A maiden dreams of loving a hero and being loved by a hero. You made my fancy real." She paused and looked down. "But a woman needs a husband, not a hero. Just a man who stays with her rather than going off to have an adventure and save some other maiden."

Her eyes closed and a tear trickled down her cheek as her fingers clenched my shoulders. She had surprisingly strong hands.

"I'm sorry," she whispered. "I wish I were the maid for you, but you're destined for more adventures and better times with other maidens." She leaned forward and kissed me on the forehead.

Ermindale returned just then. "Beornwyn wishes you, Corliss," she said, and took her place as Corliss walked away. She wiped the tear from her cheek, waved briefly from the door to the Princess's chambers, and was gone.

"You know she's right," Ermindale told me. "You and Sigurd have tasted more adventures than most of us will ever see. Terrel tells me that someday you'll tire of questing, but until then, you won't be happy with a home and wife."

She placed her fingers on my lips and pulled them into a grin.

"Smile, good bard. You'll find other maidens to save. Mayhap you'll find some to teach you new verses to *Sigurd and his Virgins*."

I gasped again. I'd never sung that song in her presence, nor would I. It was acceptable for me to scandalize a tavern wench, but not a woman of rank.

Ermindale laughed. "You didn't know the tapestries by the fire covers the wall shared with the princess's quarters? There's are holes in that wall to let her watch the court and know what's happening in her kingdom. We found them most useful while you entertained the guardsmen."

I am not often speechless. Normally, words flow from my lips like wine from a decanter. But that decanter went dry again as I tried to remember which verses I had sung in the hall and whether I'd sung the most scandalous ones where she might have heard them.

She gathered her cloth and needles. "Now I must return to the Princess. Don't be sad, friend bard. At least, don't be sad for long. There will be other maidens. Perhaps many maidens."

She kissed me on the cheek and was gone, just like Corliss.

The hall wasn't bright any longer. It wasn't home, either. I didn't want to take Ermindale's advice about quests, but I didn't want to see Corliss with Ector. I didn't want to see either of them.

A shadow filled the doorway as Sigurd returned. His gait was slow, his shoulders slumped, and his head drooped.

"You too?" I asked.

He glanced at me. "Corliss?"

"To wed Ector," I replied.

He sank onto a bench and put his head in his hands.

"I grieve for you and understand too well. Henga is to wed the smith's apprentice. They have been working together all winter and wish to continue together. She will stay here, with her father and the new smith."

I patted his shoulder. It was no comfort, but it was the best I had to offer.

A deep voice behind me spoke. "Bard, Sigurd, would you attend me?"

I turned as Elmar stepped into his private nook. We followed and reached his cell together.

"My companions," he said. "You have served me well and earned a greater reward than I may be able to grant you. I am most pleased with the husband you found for my daughter and for the kingdom you have gifted to her.

Three cups and a flask sat on his table. He poured wine into the cups.

"I would offer you a place in my castle--"

Sigurd interrupted him. "Please, no Sire."

The king continued, "Except that I know you don't want that, nor will you" he glanced at me, "wish a place in Cuthbert's court."

He handed cups to us and lifted the third to his lips. "To fair winds and warm days," he said and took a sip.

"You are two hawks. I loosed you to find a husband for my daughter, which you did most well. You fly free and you aren't suited to jesses."

He sipped his wine.

"I would give you a useful gift. Something to make your journeys easier. I will give you coin, but you have no use for more than enough to buy an ale or two."

He set his cup on the table.

"I would gift you with horses--"

Sigurd and I both shook our heads.

"I know," he continued. "Horses are not your friends."

"What I can gift you with are these." He handed us each an object wrapped in a scrap of parchment. I glanced at him, and he nodded.

I unwrapped the parchment and found a bronze signet ring bearing Elmar's rune and writing on the parchment.

I unfolded it and read. "Know by this ring and my rune upon it that I, Elmar, King of Eastmarch, am most pleased with Bard the Lutist, composer of the Sagas of Sigurd Blackaxe. I beseech my fellow rulers to show him due consideration." Elmar's rune, in gold foil, was hammered into the parchment below the writing.

I raised my eyes to the king's. He grinned. "Terrel suggested these would be the most fitting of gifts."

I nodded. A king's favor would open doors I never knew existed. I would eat at a head table and play above the salt. Tavern keepers would vie to have me perform in their inns.

Sigurd had a similar ring and notice.

"We thank you, your majesty," I finally said.

Sigurd nodded, confused. He understood the signet ring's importance and he recognized his rune on the parchment but couldn't read it. I'd explain it to him soon.

Elmar filled our silence. "You have earned this and more." He handed us two heavy pouches. "I contend that I still owe you a boon. I will deliver on my promise when you request it."

I thanked him again and we backed from his presence.

In the great room, I read Sigurd his parchment.

"That will get you a guardsman's post in any kingdom you wish," I told him. "Perhaps even Sergeant or Master-of-

353

Arms. Cuthbert would certainly be happy to house you."

He nodded. "And what will you do? Stay with Elmar?"

I shook my head. Elmar and Ermindale were wrong about me being a hawk in search of adventure. Adventure is tiring and unpleasant. But they were right that I could not stay here or with Cuthbert.

The visit to the monastery, my talk with Terrel about sins and oath-breaking, everything I'd done in the past months came back to me in a rush. I'd broken an oath when I stole my master's lute and ran off so many years ago. I'd never seen it, but that event had shadowed my life and everything I'd done until I met Sigurd.

In the past months I'd gone from stealing eggs to saving kingdoms. I'd found the honor I threw away so long ago. But my honor was tarnished and needed to be restored. It was time to confess my sins and pay the penance.

I must travel south, back to the monastery where I'd been raised. I would return the lute and the pouch I'd stolen and beg forgiveness. The trek to the monastery wouldn't take the ten years it had taken me to journey to the north, but I'd have many days of long travels. I didn't look forward to spending those days walking alone, but I needed to do this.

I haltingly explained my task to Sigurd. Why it was important to return the lute, confess to the abbot and pay my penance. I didn't expect him to understand. He had not been raised a Christian. He couldn't know the ties binding a man to the church. He belonged here in the north. He had no need to go south into the old Roman lands.

He listened carefully as I spoke and nodded when I

finally stopped.

"When do we leave?" he asked.

About the Authors

C. Flynt was the writing team of Carol and Clif Flynt. They were each other's consultant, critic, first reader and polisher, spending hours debating plot points, character motivations, likely (and unlikely) events, and doing research.

The end result is truly a collaboration.

Clif is a computer programmer, technical author (Tcl/Tk: A Developer's Guide, Linux Cookbook, The Tclsh Spot) and filk-song writer. He's been active in science fiction convention circles since the 1970s, and has proven himself inept as a fencer.

Carol was a bookkeeper, report writer and musician. She was involved in science fiction fandom, madrigal singing, Civil Air Patrol and gardening.

They shared a house in the midst of nowhere with dogs, cats, a dozen computers and friends.

www.ingramcontent.com/pod-product-compliance
Lightning Source LLC
Chambersburg PA
CBHW070403260626
47161CB00001B/257